DJ Slaughter:

Betrayal

Book VI

By: James Beltz
www.JamesBeltz.com

(Thanks in advance for your review of this book)

-Other Books in the Slaughter Series-

Book I – Slaughter: Origin Story
Book II – Slaughter: White Out
Book III – Slaughter: Skeleton Key
Book IV – Slaughter: Free Fall
Book V – Slaughter: Darkest Knight

-Other Books in the Night Trips Series-

Twisted – (awaiting publication)
Snatch – (in production)
Charlie – (in production)

Table of Contents

Chapter 1: Duality

Sam Kenny, a man with two first names, circled his opponent with the grace of a dancer. This was not a dance with choreography and trusting partnership. It was a dance of brutality. Only victory or defeat existed as possible outcomes. Win and you move on. Lose and, well, Sam didn't like to think in those terms. Winning is what got him here. Winning would see him through to tomorrow. Never consider failure and you increased your odds of success. Confidence was just as important as training and skill. Ask any CEO of a Fortune 500 company and they would tell you the same. Ask any prizefighter. Ask any member of an elite combat unit. You would get the same answer every time. Without confidence leading the way, any victory could be chalked up to good luck and fortune. Sam didn't believe in being lucky. He found the more effort he put into something, the *luckier* he ended up being.

His opponent feinted with a left jab. Instead of bobbing away or throwing a feint of his own, he grabbed his opponent's wrist with leopard-like reflexes, latching on with both hands. Sam twisted, lifting the wrist high, stepping under, taking a quick step back, and jerking down with all his might. There was no choice for the other. They either follow the pull and flip over on their back, or they end up with a dislocated shoulder, pulled muscles, and a sling for the next week or so. And lose the fight, of course. Once on their back, Sam would deliver a punishing strike to the chin and end this quickly. He hated striking a woman this way, but Sam didn't choose the rules or who his opponent would be. She might be pretty, and this duel might be a job application, but Abbi Slaughter was going to be unconscious in the next half-second.

And then she wasn't. Oh, she flipped over, all right, but she landed on her feet. It was quite the feat of acrobatics. If there wasn't so much riding on this, Sam might have marveled at her skill and complimented her on her form. What a beautiful form it was, too.

Sam doubled over at the waist and all the fight left him in a flash of pain to his groin. Nausea hit him in a rush. It was Sam who found himself on his back, clutching his testicles and shriveling up into a fetal position. Man, she was fast. Man, she could hit hard for such a tiny thing. Man, he sure did feel stupid. He groaned a response to the woman above him. "Nice one."

She smiled. "It's not polite to gloat, but that's what you get for holding back."

He glanced around the room at the other members of the team out on the edges of the sparring mat gathered to watch his "interview". They were all grinning. One was even handing over a small wad of bills to another in an apparent payoff for losing a bet. Sam felt his forehead wrinkle as he narrowed his eyes at Abbi. "I didn't hold back."

She tilted her head at him slightly. "That's what they all say, but deep inside that lump of lead you call a skull, you can't help but hold a little back when facing off against a female opponent. It's good because it shows you have a conscience, a soul. It means that despite serving as a knuckle-dragger for an elite combat team with thirty-eight confirmed kills as a sniper, you're not a psychopath. It's bad because holding back in a fight means your chances of getting your head kicked in just increased. This wasn't really a test of winning a sparring match against a weaker opponent. It was a test of your character."

Sam had rolled to his knees while she talked. "So that means I didn't fail?"

Abbi turned and walked away, replying over her shoulder as she went. "I don't have a vote when it comes to hiring muscle." At the edge of the mat, she paused to scoop up a cute olive-skinned girl, a toddler who had been hanging on to the pant leg of an older black man. After perching the girl on her hip, she turned back to Sam. "It was decided in the beginning that the people you would have to fight with in the field would all get a vote when hiring a newbie."

Sam shook his head, pointing to her husband, the man who spoke little and whom everyone referred to as DJ. "But he said I would have to spar against one of your best."

Abbi smiled at her little girl, poking the child's nose and prompting a giggle from the curly-headed kid. She spoke to Sam without looking at him. "He's sweet that way, but I'm just tech support. Now, if you'll excuse me, I have a diaper to change."

Six hours later, Sam sat on a bench outside of a set of double doors. His shirt was plastered to his torso from sweat. He had been run through the wringer in a series of drills that tested his ability to problem-solve under pressure, fire under pressure, and navigate physical obstacles in specific time frames. He had functioned as a team member in a kill house with simunition, training ammo that functioned as paintballs, proving he knew the hand signals and the proper role no matter where he was placed in the lineup. He had to demonstrate first-aid techniques in a variety of situations. In order to be considered for this position, one had to prove they didn't need to be trained from scratch. His service file said he was a seasoned warfighter. These were tests to make sure the contents of his records were not a lie.

This facility, located in West Virginia, butted up against the Monongahela National Forest. To the world, it appeared to be a several hundred-acre renovated farm. In reality, it was the location of a private combat group. They were small, but the word was they had a standing contract with many of the three-letter agencies in the federal government. This was normal. The U.S. often contracted private groups to take care of issues where it was not prudent to send in the military. That meant two things: financial opportunity and extreme risk. If you got caught with your pants down while on an op in another country, there was a good chance the cavalry wasn't coming to rescue you. That was OK with Sam. Groups that handled this kind of mission were usually well trained, equipped, and prepared for every plan to fall apart at a moment's notice.

Sam was upstairs in what appeared to be the HQ portion of the facility. On the outside, it looked like a classic red barn. On the inside, it was an insulated state-of-the-art headquarters. There were meeting rooms, offices, a kitchen area with tables for eating, and a small indoor pistol range. John Argo, the oldest in the group, and whom DJ referred to as "Sheriff," explained that lunch breaks often involved friendly shooting competitions with the winner getting dessert. This seemed like a great place for a man with Sam's expertise. But what would the vote be on his inclusion on the other side of this wall?

The door opened and Argo motioned for Sam to come in. Inside, including Sheriff, seven sets of eyes all aimed in his direction. The guy in the wheelchair, who seemed to have a major say in the day-to-day operations, was missing, as were Abbi and the geeky guy who went by the name of Carbon. Abbi hadn't been lying. This vote had been conducted by only the soldiers who went into the field, the ones who would depend on him to watch their backs.

Of the seven staring at him, two were women, built like MMA fighters. Sam had previously never been willing to go into combat with a woman. It had nothing to do with thinking a woman wasn't capable of being lethal; he knew they were. It had everything to do with knowing few women who could fireman-carry his six-foot frame two miles uphill to an extraction point if he became injured. These two certainly seemed the exception to the rule. They were broad-shouldered and beefy. They looked like they enjoyed showing a few of the men up when it came to the bench press in the weight room. When Sam had been told he would be sparring with a woman earlier in the day, he had assumed it would have been one of these two.

Slaughter was in the center, sitting at a large, round, glass-top table, looking through a file folder Sam knew was his service record. "You handled yourself well today," DJ said without looking up. "But I have a question about what I see here in your jacket. Apparently, you think it's OK to pick and choose what orders you'll follow. Care to explain why?"

Sam had been prepared for this question. He was surprised it had not come up in the beginning. "It's simple, really. The kid was being sodomized on our own base. When I complained about it, I was told that

5

was how the culture was in Afghanistan. We were in their country, and the man was a high-ranking Afghan military leader. I was told to mind my own business. I countered that by reminding my command that he was on *our* base. I was told it didn't matter. A few nights later, after having a few too many beers, I was walking by his quarters. I could hear the kid screaming in pain. I beat the man within an inch of his life and threatened to slice him ear to ear if he did it again." Sam kept his chin high, confident in his position. "Sir, it might have been different if I had been out in the field, if my team was on an op and I might give away our position or compromised the mission in some way. But this was on our base. That was on American soil, as far as I was concerned. My record shows that I have never once disobeyed a direct order prior. But on that day, I felt the order was unlawful. My command disagreed, court-martialed me, and barred me from reenlisting. I stand by my decision then, and I do so now. So, unless you guys plan on sodomizing an eight-year-old in my presence, disobeying a direct order will never come up again."

DJ stared at him, hard. "So, you just told me that you would stand by and do nothing if this had happened on mission."

Sam shook his head. "No, sir, that's not what I said. I said I might. There can't be any definitives on a hypothetical. If stepping in on behalf of a kid being abused would compromise the mission or risk the lives of my team, my brothers," he gave a courtesy nod to the two women in the room, "or my sisters, then I might not step in. Honestly, sir, without knowing specific circumstances, I can't give you a straight answer. I just know that on the day in question, the one time I disobeyed a direct order, I did so with a clear conscience."

No one moved, but all eyes were focused on Slaughter. For a moment, he seemed to be thinking, weighing the decision. Sam had been told that all the door-kickers would have an equal vote. That might be true, but they seemed to be deferring to DJ. While no one had explained the hierarchy of the command structure, it was obvious DJ was the Team Lead. Wheelchair Guy must be the Operations Commander. Abbi and Carbon were logistics and tech support. But when it came to trigger time, DJ Slaughter was the alpha dog in the room.

Finally, DJ slid an envelope from under Sam's file and tossed it over. Sam caught it, then looked at DJ, questioning. Slaughter nodded. "That's twenty grand in cash. You get paid forty for every job. We run three to five contracts a year and there's no telling when they'll be. So, you're going to want to ration that. Technically speaking, you won't be an employee. You'll be an independent contractor. Carbon will set you up with, shall we say, creative tax options. We have a bunkhouse on the property. When we go on mission, you will be required to stay there and report twenty-four hours in advance. That's *if* you pass the next phase. Starting now, you're on site for the next thirty days. We'll give you a day to get your affairs in order, but then you live here for your thirty-day evaluation. Consider yourself on probation. We do things differently than you're used to. The next thirty days will be to drill these changes into your brain and teach you a few extra skills you may not have. You will be expected to be mission-ready at the end. If you're not, you're gone. You keep the twenty, and we part ways. Understood?"

Sam nodded and shoved the envelope into his back pocket. "No need for the twenty-four hours. Got everything I own in my truck. It's good to be on the team."

Argo spoke up. "Don't get ahead of yourself, kid. You're not on the team yet. Make it to the end of the month without washing out, and *then* you'll be on the team. Welcome to boot camp all over again, probie."

Outwardly, Sam was smiling, knowing he had made it to the next phase. Inwardly, he was smiling for a whole other reason. He was now one step closer to successfully infiltrating the team. Sam Kenny was not who they thought him to be. If everything went according to plan, they wouldn't until it was too late.

Chapter 2: The Offer

DJ watched Sam Kenny dial in adjustments to his scope, preparing to move from a three-hundred-meter target to another eight hundred meters away. Most everyone just called him Probie, but DJ referred to him as Doolie. The man had two first names, or at least his last name sounded like a first name, so dual names, or dually. Like a dually truck with its double sets of back tires. Since DJ rarely heard a dually pickup pronounced correctly, he stuck with the more popular vernacular of Doolie.

DJ had to admit, the man was a gifted long-distance shooter. Using a rifle from the prone position seemed easy for the vet. Whatever he fired, regardless of caliber or action, it was about as natural to him as scratching his chin. And with that silly-looking goatee, Doolie scratched his chin a lot. From just accuracy alone, Doolie was DJ's equal. That was saying a lot because DJ could shoot. If it had a trigger, DJ felt right at home behind whatever it was. But in some ways, Doolie was better than DJ.

Not only did Doolie have an innate sense of balance for the many variables that must be juggled to achieve near-perfect marksmanship, but the man didn't need a dope book. All the combinations of elements between the rifle, the round, and the environmental conditions that all serious snipers jotted down in a book or app to refer to later, Doolie logged into his brain. Ask him a question about anything that might appear there, and Doolie could quote it to you and then back it up with results. This made Doolie better than DJ. DJ had a dope book, but most of his skill came from a seat-of-the-pants feel for what he was doing. Doolie had that natural feel for shooting, but he also had a deep understanding of the data that went into each shot.

Doolie finished his changes to the scope, made sure his rifle was level, glanced at the flag indicator at the four-hundred-meter mark for wind changes, then easily rang the ten-inch gong. Doolie immediately cleared the rifle and jumped to a standing position, at which point DJ stopped the timer on his phone.

Before he could tell the man he had just bested his previous record by over a second, DJ could make out the approaching sound of a helicopter. Whatever it was, was big. It had the slower *wump* of longer rotor blades. This was no news or police chopper. It was a heavy-lift transport of some kind. Probably military. It sounded familiar. "Get your stuff into the UTV. I think we're about to have visitors."

DJ was running the little utility vehicle flat out when he broke through the trees, just in time to see the Sea Stallion come floating over a nearby ridge. A Sea Stallion was a big Navy helicopter capable of carrying three dozen men, a bunch of their equipment, and even all-terrain vehicles for getting them closer to their objective. The bird was flying low, only a hundred feet or so over the wooded terrain that surrounded the farm. As DJ swung in front of the barn, the giant gray helicopter passed over and then banked into a long circle, scrubbing speed and angling for the field nearby. This was making DJ nervous. It was out of the ordinary and it made him wonder if they were in some kind of trouble. Had they crossed some line he was unaware of?

Brett Foster was sharing similar feelings. As DJ slid to a halt, the man was leaning forward in his red wheelchair barking orders to Carbon, yelling at him to prepare to kill their servers. The hacker had long ago set up a plan to erase their computers just in case their government friends turned into their government enemies and decided to hang them out to dry for some reason. All around him, the team had come out to see what was going on. For Doolie's thirty-day evaluation and training period, DJ had requested the entire team stay on-site to participate and let the newbie get to know the people he would be working with. All had gathered in front of the barn, watching with suspicion. A few even had weapons loaded and at the ready.

DJ snapped at them. "If we were going to be attacked, do you really think they would make such a loud approach? Put those away. Even if they've come to burn us, we don't shoot our own people. Everybody relax."

Many of the team had worried that someday the CIA would burn the team, sever their connection, and throw them under the bus. They didn't trust the CIA even though many of their contracts came from the agency. The clandestine organization would never accept blame for anything, the team grumbled. The CIA would point fingers at their operation and claim DJ and his group had acted without authorization. It was something DJ brought up to his CIA contact at the very beginning. "I'll be honest, I don't trust you guys," DJ told Alimayu Salana, their handler, when approached about the opportunity.

Ali had smiled at the time. "And you shouldn't. We lie for a living. But trust me. If I learn the CIA is going to double-cross you in some way, I'll tip you off. I owe you that much. Just make sure you have a plan to get out of the country and start a new life. I have one and I work for them. Look, it won't happen. It's never happened before. At least not since the nineties. Do me a favor and just do it for a few years. Two years is all I ask. If you don't like the way things are going: bail."

So far, Ali had been true to his word. Despite that, DJ was nervous about a giant helicopter parking on his lawn. Whatever was going on, it must be big. He was sure Ali would have quite a story to tell.

It wasn't Ali who dismounted from the chopper and headed in their direction. DJ didn't recognize him at all. He was tall and gangly, his limbs seeming slightly longer than they should be. His lenghty strides caused him to sway a bit as he walked. He had thick, curly black hair on his head, and his face was covered with even more of the stuff. Despite it all being neatly groomed, he had all the appearance of a spider monkey in a suit. The good news was that he was by himself. Aside from the three crewmembers for the Sea Stallion, he was alone. If the stranger had exited with a team of armed soldiers or people dressed like federal agents, DJ would have suspected the worst.

DJ and the rest of his extended family, the only family DJ knew, stayed where they were. No one advanced to greet the newcomer with handshakes and smiles. They might have if Ali was coming to meet them. They liked Ali. As it was, they were on edge and ready for a fight.

Spider Monkey advanced as the helicopter shut down behind him, striding through the tall grass in his black two-piece suit. He barely slowed as he arrived at the boundary of the field, easily hopping over the split rail fence separating the field from the main complex of the farm. It was then DJ began to fully appreciate the man's size. Whoever this was coming to see them, he would look more at home on a professional basketball court than in the services of the CIA. If he *was* CIA. But who else could he work for? Few agencies had the ability to call up a naval Sea Stallion for use as a taxicab. There couldn't have been more than a few hundred of them in service.

The man made his way straight to Brett. It was obvious he knew who was in charge. It wasn't the muscle-bound men and women who ran the show. It was the man in the wheelchair, and the stranger knew it. He sidestepped around the rest of the group to stand before Brett, leaning down with a polite smile and extending a hand. "The name's Seymour," he said. Behind Brett, Bradford Cashin, or Cash as he was known, eased closer. The man had worked in the FBI with Brett and was fiercely loyal to him.

Brett did not shake the hand, nor return the smile. "Shouldn't that be *Agent* Seymour?"

The man retracted his hand and stood straighter. He glanced at the others with a worried look on his face. Holding a single finger to his lips, he said, "Shhhh. No one's supposed to know that. Officially, I'm a scout for the LA Lakers." He smiled again. "You would be surprised how many people ask me if I'm a professional ballplayer."

Brett wasn't playing nice with Seymour. His distrust of the man was obvious. "ID," he commanded, holding out his hand.

The man didn't move for a moment. He merely looked around at the group, his fake smile fading from his wooly face as he sized them all up. "Fine," he said. "You would think with all the expensive gear that I know you have stashed around this place, you might want to add a smile or two to your inventory. Take it easy, guys. You don't want to bite the hand that feeds you."

Brett was agitated and he let it show, snapping his fingers as he continued to hold his hand out. "We don't know you. ID. Now."

Spider Monkey nodded, surveying the group once more. "I got you. No problem." As he reached into his jacket, seven hands shifted closer to seven weapons. DJ held up a hand, signaling them to back off. Spider Monkey suddenly seemed genuinely concerned. "Easy now, I'm pulling out my phone. Please don't poke me full of holes. This is a new suit." He gingerly pulled forth a cellphone and held it up, showing them all.

Brett's voice was stern as he addressed Spider Monkey. "That's not an ID."

Spider Monkey looked at his phone as he answered. "And I will hand it over too, but first I thought you might want verification of who I am from somebody you trust." He tapped a few buttons on his phone and DJ could hear it dialing. While Seymour waited, he handed over his wallet.

Agents for the CIA didn't carry a badge, but they did have an access card with a digital chip they used when not undercover. Brett flipped through the man's wallet and found it. He didn't pause to scrutinize it. He tossed it to Carbon and fired off a one-word command. "Authenticate."

Carbon scanned the barcode on the back with his own phone and nodded to Brett a second later. "Seymour Sinclair. CIA. He needs to change his name, though. Sounds like a villain in a Bond movie." He tossed it back as someone on the other end of Spider Monkey's call answered.

The familiar voice of Ali carried across the space. "I'm busy. This had better be important."

Seymour smiled at the phone, looking into the camera as he video-chatted Ali. "Life and death important." He turned the phone around and did a slow circle, showing Ali the group. "I have a feeling if I sneeze, these people are going to shoot me. You want to vouch for me, please? Failure to do so and you'll have to read my eulogy in a few days."

Ali laughed. "When you kick-off, no one's going to eulogize you, Seymour. No one likes you that much. DJ, are you there?"

DJ stepped forward and Spider Monkey aimed the phone in his direction. "I'm here, Ali. How come you're not the one coming to us?"

Ali shrugged. "I'm busy with something else at the moment and I guess your reputation precedes you. Look, I vouch for him. Don't trust him much, but he is who he says he is. If he's there to offer you a job, demand payment up front. Oh, and double your rate just because you had to look at his face. Hey, Seymour? Treat them right. I don't want to have to clean up any of your messes. Gotta' go."

The screen went black and Spider Monkey returned the phone to his jacket. Checking his watch, he said, "Look, I know we got off to a rocky start, but we're on the clock here." He pulled a portable drive from his other jacket pocket and tossed it over to Carbon. "You want to pull this up on a screen somewhere and let's talk? If you accept my offer, I'll need you to load onto the bird ASAP."

Carbon looked at Brett for approval. Brett looked at DJ. DJ shrugged. Two minutes later they were all standing in the ops room of the barn, staring at a video wall and hearing what Seymour had to say. What he had to say was disturbing.

He pointed to a picture of an older gentleman with neatly groomed gray hair and thin glasses. "Dr. Julius Abreo, a naturalized citizen originally from France. For the last twenty years, Dr. Abreo has been working on cold fusion. Now, in case you didn't know it, cold fusion is better than the typical kind of fusion in nuclear powerplants or submarines. For one, there is no radioactive waste generated. We have been able to do this for a number of years now, but the issue has been with containment of the reaction. The heat generated is too hot for any man-made material to withstand. We can create an energy field using superconducting magnets to solve that issue, but then you run into a whole other problem. The energy it takes to maintain the electromagnetic field is huge. You end up putting more energy into the system than the system can produce. Without going into details, Dr. Abreo recently solved this issue. Or so he says. He hasn't got around to building the device to test it yet. Additionally, his design promises to make the reactor small enough to be portable. With his new method, if it works, we're talking the Holy Grail of energy production. You can have one in your house, your car, almost anything. No more use of fossil fuels. We are talking science-fiction-like results.

"Dr. Abreo has been keeping all of his research and designs on a central drive and encrypting the data to prevent theft. Not only theft from a competitor, but theft from other countries. Yesterday, that device was stolen from the research facility where he works for the Department of the Navy."

Carbon spoke first, raising his hand as if he were in a classroom. "Excuse me, but so what? I mean, wouldn't free, clean, unlimited energy benefit us all? Oh, let me guess, oil execs are having fits with the idea and are using their cash to bribe politicians. That's why you're here, isn't it? You don't want us to just get it back, you want us to prevent the information from getting out to protect the fossil fuel industry."

Spider Monkey smiled and shook his head. "One hundred percent wrong. While he holds patents on the design, his intention has always been to release the data globally once proof of concept was complete. No, the issue is much more sinister than that." He turned back to the screen and tapped the control panel, bringing up a cascade of CAD renderings of a fantastical drawing of an aircraft that looked more like a pizza wedge. "This is why the Navy was funding his research. The power creation portion was just the first step. It would be used to create a craft that could go underwater at incredible speeds, exit to fly through the atmosphere, and even leave orbit for space flight. He was building us a UFO." He paused and looked around at the room. DJ wasn't sure what the others were thinking, but he felt as if he had been cast in a sci-fi movie. This was all a big joke, right?

Spider Monkey continued. "I know what you're thinking, and this is no joke. The energy from a portable cold fusion reactor could be harnessed to produce a non-polluting, high output thrust for propulsion. It could also generate an energy field outside of the ship similar to the one used to contain the reaction. That field would allow the ship to slip through our atmosphere at incredible velocities, as well as underwater. It could even be used to protect the hull from meteors and small debris encountered during space flight."

Argo interrupted. "How fast, exactly?"

Spider Monkey shrugged. "No one knows for sure, but Dr. Abreo believes as much as five hundred miles per hour underwater." A few in the room gasped in disbelief. "The field not only protects the ship in a sort of slippery bubble, but it reduces the gravitational mass of the ship inside."

Carbon interrupted. "You're talking artificial gravity!"

Seymour shook his head. "Not in the science fiction way you are referring to, no. But it does make it even easier for the propulsion system to make the thing move. In the atmosphere, we are talking speeds in excess of Mach 10. Outside our atmosphere, with reduced mass and in a vacuum, it would eventually make it to just under the speed of light. We could exit our solar system in days. We're more worried about the rest of these plans falling into the wrong hands than unlimited, clean power generation."

DJ finally couldn't take any more. "You've got to be kidding me. You can't really expect us to believe all of this. Spaceships and force fields? Antigravity? Now come clean on why you're really here or I'm going to let the team beat on you for a while."

Spider Monkey got real serious real fast. He shot a hard look at DJ. "Have your cyber jockey verify it." He then turned to Carbon. "Go ahead. Look the guy up. I'll wait. *Authenticate*."

Carbon blinked, then started tapping away on the tablet he carried with him everywhere. Spider Monkey crossed his arms and watched, his long arms and tall body making him look ridiculous. He resembled more a cartoon drawing than a real person. It didn't take long before Carbon found what he was looking for and sent it to the big screen, multiple news articles from entities that focused on science. "The guy is legit. He's a real scientist and recently was approved for patents on everything Agent Seymour just said. But the patents are limited in detail and vague on the drawings. I see multiple references from several physicists who seriously question his claims."

Spider Monkey addressed Brett directly. "I know how it all sounds. It's far-fetched. I get it. And who knows if he really overcame the issues like he said he did? But just a few hours after he notified the Navy he had solved the problems in the design, the drive was stolen. I'll tell you this as well. This guy, Dr. Abreo, he's already come through for us on several things the public doesn't know about. But here's one you do. Hypersonic missile technology? That was him. He came up with the design one afternoon on a coffee break! His doodles were on a napkin, and I'm not even kidding you. While the Pentagon was dragging their knuckles on it, the design was stolen. How do you think the Chinese and Russians beat us to the punch on that? So, knowing the guy's reputation, can we really afford to let our enemies get their hands on these designs?"

The room went silent, everyone looking at each other. It was Brett who broke the ice. "So how do you expect us to help you? Something this big, I'm sure you have much more useful assets than our small team."

Seymour nodded. "And we've already learned a lot in the short time it's been since the theft. For one, it was a freelance team contracted by the North Korean's who pulled this off. While we're not sure where they are at the moment, we do know where they are going to be. Our intel says the team plans to hand off the drive to North Korean agents. We have the coordinates for the location and the time for the handoff."

It was Brett's turn. "So then, why don't you go there and get them? Why do you need us? And for that matter, why don't the thieves just digitally transfer the information?"

Spider Monkey seemed ready for the question. "The drive is encrypted, as I said. It's likely the team who stole it doesn't even understand how it works. And if the North Korean scientists get their hands on it, they'll discover they don't have the resources to make that happen. The encryption is biologically based. You need an active connection to Dr. Abreo's brain. Everyone's brain waves are unique and extraordinarily complex. The man has to physically connect to the drive in order to get to the data. And while we are pretty sure the North Koreans can't work around that, it doesn't mean it's not possible. You would need a quantum computer to work through the issue. They don't have one. But once they reach that conclusion, they'll just turn around and sell it to someone who does have the expertise and the hardware. The Chinese come to mind. And they share a border.

"As to your other question, the meeting will take place in Russia, about fifty miles from where the Chinese, North Korean, and Russian borders converge. While we have assets in Russia that could get there, they would be greatly outnumbered and without the combat assets to get the job done.

"Our plan is to airdrop you over the Sea of Japan. We'll have a sub pick you up. The Vermont will get you as close to the shore as possible.

From there you will infil by RIB with a SEAL team for escort. You will make your way five miles in from the coast, and be waiting to ambush them when the bad guys show up. Exfil to the same location and the SEALs will get you back to the sub. So, are you in? The clock is ticking and we need to get a move on if we're going to be there ahead of the handoff. To sweeten the deal, we'll pay you double the normal rate just as Agent Ali suggested."

Brett shook his head, unconvinced. "We need a lot more information than that before I'll greenlight this."

Seymour nodded. "I understand that, but as I said, time's a-wastin'. Look, get your team on the bird and headed in the right direction. We can work out any details while we're in the air. At any time prior to your jump, you decided to bail on this, then do so. We can't make you. Our fallback plan will be to send the SEALs in any way. We prefer for there to not be a US Military incursion into Russia, but we'll do it if we have to.

Everyone looked at Brett. Brett shot DJ a questioning look. DJ shrugged. It took them less than fifteen minutes to load onto the Sea Stallion and leave Mother Earth. DJ wasn't going to lie to himself; he was a bit nervous about this gig. He wasn't overly fond of short notice deals with missing information. Doolie on the other hand was as happy as a clam. They needed his sniper skills, so DJ skipped the formality of the remaining week of training. Doolie was now on the team. Besides, unless he had screwed up in some major way, the kid was going to pass. It would be good to have a sniper with his skills watching their back.

Like normal, Carbon was along for the ride as their on-site tech support. Abbi and Brett would hang back and offer support from a distance. Carbon was less than useless in a firefight, but he was good to have around anyway. The trick would be hurling him out of an airplane. Their geeky team member had never jumped before. Since the landing was in water, he could just strap to someone else and jump tandem. DJ couldn't wait to see the guy's face when the door opened.

Chapter 3: Garlic Parmesan Wings

DJ sat in the back of the twin-turboprop Navy transport and looked over his team. As the Greyhound bounced through the night, buffeted by pockets of colder and warmer air of an approaching storm, he considered the people he had come to know as his extended family. There were the ones who had been with him the longest: Carbon, their genius hacker with his open disdain for corporate execs, the military-industrial complex, and all politicians, was an integral part of his group. The man was resourceful and calculating, seemingly always able to pull a digital rabbit out of his hat in time of need.

Cash used to work with Brett. He was quiet and stone-faced, seldom displaying any kind of emotion whatsoever. His cold blue eyes were a striking feature against his otherwise bland personality.

Sheriff, the black man who had once saved his life, had become their comic relief. He always seemed to know just how to issue a derogatory comment on one of his comrades that would make everyone else smile. The man was technically too old to still undertake missions such as this, but he always pulled his weight.

There was Bettie Walden, a newer member of the team. Her olive-skinned complexion was due to her Cajun roots, she claimed. There was nothing feminine about the woman. She was about as butch as they came. She was well-muscled and short in stature. Her height and build, combined with her propensity for wearing baggy clothes, made her look overweight. She was anything but. If she decked you, you would quickly realize your mistake. She tended to cuss a lot, though DJ could never tell what she was saying. All of it was in Cajun French. For this reason, DJ referred to her as Coonie. It was short for Coonass. Which was not considered profanity by her people, she promised. It was a term of endearment.

Latricia Harringer was the opposite of Coonie. Her skin was the color of night and she stood close to six and a half feet tall. Despite her size, the woman could run like a deer and could have been a track star in another life. Because of her height, when she ran, her gait made her appear to be bounding. It was for this reason DJ called her Bounder. She had braids that went past her shoulders that she pulled into a ponytail. DJ saw the long hair as a weak point in hand-to-hand combat and encouraged her to cut it shorter. She had replied that if anyone touched it she would break them in half. DJ believed her and dropped it. To say she could handle herself was an understatement. She had beat every team member on the sparring mat. Including Abbi.

Lastly, there was the new guy. Doolie was proving to be a good fit for the team. He got along with everyone, could shoot, and had an incredible memory for details. While this would be his first mission with the team, DJ had a good feeling about him.

Carbon sat across from him and called out over the roar of the engines. "Look, I'm telling you, you don't need me. Seriously, this is not a mission where tech support is needed. You can do this without me. Just let me ride back to Tokyo. I can figure out my own way from there."

It was Argo, sitting next to Carbon, who responded. "Dude, it's not that bad. Besides, with the cloud cover and no moon, you'll never see the ocean rushing up at you at nearly two hundred miles per hour." Argo smiled broadly at Carbon and the hacker looked like he might pass out.

DJ laughed quietly to himself. The plan was a low open over the water to prevent too much separation from each other once they hit the ocean. In the near blackout conditions, they would have a hard time finding each other normally, so each person was wearing a transponder and a small display on their wrists. Their gear was stored in two boxes designed to float and was also tagged. On touchdown, they would use the transponders to swim toward the boxes as a rendezvous point. The next step was to wait. The sub would be nearby and submerged. It would pick up their transponder, navigate until close, then break the surface. The onboard SEAL team would scoop them up in a couple of RIB boats and bring them in. Piece of cake, DJ thought. All his team were swimmers, save for Carbon, but he could use his flotation vest to float and DJ would tow him along behind.

The light in the cabin flipped to red and the call came out for three minutes until drop. DJ stood, grabbed Carbon, and turned him around. It took only moments to strap his harness to Carbon and then they shuffled toward the loading ramp and their gearboxes. Two crew members from the aircraft were stationed near the end with harnesses strapping them to the aircraft. In front of him, Carbon started saying something, but not loud enough to be heard. When the loading ramp suddenly began lowering and the air began twisting through the cabin, Carbon stiffened and began to shout. "No! Cut me loose! I'm not doing this!"

The call came to jump, and the crew members released the clamps on the gearboxes strapped on top of one another. A second later and the bundle was ripped out of the rear of the plane by a smaller chute, vanishing quickly into the night. DJ stepped forward to follow but Carbon began twisting like a snake in front of him, screaming at the top of his lungs. "No, no, no, no," he repeated over and over again, followed by one longer "NOOOOOOO," as DJ stepped from the Greyhound. Carbon continued his one-word shout until he was completely out of breath. There was a brief second of silence from the man who had gone rigid, strapped to DJ as if he were a one-hundred-and-seventy-pound statue incapable of anything but making noise, then the screaming began all over again. DJ said nothing to the man, enjoying the moment, savoring every detail for later. When this was all over, the team would relax back at the barn, remembering what they had done, celebrating another victory. When they did, DJ would regale them with the tale of Carbon's antics as he plummeted from twenty thousand feet over the Sea of Japan in the middle of the night.

There were three more lengthy screams before DJ finally pulled the chute, slowing rapidly through the air. Just before they struck the water, DJ pulled the release pin on the chute, falling the last few feet into the ocean and allowing the chute to carry farther away from them. The last thing they wanted was for the chute to tangle with them in the water.

The cold ocean closed over them, and like magic, Carbon's petrified screams were silenced at once. It was almost instantly replaced by kicking and thrashing. DJ didn't fight him. He released the pins shackling them together and kicked away. He wasn't worried about the poor man drowning. They were both wearing auto-inflating life jackets. As soon as they hit the water, the compressed air cartridges did their job and filled the preserver nearly instantly. Carbon was already on the surface and thrashing the water in a panic when DJ's heavier body emerged from the cold, black water. DJ could barely make him out in the dim light, but it was sure funny to see. He let him go on for a moment more before finally admonishing him. "You're wearing a life jacket, you big baby. Stop fighting it and just sit there and float."

At last, Carbon seemed to understand he wasn't going to die. The hacker sputtered as they bobbed on the swells. "I don't understand. Why couldn't we have just boarded the sub in port?"

DJ laughed. "Because the Chinese watch our ports with satellites and the Vermont is supposed to be patrolling the Indian Ocean over seven thousand miles from here. That plane we just jumped from-"

Carbon cut him off. "*You* jumped! *I* was nearly assassinated!"

DJ sighed. "That plane would have looked like any other patrol craft in the air. We don't want to tip off the Russians we're about to invade them, remember?"

Carbon scoffed. "What I remember is that we *used* to be friends."

DJ consulted the small digital display on his wrist and quickly located the others. He also spotted the one identified to be their gear. DJ retrieved a length of paracord from a cargo pocket. He tied one end to himself and the other to Carbon. Ten minutes of relaxed swimming and the two of them reached their destination. Carbon latched onto the box for extra buoyancy. They were the third to arrive, but it didn't take long for the others to show.

Carbon was still clearly not happy. "How long do we have to wait? I thought the water would be warmer. It's summer after all. Seriously, guys. This sucks. We're just sitting out here waiting for the sharks to just pick us off. I'm telling you. I did research. Do you know how many species of sharks call this body of water home? We're nothing but a floating buffet out here. And what if the sub never shows? What if they're a hundred miles away waiting in the wrong location? What are we going to do then? I mean, why couldn't we have at least brought our own boat? And do you know what this saltwater will do to my gear if this box leaks?"

Carbon would have continued to jabber away were it not for Coonie shutting him up with a single question. "Hey, Carbon, you know sharks are attracted to noise, right?" Carbon's mouth clamped shut in mid-sentence and the whole team laughed.

After a long few minutes of silence, bobbing in the Sea of Japan, waiting for the inevitable RIB boat full of SEALS, Carbon broke the night with one last, whimpering statement. "I hate all of you."

Brett sat in their operations center at the farm. Something was bugging him about all of this, but he couldn't put his finger on what it was. There was nothing definitive about what it was. It was just a gut feeling that something wasn't right. Looking at their closed-circuit camera feed of the property, that feeling was growing stronger. Two black SUVs were making the trip down the long drive to the barn. He turned to Abbi who was looking at a computer screen. "We have visitors," he told her flatly.

Across the room, playing with an activity set for toddlers, little Cassie was busy trying to put the correctly shaped blocks into the right holes. Abbi looked at the screen, then glanced at her daughter, slight concern crossing her face. "Where's the team?" she asked.

Brett sent an image to the video wall. "They just made their jump. Carbon will send us confirmation when the sub picks them up. So, that's not bad news coming down the driveway. I'll go meet them. Stay here." As he rolled to the elevator that would take him to the ground floor, he issued a command. "Prepare to burn our servers just in case. And get a gun. I've been having second thoughts about all of this. Something feels off."

Abbi stood and called after him, worry coloring her voice. "What have you been thinking?"

Brett hit the button on the elevator door and then entered. "I have no clue. But maybe you better do some more research on that scientist. Find his last known location. And see what you can find out about Agent Seymour."

By the time he rolled out the front door of the barn, two men were exiting the vehicles. Both were wearing jeans and short-sleeved button-ups. The one closest gave a courtesy nod and spoke. "You must be Brett."

Brett checked them both out. He could see slight bulges at their waist under their shirts indicating they were armed. "Did the wheelchair give it away?"

The man smiled. "We were sent by Agent Seymour. You can call me Bill, he's Ted. We're here to help you on your most excellent adventure. We're going to sit with you while you monitor the mission. If you need anything or your team gets into trouble, we're supposed to coordinate a response."

Brett smiled and shook his head. "Sorry to have you waste your time, but I think we can handle it. Have a good trip back home."

Bill smiled and glanced at Ted, then back. "Sorry, Brett, but it's not really an option. I'm sure you can appreciate just how sensitive an op this is. We're here to help make sure it's successful." He produced a folded sheet of paper from his shirt pocket and held it up between two fingers. "For starters, how about an access code for satellite time. I know you would enjoy a bird's eye view of everything. It'll give your team advanced warning of anything in their path."

Brett hesitated. There was really nothing odd here. The CIA had occasionally demanded access to the team as they operated. But in the past, it had been from someone they trusted. Brett didn't know who any of these new players were. Even though Ali had vouched for Seymour, something still felt off. Their attitudes were condescending. Their smiles were fake. And Brett didn't trust anyone he didn't know. Still, he wasn't sure if there was anything he could do about it now. Maybe he was just overreacting. Maybe he was just becoming paranoid with age and the environment he worked in. Brett spun the chair around and headed for the door. "Come on," he said. "We'll get you set up in the ops. But a word of warning: this is a family-owned business. As such, there's a baby upstairs. Look at her wrong and I won't be responsible for what the mother does to your face. Any plastic surgery bill incurred will come out of your own pockets."

———————

DJ was the last one up the Jacob's ladder and onto the hull of the Vermont. So much for SEALS scooping them out of the water on RIBs, he thought. The giant black submarine eased out of the water twenty feet away from where they floated. For a moment, DJ didn't even know what it was. It rose from the water like a leviathan, quiet, stealthy, ominous. One minute they were all alone. The next they were looking at a black mountain of steel rising from the depths. It scared Carbon half to death, prompting a long string of profanity that didn't even make sense. A moment later and a latch opened from behind the sail, the iconic tall tower that protruded from every submarine. A voice called out to them, asking for DJ by name. He answered and the voice told him to hold on a sec. Next came a host of red-lensed flashlights bathing them in crimson, followed by tossed ropes attached to life preservers. One by one they were hauled to the side and up the rope ladder.

They were told they needed to hurry. They were warned from making too much noise while boarding, and to get down the hatch as quietly as possible. The crewmen who helped them even took extra care to keep the gearboxes from banging against the hull when bringing them on board, lifting them high, and handing them carefully to each other in a chain toward the opening.

The sailors scurrying along the hull carried an air of concern and DJ asked why they were on edge. One of them grabbed his arm and helped him to the hatch, speaking quietly as they went. "We've got an enemy sub in the area. It's what took so long to get to you. A Russian Yasen-M has been patrolling the coast. We don't think they know we're here, but we lost contact half an hour ago. The thing just vanished. We need to dive as quickly as possible."

DJ watched as the equipment boxes were lowered through the hatch carefully, handed down the ladder to more sailors who were perched along the length. Finally, he carefully descended into the sub, the sailor he had been talking to following close behind and securing the hatch above him. At the bottom, the sailor nodded to an officer whom DJ recognized as the XO. His name badge said, Watts. He was a seasoned-looking black man with a serious expression on his face. Watts raced up the ladder and double-checked the hatch, then nodded down. As soon as he had, the sailor next to DJ called out over a small walkie-talkie. "Control, Auxiliaryman of the Watch. Plug Trunk Hatch secure."

He waited for only a second and then a man's voice came across a speaker mounted above their heads. The voice was low and the volume minimum. "All stations, control, commence emergency dive." This was almost immediately followed by a whooshing sound of air and the sub tilting forward sharply.

The Auxiliaryman gave orders to the soaking wet team dripping in the hallway, keeping his voice low. "Everyone listen up. I will lead you to your berthing assignments so you can change into something dry, but we have an enemy sub close. I need you to talk softly and keep from banging anything around. I also need you to remove your footwear. Until further notice, socks only." No one moved. The team looked at each other with uncertainty, the unfamiliar environment bombarding their brain with questions. The Auxiliaryman repeated his command more sternly. "Boots off, now." Hesitation left them and everyone sat to remove their boots.

Coonie was the last to sit, she stood on the other side of the auxiliaryman looking up at him with a smile. "I like a man who's bossy." She then slapped him on the butt and winked. A look of horror washed over the surprised man's face.

He looked first to his XO, then to DJ, and back again to Coonie. "I, umm, ma'am, I'm gay."

Coonie shook her head. "Of course, you are. Why are all the cute ones hitting for the other team?" She sat and removed her boots.

As DJ began unlacing his boots, the XO, who had elected to remain silent until this point, picked his way through the hallway, reassuring them as they went. There was an edge to his voice. "We're on a fifteen-degree dive. It won't get too steep. And remember what you were told about keeping quiet. I would hate to launch you from a torpedo tube for failure to follow orders." It was clear to DJ that none of these people wanted a bunch of civilian contractors on board. As a former corpsman for the Navy, DJ understood completely. They had invaded these submariner's home. To add salt to the wound, they weren't even military, to say nothing of being distrustful of the CIA. He would order his people to stay out of the way and keep quiet. Hopefully, they would be gone and out of these people's hair as soon as possible.

Carbon sat at a table in something resembling a cafeteria, only smaller. It was where the crew of the sub gathered to eat. Since it was in between normal mealtimes, the only ones present were his team and the cooks in the tiny kitchen. They had changed clothes and gathered here to go over finalizing their plans for the ambush. When they entered, a cook wearing coveralls and a hat with a logo of a cougar in front of a mountain, emblazoned with the words "Catamount Tavern," asked if any of them wanted something to eat. Carbon was the only one who spoke up and said yes. It was pizza night, the young man said. They still had some leftover garlic parmesan wings and a few pieces of cheese pizza left. He could reheat them and set them out. Carbon was eager and readily agreed. Maybe there was something good to be salvaged on this god-forsaken trip.

He had been bounced around in the back of a small cargo plane with seats that had to be the most uncomfortable and cheapest the Navy could buy. He had been strapped to an uncompassionate DJ Slaughter and forced out the back of the thing. The freefall was loud, windy, and black. Carbon had been certain they were going to splat into the ocean in the mother of all belly flops. The landing in the water wasn't a bone-cracking impact; it had been far worse. The idiot he was strapped to had cut him loose without warning. He had then become convinced he was going to drown. When he bobbed to the surface and was forced to float and wait, he had been positive the shark from Jaws would swallow them all whole. Now, he was finally dry and warm but had been told that if he so much as sneezed, a Russian submarine with a name he couldn't spell would blow them all up. This was the suckiest mission ever. Usually, he was tucked safely out of the way, employing the technical skills he was good at in the back of some van or an apartment nearby, while the rest of his team went and grunted like Neanderthals and played with their big guns. Pizza and wings wouldn't make the memory of what it took to get here go away, but it would at least make him feel less like the victim in some movie where he had been kidnapped for a ransom.

DJ and the others were looking over satellite images on Carbon's tablet, discussing where to deploy in preparation for the ambush. Carbon sat silent like a good little hacker and waited for his wings. He would get some of those wings, too. If any of the others tried to hog it before he could get his hands on a few, they would pay. Not that he would attempt anything physical. He wouldn't stand a chance. But he could threaten to scream like a baby with a wet diaper, invoking an attack by that hidden Russian submarine, if he didn't get some of them wings. DJ had said that Navy submarine cooks were some of the best out there. Many of them went on to make five-star meals for the Pentagon and catered White House dinners. They even cooked for the President. Yep, he was getting some of them wings. Yes, he was.

Carbon watched the young cook do his thing across the room and on the other side of a serving counter. He worked quickly but quietly among his peers, who seemed to be prepping for a future meal. There was no pan clanged, no door closed too hard, no timer with a bell set. He was obviously well versed in keeping noise to a minimum when required. After what seemed like an eternity, the kid started over with a tray of pizza slices arranged on paper plates. Carbon assumed it was to prevent the clatter of dishes. As the young man made his way around the counter, the sub suddenly banked like an aircraft, going into a hard turn. Carbon felt a knot develop in his chest, knowing the pizza would end up on the floor. Surprisingly, the kid tilted over against the turn, remaining upright and solid in his footing. The sailor must be used to this, he thought.

As the kid set down paper plates in front of them all, making sure Carbon was one of the first to get his share, DJ pointed to the map turned towards their newest team member. "Doolie, I want you to take an alternate route in. Follow this ridgeline and set up overwatch on this hill. I want you to get there ahead of us so you can radio back anything you see."

The young cook, apparently eager to chat with his visitors, turned to Sam at DJ's mention of the odd nickname. "Doolie? Is that short for something?" he asked quietly, a pleasant smile on his face.

Doolie pointed to DJ. "Our team leader has a habit of giving everyone nicknames. My name is Sam Kenny. Since I have two first names, he calls me Doolie."

The kid smiled. "I have two first names, too. Evan Thomas." He then turned to DJ. "So, what would my nickname be?"

DJ smiled at the sailor. "That's easy. E.T."

Across the room, a chuckle could be heard. Turning, Carbon saw another sailor leaning across the counter, listening in. The new person then turned to the other cooks in the narrow kitchen. "Hey, everyone. PO3 Thomas has a new nickname. E.T. Makes sense, right? He's always the first one to call home when we hit a new port."

Evan shook his head. "I should have never opened my mouth. That's going to stick around a while."

Carbon quickly lost interest when the sailor in the kitchen set a plastic tray loaded with wings on the counter. This was his chance. If he could get to the wings first, he could ensure none of his teammates denied him the deliciously prepared barnyard delicacy. He stood quickly, maneuvering around DJ, and making a beeline for the counter. That's when tragedy struck. He tripped, went sprawling, and knocked over three chairs in the process. He and the chairs went clattering across the crew's mess, making a tremendous amount of noise. Too much noise. Carbon's heart dropped into his socks.

PO3 Thomas held up his hands and hissed to them all, "No one move!" he darted silently to a corded phone hanging near the counter. He snatched the handset, tapped a few buttons on the dial, and then spoke. "Sonar, sound transient. Ten seconds ago, one of our visitors knocked over a few chairs in the crew's mess." He hung up the phone and turned to face the group.

Carbon, still laying on the floor, too scared to move, whispered from the floor. "Did I just kill us?"

E.T. shrugged. "We'll know soon enough."

Chapter 4: The Nutcracker

The Captain of the Vermont was furious. Quiet, but furious. Captain Markel stood in the crew's mess with his arms crossed and his brow furrowed. "What part of quiet do you not understand?"

DJ stood. "Sir, it was an accident. The man tripped."

The captain stepped closer. "Is that supposed to make it better? Your little accident has us hovering about fifty meters above the ocean floor at a dead stop. Our sonar picked up your accident. If we picked it up, you can bet that Russian heard it too. So, now we have to sit here playing hide and seek, waiting to see if the other captain is too stupid to give himself away. You not only compromised your mission, making meeting your deadline almost impossible, but you compromised this submarine and all one hundred and thirty-three souls that call it home. And for what?" He focused his glare on Carbon. "Hot wings?"

DJ tried to apologize again. "Sir," he started, but Markel cut him off.

"No, you zip it. We are six miles from your drop-off point, but it might as well be six thousand because I can't risk moving. I can't do a slow surface because the Russian is too close. I can't dive because we're in water less than three hundred feet deep. We're already parked on the bottom. And I can't sprint for the internationally recognized boundary for territorial waters because it's too far away. The last time we caught a sniff of that Yassen, it was only ten miles out. So we're stuck here, doing our best imitation of a shadow."

DJ was now worried. If they didn't make the rendezvous location on time they would lose the data drive. "Sir, if we're this close just drop us off here. The SEALs can run us to the shore. Surely a RIB can make it there and back without fuel being an issue."

The captain shook his head. "Three things are horribly wrong about what you're asking. I can get us to the surface quietly, but if the Russian is closer than we think and happens to be looking through his periscope, we'll be seen. Secondly, we don't have a RIB on board. Do you really think you could fit one down that hatch? We do have a couple of inflatables, but running the outboard would alert the other sub. That leads me to number three. What SEALs?"

DJ blinked. He was told they would be responsible for infil and exfil, getting them to the shore and back to the sub. He hadn't seen any since arriving. DJ had just assumed that since they were only performing escort duty, and the fact that DJ and his team were civilian contractors, they had elected to stay away until it came time to depart. "We were told a SEAL team was onboard and would get us in and out."

The captain smiled. "Then your CIA friends lied to you. You're on your own, buddy. But relax, you won't be going on any mission anyway. We're going to pretend to be a hole in the water until I think it's safe to move again."

At the mention of no SEALs, his team began grumbling and muttering under their breath. "We should have never trusted anyone but Ali," he heard Bounder say.

DJ snapped his fingers to silence them. "Sir, do you know the mission we're on?"

Captain Markel nodded. "You're supposed to rescue some spook who got themselves in hot water. Well, the CIA can figure out another way to rescue their friend. I'm not risking this entire sub for the life of one spy."

DJ shook his head. When this was over he was going to snap Agent Seymour's neck. "Looks like the CIA lied to you too. At least let me explain why we're really here. It's your boat, I get it. Your word is law here, but please let me explain to you the mission we're really on."

The Captain looked at him and the team. DJ could tell he really wanted to tell them all what to do with themselves. He had been forced to take on operators who weren't in any branch of the service. He had been ordered to do the bidding of the CIA. Not to mention one of them clumsily made a racket on his boat and placed his entire crew into harm's way. He wasn't happy. He was rightly and royally pissed! But DJ and his team still had a job to do. It was a job that meant securing America's secrets and keeping innocent citizens safe from other countries. If there was a chance of getting the captain on his side, he had to take it.

Captain Markel nodded. "Explain your mission, but understand it doesn't change the situation we're in."

Abbi threw the satellite image onto the giant screen for Brett and their agent invaders to see. Her desk sat in a back corner. Behind her was an arrangement of things that looked out of place in this state-of-the-art operations center. There was a shelf with diapers, baby powder, creams, and ointments. A changing table decorated with tiny comical ducks was placed underneath. A playpen sat in the corner, and one of those automatic swings that ran on batteries, currently swinging Cassie who was fast on the way to nappy time, stood nearby. There was even an activity center for tots and a small box of toys. Her little corner of the room was more a childcare center and less high-tech gadgetry. That was fine by her. She only needed her three screens, a mouse, and a keyboard to perform her part of the missions these warriors went on.

She was sure some would find her role here odd. Not so much the baby, but the fact she participated at all, or why she even tolerated her husband to go guns a-blazin' into parts unknown. She had long ago come to terms with who DJ was. It was how she had been introduced to him. It was how she had fallen in love with him. She knew him to be a warrior. She knew there might come a day when that warrior didn't return home. If that ever happened, she would weep. But she suffered no regret about sticking with him. She either loved him or she didn't. And if she did love him, she had to accept him for who he was. Every part of him. The dark and brooding parts, the violent and dangerous parts; none of that could be removed without changing who he was. Love was an all-or-nothing thing. And, oh, how she dearly loved her man.

All eyes stayed focused on the satellite image, even though there was nothing to be seen. There was still plenty of time left before the scheduled meeting of bad guys and the exchange of the data drive. Soon, her team would beach a small boat onto the shore and set up their ambush. For now, they were somewhere under the Sea of Japan, making their way towards their target. Until they emerged from hiding, they were out of contact.

With Brett and the others focused away from her, she set about doing the other thing Brett had asked. She concentrated on learning more about Agent Seymour. Something wasn't sitting right with Brett, and she was zeroed in on finding out why that was. The first thing she did was send an email to Agent Ali, asking if he knew anything about the mission they were on. She didn't have to wait long for the reply. He didn't, Ali said. She sent him a few details and asked if he could corroborate any of the information. He said he would check but was out in the field at the moment. It might be a while before he could find out anything.

The second thing she did was attempt to breach the firewalls in place at the CIA. She wanted to do some sleuthing on the agent himself. Was there anything in his file that might flag him as a threat? Had he been sanctioned for anything in the past? Had he been involved with any missions that her team would find lacking a sense of morality? The CIA, after all, had been involved with drug running to finance conflicts in the past. Couldn't they be doing something similar now?

She set her custom-designed program running to break in, and minimized it into the background as one of the agents stepped around to see what she was working on. She glared up at him and thought of punching him in the testicles for the intrusion into her space. They were hanging right there, just begging to be used as a speed bag. Instead, she fired off a venomous comment. "Do you mind? I don't like people I don't know looking over my shoulder."

The idiot, who proclaimed himself to be Ted, smiled innocently at her. "I was just wanting to know if you heard from your team yet. Why so defensive? You're not hiding something, are you?"

Abbi clenched her fist, preparing to teach the spy a lesson he wouldn't soon forget, doing everything in her power to restrain herself. "One, you need to lower your voice before you wake Cassie. Two, when I hear from the team, you'll know it because it will come across the speakers in the ceiling. Three, I'm not the spook in the room. You are the ones who conceal things for a living. And four, if you don't back out of the way, you'll find yourself wheezing on the floor and regretting your decisions."

Ted looked down on her. It was the same look she had seen from sexist men her entire life. "Take it easy, sweetheart-" She wasn't sure what the rest of that sentence was going to be, because she cupped his balls in her left hand and squeezed. She stood quickly and followed her move with an open-palmed jab into his face, feeling the man's nose crack with the blow. Still squeezing with her left, she grabbed his shirt collar with her right and twisted him to the floor. Her left hand tightened around his manhood one more good, hard time, and then she released. She stepped back and glanced at Cassie, still out cold in the swing.

Returning her attention to the man on the floor, she said, "Call me sweetheart one more time and I won't be so gentle." Both Brett and the agent called Bill were across the room, their mouths slightly agape with dumbfounded looks on their faces. She shrugged. "I warned him. He didn't listen."

Ted lay writhing on the floor, one hand on his groin and the other covering his bleeding face. "You broke my nose," he exclaimed.

She gave him a sarcastic version of the same smile he had offered her only moments before. "Relax, *sweetheart*, it's an improvement."

Chapter 5: Complications

DJ sat with his team, bobbing in two inflatable boats, watching the massive hull of the Vermont slip silently below the waves. The Captain had listened as promised. In the end, he took a chance, surfaced, and let them off. DJ was warned, however, there may not be a recovery for him when this was all over. He was also told they may not make it to the shore alive. The plan was to sit here for fifteen minutes and let the sub slip away. They would then start the small outboard motors and head for the shore. However, if the Russian sub was closer than they thought, and if they took a peek through their periscope, they would likely call it in. This would mean a patrol boat would intercept them before they even got close to the shore, or a platoon of soldiers would be waiting on the beach to pick them up. None of those scenarios were ideal, but his team took a vote and decided to go for it anyway. The idea of the data drive not being recovered and all of those secrets being auctioned off to the highest bidder was not something they could live with.

DJ checked his watch. It was a little after three in the morning local time. If they managed to not draw the attention of the Russian navy, they were going to be pressed for time to make it to the shore and into the trees before daybreak. It was going to be close. The seas were rough for their tiny boats so it was slow going.

Carbon sat clutching a waterproof backpack, his night-vision goggles making him appear like a frightened praying mantis. "Can't we just go already? Our submarine is gone. They'll never know."

Cash shook his head. "Yes, they will. As soon as we fire up these outboards the sonar will pick it up. The Captain asked for fifteen minutes to get to the bottom. We break our word and he likely won't be here when it's time to go. You want to risk that?"

Coonie chimed in. "The Captain already offered me twenty dollars to leave you behind. I don't think you want to make him madder than he already is."

Carbon smirked at her. "Twenty bucks? Really? That's all I'm worth?"

Connie shook her head and smiled. "Oh, no. I told him you were worth at least fifty."

They waited the allotted time and then headed for shore as fast as the boat could handle it. Thankfully, the swells were with them making the ride smoother than expected. They kept an eye out for other vessels, but saw none. It wasn't long before they could hear the breakers crashing onto the shore. Soon, they were riding one in and beaching their boats. Their GPS kept them on track, and they managed to land precisely where they had intended. Fortune continued to be in their favor. The beach was devoid of life. They wasted no time on arrival. They hoisted the boats and ran for the tree line, burying them in the undergrowth as best they could.

DJ pointed to Doolie. "Alright, Two Names, time to prove yourself. You get a twenty-minute head start. Get to the top of the ridge and get me eyes on that valley and the meet point. We'll wait and then head in. Hopefully, none of these guys are early. Let's hope our luck stays." He directed his next comments to Cash. "Get our comms connected to home. See if Abbi was able to get us an ISR feed for an overhead view." Lastly, he turned his attention to Carbon. "Get your bird in the air."

The bird in question was a specialized drone first put in place by the Navy SEALs. It was a small fixed-wing aircraft fitted with a laser scanner and high-res camera. A battery-powered propeller pulled it through the air when required, but it was specially designed to float on air currents and updrafts like a large, winged bird. In fact, it looked just like one. It was called the Falcon.

The Falcon's primary objective was to soar in the sky mimicking an actual bird. It was even equipped with synthetic feathers that adorned the wings and tail to be both convincing and to enhance flight. A small computer gathered sensor data to process air movement around it. It used this to bank and soar with the winds and updrafts. From twenty-five yards away, it was completely convincing.

SEAL teams and other Tier 1 echelons of the Special Forces utilized the Falcon to gather intel by flying over targets. With its camera, it could zoom in to identify enemy combatants below. With its laser scanner, it could range targets from a distance for guided munitions, or with multiple passes from various angles it could send the information downstream. An accurate computer model of a set of buildings, or a ship, could be used for infiltration assessment. If connected to a 3D printer, they could even build a scale model for assault planning with teams. None of that would be needed here, only the high-resolution camera. Still, it was a specialized tool and Carbon took it on every mission. He even named it Fred.

While Cash and Carbon set up the gear, DJ directed the others to fan out and form a perimeter. It was wasted breath. This wasn't their first rodeo. They were already in motion, slipping through the trees like wraiths.

Latricia Harringer, aka Bounder, paused against a mossy trunk and looked around. There was a thin, but well-worn path before her. Following it left would take her back to the Sea of Japan. She could still hear the waves beating into the shore in the distance. There was a small town nearby. Perhaps this was a trail used by the locals for accessing the beach? She peered first left, her night vision goggles rendering the world in grainy green. There was nothing. To the right revealed two figures, also wearing night-vision goggles. Both were dressed in military fatigues. Both carried Russian AK rifles. Though, oddly, one of them had a second slung over his shoulder. They seemed shocked to see her. The soldiers were rooted in place, unsure of what to do. They were young. They had likely never seen combat. For a quiet second, she almost felt sorry for them.

While taking the lives of the ones involved in the exchange of the drive was encouraged, it had been impressed on them to avoid killing anyone else unless absolutely necessary. Including the Russian military. But what else could she do? If they escaped, every Russian with a gun would be combing these hills. The mission would be compromised. Worse, their weapons were not suppressed like hers. If they even got off a single shot this op would be over before it even got started.

She was well trained, expending great amounts of ammunition. Even easier, her targets weren't moving, standing completely still like two silhouettes at the practice range back at the farm. They were twenty-five meters away. What she did next didn't even require much thought. She snapped the gun up and fired two quick rounds. The .300 Blackout was meant for moments like this. The heavy thirty-caliber rounds made more noise impacting their skulls than her weapon did in firing them. The event was over between heartbeats.

DJ wasn't going to be happy, she thought. She would need to hide the bodies and then check for a radio. Cash spoke Russian. She would hand it off to him and he could monitor any transmissions to see just how screwed they were. But first, she needed to call the boss and inform him of what happened. She opened her mouth to speak, but words never came out. She caught just a hint of movement from her peripheral before she was tackled from the side. She had a fleeting thought, connecting the image of the Russian with two weapons, the second slung over his shoulder. She caught an odor as well before she impacted the ground. It was foul. The smell of bodily waste? Had this third soldier been taking a crap in the woods while his friend held his weapon?

She had certainly been hit harder while on a sparring mat, but in the uneven terrain, she lost her footing and went down on her shoulder, impacting something hard. A rock, maybe, or an exposed root. It took the breath out of her and she felt her arm pop out of the socket, dislocating her shoulder. She instantly let go of her main weapon, her left hand numb and tingly. The AR platform rifle was still strapped to her, but now a body was on top of her, pinning it to her chest. She was struck twice in the face, knocking her goggles down below her chin.

Latricia was wounded, in a bad position below her adversary, and fighting blind. She tried to block the flurry of blows that came at her then, but her left arm wouldn't respond to her commands. If she couldn't find a way to grapple with her opponent effectively, finding an opening or some pressure point to utilize, the person on top of her would beat her into unconsciousness. Carbon had been right. This mission really did suck.

Argo took up a position at the rear, backtracking to the beach, eyes open for hostiles on their six. The breakers made an oscillating and constant roar, masking out the sounds of people, so he made his approach slow and careful. Still hiding within the shelter of the pines, oaks, and elms, he peered out at the beach and was disturbed by what he saw. Two military-looking SUVs approached, running parallel to the water and just inside the flat, wet strip of sand and rock close to the shoreline. They were following each other close and cruising slowly with their lights off. The sun was just beginning to paint the horizon a deep purple, so there wasn't enough ambient light to drive by. This meant the occupants were using night-vision goggles similar to his. Not a good sign. At the closest point to him, they stopped, the noise of the waves covering the sound of the engines. As he watched, eight doors opened, and eight people exited wearing the camouflaged uniforms of the Russian Army.

They didn't seem to be looking for anything in particular; they just got out and congregated in a group. Two of them fired up cigarettes. Three of the soldiers propped their AK rifles with their long banana-shaped magazines against the vehicles. They weren't alarmed by anything, nor did they seem to be looking for the team. It was apparent the approach to the shore was not seen by the Russian sub and radioed in. They seemed to only be socializing. Maybe it was just a routine patrol.

Argo triggered the mic on the strap around his neck. "Hey, boss. We got a problem. I've got eight guns on the beach. They just rolled up in two trucks."

DJ responded on the other end. "Are they looking for us? Talking on a radio?"

"That's a negative," Argo replied. "They're all relaxed. It's like they just paused on their way somewhere to stretch their legs. But the trucks were in blackout and they're wearing night-vision."

There was a pause before DJ replied. "All of them?"

Argo slipped the goggles down and went for a pair of heat sensing/night-vision binoculars. The soldiers jumped closer, their bodies colored in shades of red and orange as the optics picked up the heat. "Every one of them. They're armored up too, wearing plate carriers. They don't have the service issue AKs either. I count seven AKS-74Us and one SV-98. These aren't your run-of-the-mill grunts."

DJ's tone changed on the other end. It was suddenly more tense. "Spetsnaz. If they aren't looking for us, what are they doing here?"

Argo chuckled. "Smoking cigarettes and watching the sunrise. They're not amped up at all."

Another pause by DJ. Then, "Let me know if they move. Carbon's having problems with the Falcon. We'll move out as soon as we can."

Argo looked over the soldiers one more time. "I just had a bad thought. Suppose these guys are perimeter security for the meet going down soon?"

Coonie jumped in on the comms, voicing her opinion from her hiding spot. "Nah, can't be. That would mean our spy friend lied to us again, and this meeting is happening with the Russian Army and not some contractors. I mean, what are the odds Agent Seymour would lie to us twice?"

DJ replied, a hint of anger in his voice. "If that's true, then this will be a wasted trip. We don't have the manpower and I'm not taking on an entire country."

Argo chuckled quietly to himself. He knew DJ too well. The man was a fixer. He appointed himself to right every wrong he confronted. There was no way the man was going to pack up and go home. He might send the team off, but he wasn't going to let this go until he had possession of the drive. Then, and only then, would he head back to the farm. And he wasn't going to let the lies from Agent Seymour go either. Argo felt sorry for the spook. But only just a little. The spy deserved what was coming to him.

He hit the mic again. "Coonie, you got any Russians on your end?"

She replied quickly. "Just trees. Lots of trees and skeeters. If I had me a good cup of Community Coffee it would remind me of home."

Argo nodded and called for Sam. "Doolie, you seen anything?"

Sam answered, his breathing hard from his trek up the steep hill. "No bad guys on my end. Give me a few more minutes to make it to the top. I'll give you the lay of the land. We heard from the farm yet? If they were able to get us a sat feed, that would be better. If Fred's broke, we could use ISR."

Right on cue, Abbi broke in on their comms. "Greetings from West Virginia. You guys are late. I do have a satellite feed for you. Two of Seymour's friends showed up at the farm with satellite access. They're listening in so feel free to bad mouth them all you want. I'm not sure if we're going to get any more help from them, anyway. They're a little mad at me at the moment, but more on that later. I need you to listen up. You're surrounded. I have bad guys around you in a three-mile perimeter. Numerous heat signatures. I even have a few armored personnel carriers. The kind with the big guns on top. I don't know how you managed to get inside the circle without getting caught, but if you so much as sneeze, from this point on my marriage will be long distance only. I doubt very much if our CIA friends will send in a rescue team to a Siberian prison. My advice is to stay where you are and wait for them to leave. The phrase *overwhelming odds* doesn't even begin to describe what I am looking at on my screens."

For the first time, Argo was worried. They would certainly not stand by and do nothing. DJ was too driven. There was no such thing as a lost cause for the man. He didn't know the meaning of the term. And there was no way his team wasn't going to back him up.

Argo called out to Bounder, asking for a sitrep.

There was no answer.

Latricia's hands were bound behind her back. She was nearly blind, staggering through the forest in blackness. Her weapons had been removed. She was dizzy and nauseous, with the taste of blood in her mouth. She likely had a mild concussion. As she was shoved down the dirt path, pistol pressed against the base of her skull, moving steadily away from her team, she knew just how much trouble she was in. She could only assume she was being led to where the soldiers had come from. There would be more of them, she was sure. They would discuss the implications of her being here in these woods. Then they would sound the alarm. There would be an all-out search for more of her kind. They would close in on her team. They would be tortured, questioned, and killed. She could not let that happen, but she was unsure of how to prevent it.

The man behind her shoving her down the trail had not used a radio. Right then, she still had a chance. If she could somehow overcome her captor, she might avert a catastrophe. But how? She could barely make out the darker shapes of trees as she stumbled along. Her hands were locked behind her. Her shoulder was dislocated. Curious, she tested her bonds. They felt plastic, like zip strips. Under the right conditions, she could break them. But not with one arm out of socket. And how to deal with the gun to her head?

She lost her footing and went down. She did her best to roll with the fall, but failed, gritting her teeth, and groaning from the impact, her shoulder the receiving end of a thousand daggers of pain. Her captor grabbed her by her ponytail of braids and hauled her back to her feet. She wanted to scream in pain. She couldn't. Sure, it would alert DJ and the others to her situation, but it might also alert whoever awaited her on the other end of the path. She wanted to shout in anger and launch herself at the brute behind her. She couldn't. The hard truth was she wasn't physically able.

Her brain turned over every possible scenario she could think of, searching for a way out. It wasn't there. It didn't exist. Without warning, she was shoved out of the trees and onto a gravel road. She was out of time. She could see better here, though barely. The canopy above her thinned, and she could make out a large truck, but precious little else. The sun was beginning its climb from beyond the ocean behind her, but it was still past the horizon. Soon, dawn would bathe this forest in dappled light. But for now, it was still too dark to see much of anything.

A voice spoke in front of her, gruff and deep. She could not make out what was said. She didn't understand Russian. Someone fired up a lighter in front of her, sticking the end of a cigarette into the yellow flame. Counting the soldier behind her, there were three of them. Her captor spoke, furious and hissing. She wasn't sure what he was saying, but she caught the gist. He was explaining what had happened. In the glow of the cigarette, she could tell the other two were surprised. Surprise was replaced with anger. She had killed their comrades, their friends. The one smoking turned and opened the cab door, reached inside and dragging out a handheld radio. This wasn't good, she thought. He was about to report in. The mission was dead; her team would be found.

As he held the radio up, preparing to speak, she heard a familiar sound. Metal slapped against metal, along with what sounded like a brief release of high-pressured air. In the silence of the wooded road, it was far louder than anything depicted in movies, but there was no doubt what it was. She was quite acquainted with it as a part of her life. It was the sound of .300 Blackout with subsonic rounds being fired from a suppressed AR15. The man with the radio tipped forward, his forehead colliding hard with the frame of the truck door. She relaxed her knees and dropped into the road, desperate to avoid being collateral damage. Two more identical sets of noises and the other two lay dead about her.

She wheezed out a thank you through gritted teeth, her shoulder screaming in pain. "God bless you, DJ Slaughter. I am so thankful you can shoot."

The reply made her grin from ear to ear despite her suffering. Bettie Walden, the short and stout redneck woman from Louisiana, answered instead. "Only a coonass could run through these woods without making a sound. That ape-sized fool is still somewhere behind me."

Chapter 6: Hammer Time

After DJ popped Bounder's shoulder back into place, he looked her over for other injuries. Other than having a fat lip, swollen eyebrow, and other contusions, she was OK. She was definitely still in the fight. When Bounder had gone silent, Abbi had used the satellite feed's thermal imaging to locate and rescue her. He stood with Coonie on the gravel next to the Russian truck, considering their options. The Sheriff and Carbon were back with the gear, and Doolie Two Names was on the ridge surveying the meet point. They were awaiting his orders. He wasn't sure what orders to give.

Nothing was looking like it was supposed to on this operation. A meeting was scheduled to go down in just a short while. A small team, contracted to steal a data drive loaded with top-secret plans, was supposed to hand it off to a unit of North Koreans who had crossed the porous border into a narrow strip of Russia. DJ was supposed to ambush that handoff, take the drive back, and slip out to sea to meet up with the Vermont. So far, none of that was close to reality.

The Russian Army had set up a perimeter surrounding the meeting location. This could only mean the handoff was happening with the Russians and not the North Koreans. DJ and his team had either been lied to by Agent Seymour, or the contracted thieves found a more lucrative financial opportunity by selling the drive to the Russians. In either case, DJ and his small group were outnumbered and surrounded. Their exit was cut off, and even if they could fight their way through and make it back to the ocean, they would never make the six-mile journey without being intercepted. Even if *that* were possible, the Vermont might not even be there waiting.

Brett and Abbi were on the other end of the comms safely ensconced at the farm, instructing them to lay low, wait until the meeting was over, and then bug out after the hand-off had concluded. The two CIA agents with them were heard pitching a fit in the background, saying something should be done, reminding them this was what they had been contracted to do, threatening them with a promise never to use them again. DJ's team on the ground with him remained silent. He was in charge. Whatever he decided, they would follow his lead. The problem was, the choices only presented bleak options. What they needed was a Plan B.

DJ looked at the truck, the two female warriors with him, and down the road towards the meeting location. decisions, decisions. Go into hiding, or face off against overwhelming odds? DJ wasn't opposed to hiding. Certain situations demanded it. Still, at the moment, it didn't feel right. Compounding that feeling, something was beginning to nag at DJ, chewing on the back of his brain like a dog with a shoe. Something wasn't right. Something was off. He needed to see this through and uncover the mystery of what it was.

DJ keyed his mic. "Doolie, head back and meet up with the others. Sheriff, I think it's time to drop the hammer."

Argo's reply came across the earpiece tucked in DJ's ear. "I have been waiting for months to say this: *Stop*! Hammer time!"

Russia sucked when it came to building roads, Do Hyun thought. Still, it was better than where he was from. North Korea had to be the worst. It was the first thing that amazed him after sneaking out of his home country. The roads almost everywhere else were spectacular by comparison. Oh, sure, the streets were pristine around the capital city of Pyongyang. Image was everything to the potbellied dictator. But leave the city and it all deteriorated quickly. Roads that were considered highways in North Korea, were like dirt tracks in America. Unless they were direct routes to a military base, North Korean roads saw almost no state maintenance.

Do Hyun had become something of a connoisseur of roads since becoming a spy for the tiny country. He rated all he traveled, critiquing them on smoothness, drainage, width, etc. The one he was on now, meandering its way through the tree-covered hills of eastern Russia, was a three on his scale. Although it was listed as a main road on the map, it was nothing more than a two-lane gravel path. Few people used it, preferring the four-lane concrete and asphalt highway running parallel just a few miles from here. The only reason he chose this route was because of the meeting he was attending. It was at an intersection just up ahead, where two dirt and rock paths happened to bump into each other in the middle of thick forests.

Do Hyun wished he could take advantage of the cell phone-sized data drive he had in his possession. It was worth a great deal more than he was selling it for. The only problem was he didn't have the cash or resources for breaking the encryption and obtaining the information locked inside. And even if he tried, word would get out. Someone would talk. Every criminal entity would be out to kill him and take the drive for themselves. It was bad enough that Do Hyun was soon to become a wanted man by his government, but to have every greedy person with a gun hunting for him was more than he could handle. No, this was far better. Sell it to the Russian, and he and the other five members in this rusting van could retire to an island somewhere. Sand, sun, bikini-clad women, and unpronounceable drinks with brightly colored umbrellas were all he craved. Let the Russian deal with cracking the code. Word would get out, as it always did, and North Korea would put a hit out on the man. When that happened, all attention on Do Hyun would vanish. At least he hoped.

The road ahead curved and he arrived at the intersection. He was the first one here. This was good. It meant the Russian had not the time to set up an ambush. Even if he had, Do Hyun had a failsafe to make sure he walked out of here alive with his suitcases of cash.

They parked in the middle of the road just shy of the intersection and exited from the van, waiting for the other party to arrive. They didn't have long to wait. Soon, Do Hyun heard the sound of approaching vehicles. When they pulled through the tunnel of trees in the dim grey of early morning, his pulse doubled. This was it. They were leaving here rich, or they were going to die in the eastern forests of Russia, no one knowing what happened to them.

There were three vehicles in the small convoy. The first two were military trucks. They sat high up on off-road tires, a single cab in front, and a canvas-covered bed behind. They were the types used for troop transport or hauling supplies. No doubt there were ten to fifteen armed soldiers in the back, all cold killers with itchy trigger fingers. Wasn't that the American expression? Being outgunned didn't concern him. It was the occupant in the third vehicle, an expensive silver German luxury SUV, that had his attention. The man inside would dictate how this meeting went. He would try to take the drive by force, issuing commands to his small army to open fire, or he would produce great piles of cash in bags and honor his end of the deal. Do Hyun would find out soon enough.

The first truck stopped just short of the intersection on the opposite side, pulling over as far as it could. The second performed a similar move, parking even with the first on the weed-covered shoulder. The SUV idled slowly into the middle slot in the center of the gravel track. As expected, soldiers swarmed out the back of the two trucks with AKs, helmets, and plate-carrying vests with ammo pouches in front. If they decided to open fire at once, Do Hyun and his crew would be turned into mounds of red goo in short order.

The soldiers formed a wall of armament in front of the vehicles, a skirmish line. Only then did the driver's door of the SUV open. An officer stepped out with creased pants and pressed jacket. He placed his hat on his head and then opened the rear driver-side door for General Alexander Abramov, the man who had offered great sums of money for the small box still sitting in the van.

General Abramov stepped forward and the wall of guns in front of him parted to allow him through. He was a lengthy man with chiseled Slavic features. He stood proud in the middle of the road with his piercing blue eyes and his practiced air of authority. He surveyed Do Hyun's small team for a moment, then spoke in Russian. "You have my drive?"

Do Hyun smiled and gestured to the line of soldiers, answering in Russian. "So many men. One would think you have come to take the drive and not pay me. That would be less than honorable."

The general smiled. "Now why would you lie to yourself like that? Neither of us are honorable men. I have your money." He held up a hand and motioned over his shoulder. Behind him, his driver lifted the rear hatch of the SUV. A moment later and he walked forward, shouldering three large duffle bags. The man passed through the wall of soldiers until he was standing in the center of the intersection. He dropped all three, turned, and retreated back to the driver's door of the SUV.

Do Hyun nodded to one of his men. His partner-in-crime walked quickly to the bags and unzipped one, reaching in and grabbing a stack of bills. He held the bundle of euros up for Do Hyun to see before dropping it back in. He started to sling one over his shoulder, but the Russian raised his voice. "Not yet. I have shown you mine. Now you must show me yours." His friend retreated from the bags and walked back to the side of the van. Sliding open the rear door, he retrieved a small black case and returned to the middle of the intersection. He unlatched it and held it open, waiting. This was where it got tricky, Do Hyun thought to himself.

This time the General's driver produced a small laptop computer and a coiled green cable from the backseat. He returned to the middle of the intersection and connected the drive inside the box to the computer, looked at the screen for a few seconds, then turned and nodded to the General. The General nodded back and motioned for him to bring it over.

It was time for Do Hyun to make his play. He called out in Russian while raising a small cylindrical device he had concealed over his head. "Not so fast, General. I am sure you would never consider killing us and taking the drive, but to be certain one of your men does not take matters into their own hands, I have implanted an explosive into the box. If I press this trigger, not only will it destroy the device, but it will make a mess of your driver. The bomb is now armed." A small red light began flashing on the front of the box and Do Hyun's partner closed it and latched it closed. "Open the box, and it goes off. I press this button and it goes off. We will take your money and drive away. Try to follow us, and I press the button. Shoot at my van, and I press the button. If for any reason I think I am in danger, I press the button. I think you understand."

General Abramov laughed. "And just where do you think you will escape to?"

Do Hyun lowered his hand. "Do you not think I have planned for an escape much as I have planned for your deception? General, I have read your file. I know you to be an intelligent man. That drive is worth many more times what is in those bags. Be smart. Let us both walk away from here wealthy men."

The General didn't have time to respond. Another truck approached from the east, from down the twisted and pitted road that led towards the ocean. It bounced and rocked along slowly, just another Russian military truck like the two before him. As if the other two loaded with soldiers wasn't enough. This wasn't going how he had hoped. Still, he had to believe the General in front of him would not sacrifice the drive still waiting in the intersection with his comrade and the General's driver. Unless, of course, Abramov believed him to be bluffing. It would be a mistake. Do Hyun never bluffed. In his experience as a spy, bluffing seldom paid off.

The truck, its wheels grinding into the gravel, came to a slow halt just before reaching the intersection. Unlike the others, the engine didn't shut off as another Russian soldier exited the driver's side, slinging his AK over his shoulder and adjusting the low slung pistol strapped to his leg. He held a hand up and took two steps closer. A quick glance at the General and his men told Do Hyun something was off.

Abramov barked at the newcomer, agitation in his voice. "Why are you not at your post?"

The man looked at them both and then replied to the General in perfect English, another language that Do Hyun spoke. "Sorry, I don't understand Russian. I know the military leadership makes learning English a requirement, so I assume you understand me." He then focused on Do Hyun. "Can you understand me as well?"

Do Hyun nodded as Abramov advanced a step, clearly both curious and angry. The Russian replied to the newcomer in English. "I would have thought the CIA would have required you to learn Russian. Especially if they were going to send a spy into my country. Spies are shot here in Russia, especially when they are caught wearing the uniform of the Russian Army. Before I make that a harsh reality for you, I am curious as to why you so foolishly interrupted my meeting."

The stranger smiled and nodded, but held up a finger, signaling the General to wait a moment. He then turned to Do Hyun. "My name is DJ but I am no spy. I've been hired to recover the drive. I'm here to help you out. You know he's not going to let you leave here with that money, right?"

Do Hyun glanced at the General and back. "The drive is wired with a bomb. I press this and he loses it"

The American nodded and addressed both Abramov and Do Hyun. "I can make both of you a better offer." One where the thief and the Russian both get what they value most. He pointed to Do Hyun. "You get to leave here with the money," he then pointed to General Abramov. "And you get to leave here with your life."

The Russian was incredulous at this lone stranger facing down over a dozen armed commandos. He turned to his men. "Kill him." His men raised their weapons as one and pointed at the lunatic American. They never got off a shot. There was a brief moment of a whooshing sound, and Do Hyun caught a glimpse of something racing from the heavens, just a blur of motion. Whatever it was crashed through the hood of the luxury SUV. It was instantly followed by an explosion, sending flames and shards of metal into and through the group of men in front, killing them in an instant and rendering both trucks alongside useless.

The shockwave tore across the intersection, knocking both the driver and Do Hyun's friend flat. Do Hyun and the rest of his men were sent staggering backward from the blast. He recovered his footing and focused on what was left of the Russians. Their bodies were scattered about, broken, lifeless and charred. The SUV was split nearly in two, and all three vehicles were burning. In the middle of the intersection, his fellow spy was dead, a piece of what looked to be an AK47 barrel protruded from his face. The driver was moving, his legs slowly kicked the gravel and a moan could be heard. It didn't last long. The unmistakable sound of a suppressed weapon fired from Do Hyun's right and the man flinched and moved no more.

Do Hyun turned to face the American, raising the trigger to his bomb. "I'll do it. You will get nothing."

The man casually lowered his silenced pistol to his side and shrugged. "Doesn't matter to me if it's destroyed, but I *am* under orders to bring it back. I get paid either way, but still, I'm obligated to try. This can still end well for you but we're running out of time. There's likely to be over a hundred more of those guys headed here now. I would like to be gone when that happens. All you have to do is drop that trigger, grab your money, and head out of here. I only care about the drive. You have five seconds to decide or you die too."

Do Hyun glanced at the man's weapon held low and next to his thigh, pointing at the ground. He looked at his own men, all had pistols out and ready. "Do you really think you can kill me before I hit this button?"

The American regarded him for a moment. Then, "Do you know what the apricot is?" Do Hyun blinked. What was he talking about, he wondered? Was he insane? The stranger continued. "There's a place where your brain stem connects to your spinal column. Snipers for the ARMY Rangers call it the apricot. Shoot you there, and you won't be pressing any buttons."

Do Hyun glared at the man. "You really think you're that fast, that accurate, that you can shoot me in this apricot from twenty-five meters away?"

The American shook his head and pointed to his left. "No, I'm going to kill the rest of your friends. The guy hiding in the bushes with the AR15 will shoot you. Three seconds."

Do Hyun looked to where the man pointed. There, deep in the shadow of low hanging branches, a man-sized shape stood next to a tree, pointing a rifle at him.

The American spoke again. "Last chance."

Do Hyun paused, thinking. And then he thought nothing ever again. There was just darkness. Impossible darkness. Do Hyun floated alone in an inky black darker than night. The world was gone forever.

Chapter 7: Death & Betrayal

DJ managed to take out all the others but one. Cash ended him in the same manner as he had the ringleader with the trigger for the bomb. "Get a bag of that cash," he instructed his stoic teammate. "We never know when that will come in handy. Take the other two and scatter it out on the road."

DJ didn't go out of his way to confiscate money from the people they killed but leaving duffle bags of euros lying in the middle of a remote section of Russian wilderness just seemed foolish. This wasn't the first time they had done it either. There was plenty of opportunities to spend it on gear, bribe the locals of whatever country they were working in, or even to pad their retirements. If he were greedy, he would have told Cash to grab all three. That wasn't prudent. They would have trouble transporting so much money, and the other bags of scattered cash might come in handy in slowing down the troops on their way in. Seeing large sums of money just lying on the road could be a distraction. Any minute DJ and his team could delay a pursuit might mean the difference in life or death.

DJ snatched the box with the drive. Next, he raced over to the body of the North Korean and retrieved the detonator as well.

Cash seemed concerned. "Is taking that thing really wise?"

DJ nodded, heading back to the truck. "Carbon may need it to figure out how to disarm the bomb." The small cylinder had a button protected by a flip-over cover. He closed it as soon as he picked it up. The last thing they needed was to blow themselves up on the way out of here.

He started the truck, then pulled forward into the intersection and did a U-turn to head back to the beach, glancing at the smoldering remains of the dead Russians as he spun the truck around. The Hammer had certainly done its job. Too bad they had only elected to carry one with them.

The Hammer rocket was a recent addition to their armament, courtesy of Agent Ali. It could be fired line-of-sight, or it could be launched from behind cover and guided in with a laser targeting system, which was what had been done here. The Sheriff had fired it from near the beach, aiming it into the sky, and Carbon had guided it in using the repaired Falcon drone circling overhead.

Before that could happen, the rest of the team had to take out the Russian commandos on the beach. They were too close and would have spotted the rocket launch, giving away the team's location. Coonie, Bounder, Doolie, and Sheriff easily took out the eight Spetznas relaxing by their truck. The element of surprise was a powerful weapon.

The road DJ was on dead-ended before reaching the ocean. They had to navigate the same thin trail Bounder had been dragged down to reach the beach. The rest of the team was ready and waiting on the shore with the gear loaded and the Zodiac inflatables ready to shove off. Even though it was now approaching 0630, the plan was to head out to sea and hope they weren't spotted in their small craft. They would turn on their transponders so the Vermont would be able to detect them with their towed antennae array.

DJ and his team would travel the six miles out to sea and then wait. He didn't know if the sub would be waiting for him, nor did he know if it would risk breaking the surface in the daylight. They might have to float all day hoping to not be found by a Russian patrol boat. If that were so, Carbon was going to be a nightmare to live with, a chatterbox of complaints. He would need to keep the hacker's brain occupied.

DJ handed off the box with the drive to Carbon as soon as they reached the beach, giving him instructions to see if he could break in. He didn't trust Agent Seymour to be truthful about the contents. They had already been lied to. The claim about having a SEAL team escort for infil and exfil had been egregious enough. DJ was pretty sure the man had already known about the Russian general too. The agent had sent his team into an impossible situation with a small force. There had to be a reason why, and he wanted to know what it was before they got back. DJ warned Carbon of the explosive. He instructed Carbon to see if he could hack in, despite having been warned it would take a quantum computer to do so.

For no other reason than DJ just didn't want to deal with Carbon's complaining, he had the hacker, Sheriff, and Bounder in one boat with Doolie driving. DJ, Cash, and Coonie took the other one with the gear. Coonie offered to drive, but DJ was in a foul mood and took over the rear seat with the outboard motor. He checked the gas tank. If he calculated correctly, they would get to their meet point with a quarter of a tank to spare. They wouldn't have enough to make it across the Sea of Japan, but they could limp back to shore if the Vermont never showed.

Seas were rougher than he would have liked. It slowed their progress, but it also helped to conceal them from other boats that might appear on the horizon. As DJ led the way, he occasionally glanced back at the other boat to make sure they were keeping pace. He could make out Carbon hard at work trying to accomplish his task. DJ wasn't sure if this was wise or not. The first hurdle Carbon had to overcome was to disable the bomb. Trying to disarm an explosive device while bouncing around in a boat seemed foolish, but DJ knew the hacker would never tackle anything he couldn't handle. If Carbon was working on it, it must mean the task didn't require tiny tools and a delicate hand. It was probable the hand trigger could turn it off as simply as it had been turned on. Regardless, DJ trusted Carbon's abilities and instincts.

Carbon sat in the middle seat and waited until they were well away from the shore before looking at his new treasure. He lived for new tech. The creativity of others inspired him. Combine that with his love of uncovering secrets, and he had trouble restraining himself for too long. The explosive itself wasn't that sophisticated. It appeared to be activated by a simple radio transmitter. When he unscrewed the bottom of the trigger and removed the battery, the light on the front of the box stopped flashing. Apparently, proximity was the key. If the radio connection was broken, the bomb ceased to function. He slipped the trigger and the battery into a vest pocket and examined the storage container more closely. It was a thick case made of an impact-resistant plastic/polymer combination. It was the kind meant to ensure the protection of the gear stored inside even if it was tossed down the side of a mountain. He could see no other indication on the outside of the box that any secondary triggers had been wired to the hinges. He took a deep breath and popped the latches.

Next to him, Argo took in a deep breath and slapped a hand down onto the lid, worry lines becoming more prominent in his leather-like face. "You sure about this, kid?" he asked. "Why not wait until we get it back to the sub. Let yourself get a better look. And why risk getting it wet?"

Carbon glanced at him and grinned. "I know what I'm doing, Gramps. Chill." Argo hesitated before removing his hand, those worry lines still deeply furrowed.

Carbon flipped the lid open without worry. His reasoning was simple: The design was all about letting the men who delivered it escape before the recipients could open it. With the light on the front no longer flashing, it would signal whoever had possession of the box it was now safe to retrieve the drive inside. Sure enough, Carbon found a plunger inside that would have been depressed with the lid closed. Opening it prematurely would have completed the circuit and turned their small craft into floating debris, and their reducing their bodies to chum for the sharks.

Carbon laughed. "See, I told you I know what I'm doing." The inside was lined with dark gray foam, cushioning the contents. The data device inside was nothing more than a standard-looking portable hard drive. Which was curious. Agent Seymour had made it sound like the thing was state of the art. This looked like something he could have ordered online and had delivered the next day. It surely didn't mean there wasn't some serious encryption technology going on inside. Maybe the drive had been disguised to fool the casual eye? There was only one way to find out.

He pulled out his tablet. The case it was in served to protect it from the water, sand, and other debris. The first thing he did was to see if the drive had a power source by looking for an EM or electromagnetic field. It did. A quick search found it was WiFi-enabled as well. This meant no cables needed to be connected to access the contents. Carbon went ahead and resealed the protective box to keep it from getting wet. Leaving it sitting on his lap, he linked to it easily with his tablet and began to search. What he found surprised him. There was encryption on it, but not anything that would require a quantum computer as was promised. In fact, he was certain he could crack it easily. This both intrigued him, feeding his curiosity, and scared the bat crap out of him. Was DJ right? Was this mission all one big lie?

He applied one of his programs to attempt to crack the code and allow him in. Turning to Argo, he said, "Something's not right. This is too easy. I'm starting to think maybe the people who tried to sell this to the Russian were lying to them. There's probably just recipes or some grandmother's diary on here."

Shockingly, without much wait, he was suddenly in. He blinked in surprise and began looking through the contents. There was a series of folders with unique names. They were names he recognized. There was also a simple text file. He open it and nearly fainted at what he saw. Carbon sat there staring, not moving, dumbfounded. Argo watched him, waiting. Finally, after a long few seconds, Carbon turned to Argo to tell him what he was looking at when something in his peripheral caught his eye.

It was Sam. He was pointing his pistol at him. "Drop it at my feet," he ordered, the promise of murder smoldering in his eyes. Carbon didn't even hesitate. He did exactly as instructed, dropping the case onto the bottom of the boat at Sam's feet. It was only then he noticed Argo was aware of the betrayal too. A glance at the older man showed that he was angry at Carbon's obedience. But what else could Carbon do? He was no hero. He was no warrior like the rest of this bunch. His battleground was a field of ones and zeros. Yet the look in Argo's eyes told him everything. He had just given up the only leverage they had. Sam was going to kill him now. The intent was evident in the man's heated stare. Their newest recruit had shed his polite persona. What sat at the back of the boat, working the throttle on the small outboard, was a villain who operated with no remorse. He was going to kill Carbon, Argo, and Latricia. His weapon was silenced. DJ and the others just up ahead wouldn't hear a thing. Sam would then power up behind them and shoot them all in the back. He was nothing more than a thief. A murderous thief.

And poor Latricia. She was sitting at the bow, eyes focused ahead, clueless of the treachery behind her. She would never see it coming. Carbon's eyes cut to the rolling waves. Not long ago, he been convinced he would die out here. Then, his focus had been on the silent predators who called these waters home. He had been wrong. It would not be the sharks that ended his life, it would be the traitor pretending to be their friend.

The boat hit a larger swell and the bow rocked up and then down. Carbon watched as the action caused Sam's aim to first drop, pointing at Carbon's waist, then rise again to point over his head as the inflatable crested the wave. It was then that Argo moved. His friend did not go for his gun. There was no hope for that. No amount of speed could have allowed him to draw and fire. Instead, Argo lunged sideways, embracing Carbon in a bear-like hug, and shoving them both over the side. Before the cold water enveloped him, Carbon saw the pistol recoil twice, heard the muffled bark of the report, felt Argo grunt from pain. Then, Carbon reflexively closed his eyes as the deep blue of the Sea of Japan closed over his head.

———————

DJ had been shot many times. Too many. He had been fortunate so far. He was fortunate again. He felt the impact of a round between his shoulder blades. The synthetic plate on the back of his vest protected him, doing its job, keeping him alive. It didn't mean the strike didn't hurt. It did. A lot. A trip to a chiropractor would be in order after they got back. Still, from his experience, he could tell the bullet was on the smaller side and slow. A larger thirty caliber round from an AK, for example, would have knocked him flat, broken a rib or two, and had him trying to remember how to breathe. He was thankful.

DJ shoved the outboard motor throttle away from him to the right, causing the boat to make a hard left. Turning his head to find the source, he was shocked into inaction. The second Zodiac was empty save for Doolie, and the newbie was firing his sidearm at him. They had been betrayed from within. Doolie had killed the others and was now focused on the first boat. DJ's brain was torn between wanting to know why and fighting back. A second bullet whipped past. A third punched through his boat and whistling air could be heard. A fourth caused Coonie to curse. A fifth struck the water in front of him, then skipped through the boat and grazed his leg, causing him to wince in pain. More leaking air could be detected.

DJ snapped out of it, released the throttle, and drew his trusty pistol. His first shot went wide. His second went low and into the water. The rolling ocean and pitching boats provided unstable platforms for the shooters, with moving targets that bobbed unpredictably. His third passed just left of Doolie's head. An answering round just nicked the front of DJ's gun. Sparks flew and tiny shards peppered the side of his face. The gun was twisted violently in his hand from the impact and burning pain flashed through his wrist, spraining it. DJ dropped the ruined weapon and reached for his rifle. As he did, he could hear Cash and Coonie finally start firing back. He also heard the other boat motor rev to peak power as Doolie decided it was time to go.

Their boat was doing a slow spin in the ocean, and when he brought his weapon up, both Cash and Coonie blocked his view. Doolie was at full throttle and racing away. DJ snatched the throttle back and twisted, eager to pursue, but it was Coonie that gave him pause. She pointed to the right and shouted. DJ's head twisted in response. At first, he saw nothing. But then he caught sight of two bodies floating in the water fifty yards away at the peak of a swell, arms waving.

DJ couldn't pursue. He had friends in the water. Friends who might be bleeding out and dying. He barked at the other two to patch the boat, and then pulled on the outboard to turn into the direction of his floating teammates.

The Zodiac was equipped with a compressed air cylinder for inflating the raft. If the pressure valve sensed a leak, it automatically began to pump air into the raft. The boat was also outfitted with a patch kit. There were several large squares that looked like rubberized Band-Aids. Their sticky surface would bond even if they were wet and soaking. Both Cash and Coonie got to work and DJ steered towards his floating friends.

He lost sight of them for a moment as they passed on the other side of a wave. When they came back into view, he could tell their issue was serious. Carbon was frantically waving with one arm. The other was wrapped around Argo. The Sheriff wasn't moving. He was floating in a relaxed state with his head leaned back onto Carbon.

DJ gunned the throttle, urging the craft to move quicker. When he finally reached them, DJ could feel his anger pushed to the boiling point. Carbon was OK. Argo was breathing and awake, but there was a pool of blood in the water around him. He had been shot. Maybe multiple times. The Sheriff pointed weakly to his left side but said nothing.

DJ and Cash hauled the wounded man over the side and Argo let out a long groan of pain. Once in the boat, DJ rolled him onto his back, the man's legs hanging over the side. He began to examine his friend and found two bullet holes in his left side below the ribs. The vests they wore offered no protection under the arms. That was precisely where Doolie had chosen to shoot him. The wounds were low and toward the front. There was a chance nothing vital had been hit. It all depended on the angle of the wound tracks.

Coonie finished patching the boat and hauled Carbon in next. As DJ worked to free the Sheriff of the vest, he snapped a question to Carbon. "Where's Bounder?" The wide-eyed hacker said nothing. He simply shrugged.

Coonie stood in the rocking boat, balancing herself with the rocking waves, scanning the ocean. "Lost Sam. Don't see him at all." The pitching sea made it hard to spot things on the surface. It wouldn't matter even if they *could* see him. Loaded down as they were, they would never be able to catch up. "There!" she exclaimed, pointing behind to the rear. DJ turned, expecting to find the traitor skipping across the water like a smooth stone in the distance. Instead, he saw a floating body. An unmoving, lifeless body.

DJ whipped the boat around. He feared the worse. He got exactly that. Latricia was dead. She had never seen it coming, clueless of the fate that awaited her. The bullet entered the back of her head and exited from just above her right eye.

DJ was as mad as he had ever been. He had not experienced this level of frustration in some time. Every one of those moments had been associated with the death of someone close. He found himself clenching his fists and gritting his teeth. The rage was building in him, making his face warm. His heart was pounding. There was no way to release it. He was surrounded only by those he cared for, and miles upon miles of water. He looked around, seeking something to break. It was then he noticed Cash was bleeding from the arm. Coonie had a nasty gash on her cheek, a narrow miss for a headshot by their traitor.

But why? Why had Sam Kenny done this? To sell the drive to some other party? And how did he possibly think he could get away? The only place within range of his tiny boat was a Russian fishing town on the coast. He might not even be able to reach that. Could he speak Russian? It hadn't been included in the man's file. There was no escape for the man. Dressed as he was, armed as he was, Sam Kenny would be captured or shot as soon as he could make landfall. Especially now that the entire Russian Army was looking for them.

There were too many questions. There were no answers.

DJ pointed at Carbon. "I know the comms package was on the other boat but use your satellite phone and call the farm. I need to speak to Brett."

Chapter 8: Murder, Capture, and Escape

Abbi didn't like how she had lost contact with Ali. True, the man had said he was busy, but he wasn't considered a field agent anymore. He coordinated things. He didn't go on missions. What could be going on that was intense enough for him not to spend ten seconds and reply? The longer this waiting stretched on, the more she became convinced that something much bigger than what they could see was bearing down on them like a fanged monster. The longer the wait, the more distrust she had for the two agents who had invaded their farm under the claims of "helping." Don't even get her started on Agent Seymour. The man was hiding something. She was now sure of it. And where had he disappeared to? He had sent her team off on their objective but didn't make the trip with them. Why wasn't he here instead of Bill and Ted? With something so big at play, she would have thought the man would have wanted to stay close to the operation in some way. Where was he? What was he up to? Was he really who he said he was, despite the assurance of Agent Ali?

To learn more about who the mysterious Agent Seymour really was, Abbi had a program running in the background designed to break into the CIA's classified personnel files. To make this process faster, she had hacked into MIT's supercomputer and employed its big brain to crunch her custom code. She wasn't sure how long it would take, but it couldn't come soon enough. The mystery was killing her.

The men in the room were all focused on the large screen, watching the team with a commandeered satellite as they made their way out to sea to meet with the Vermont. There were no other vessels close, and it looked like they would have no issues. That's when things abruptly changed and spun her life around. Two people were falling into the water out of the rear boat. Abbi hastily stood from her desk and walked to stand with the others, suddenly anxious for an entirely new reason. Before she could stand even with the others in front of the wall-sized screen, whoever was in the front of the boat fell forward into the water and the raft ran over the top of them. Abbi's heart was galloping in her chest and a knot appeared in her stomach. The camera view wasn't close enough to distinguish who was who in the boats. The satellite was of an older design and the resolution was not as good as some of the more sophisticated models in orbit. Additionally, there was sporadic cloud cover often rendering the image hazy as it struggled to see through the partial covering.

Brett was sitting on the edge of his wheelchair. "Who was that?" he demanded. Abbi didn't respond. She didn't know. He had as much information as she did.

She found herself easing closer to the screen, squinting her eyes, struggling to make out the identity of the occupants. As she watched, it appeared the one driving the second boat was pointing at the group in the first. No, they were firing! Whoever was driving the second raft was shooting at the occupants of the first! It made no sense. She looked on in horror, aware that a moan of despair had escaped her lips. She couldn't help herself. She couldn't tell who was who, or why one was killing the others. In shock, she could only watch as the first boat took a hard left. The one driving the lead boat began firing back. It was DJ. She was sure of it. Suddenly he seemed to recoil and hunch over. He had been hit!

Anger, fear, and confusion welled up within her and she shouted at the screen, her hands wrapped into fists, desperate to help in some way. But she couldn't. She was stuck here, thousands of miles away on the other side of the planet, powerless to do anything but watch and pray.

The others in the first boat seem to finally realize what was going on and began firing at the lone member of the rear raft. Whoever it was, veered off and began powering away. The screen flickered for a moment and then went black. A pop-up window appeared in the middle of the screen that read: Connection Lost. Brett shouted at her, "Get it back!"

She spun on her heels, prepared to do just that, but froze. In her focus, she hadn't noticed both Bill and Ted had backed away from the screen. Bill had his pistol out and pointing at them, a smile on his demented face. Ted was all the way to the rear of the room, standing behind Abbi's desk. One hand was still on the keyboard of her computer. The other was wrapped around his own gun. It was pointing at the still sleeping Cassie, clueless of the chaos that had descended on the world around her.

Bill chuckled softly at seeing the desperate fear wash over her face. "Well, I guess we don't need you two anymore." He sighted down the barrel at Abbi's face. There was no concern for her safety. She had forgotten about what had happened on the screen behind her, her worry for her team and husband a distant memory. Her only thought was of Cassie. Would they kill her? If not, who would care for her? Would DJ be able to find his way to his daughter? Just when she was sure Bill would pull the trigger, a ringing phone broke the silence of the room like a hammer does glass. He paused and held up a finger to her. "Hold that thought," he said. He fished his cell phone out of his jacket pocket and answered. "This is Bill." There was a long moment as he listened to the other end. Then, "I see. Understood." He hung up and put the phone away. "Well, it seems that since some of your team survived you still might have some value." He shifted the gun to Brett. "You, however... Well, let's just say three's a crowd." The gun went off twice, impossibly loud.

Abbi jerked her head to the left to see Brett looking down in wonder at the two bullet holes punched through his starched white dress shirt, and the expanding circles of red around them. She was crouching next to him then, shouting his name, a taloned fist of pain clutching her heart.

He looked up at her, sorrow in his eyes. He spoke then, softly, almost a whisper. "Whatever happens next is my fault. Should have never taken the job. I'm sorry."

She gripped his hand, fury, and sadness rolling through her. "It's not your fault. And I promise you, they'll pay." He offered a weak smile, tears forming at the corner of his eyes. Then, gradually, bit by bit, they glassed over, the light to his soul dimming. It was the same look her mother had given her long ago as she lay dying in Abbi's arms. And then, Brett's eyes closed forever.

A single tear tracked slowly down his left cheek.

Brett Allen Foster was dead.

Alimayu Salana finally had an opportunity, his first chance at escape. All he had been hoping for until now had been a chance. That was all he had here. A chance. He had been captured, fairly easily, too. One never expected an attack to come from within, from someone on your own side of the playing field. Certainly not from your own organization. Never from a friend. Yet there he was, tied to a chair, beaten and battered by someone he had once called a friend.

It had started simple enough. "Hey," Seymour had said one day over coffee. "Guess what I found out." From that started a conversation about acquired intelligence concerning a foreign power. It transitioned into a "what if" scenario. It was followed by "imagine if". Ali had played along, sure his friend was just playing the same game many did when fantasizing about winning the lottery. He didn't think there was anything to it. By the time he realized the other was serious and offering Ali a chance to join the team, it was too late. Seymour had concluded Ali wasn't going to be a team player, and since Ali knew too much, he had now become a liability. Liabilities could only be handled one way: a bullet through the ear.

Still, he had not gotten what he expected. He had been tied to a chair, beaten, forced to assure Brett and his team that everything was on the up and up, and set aside before his planned murder just in case he was needed in some way. Ali was sure that time was almost up. Ali had served his part, nothing had materialized where he might still represent some value, and his execution would happen very soon.

Up until now, he had been biding his time and searching for an opportunity to escape. It had finally presented itself. For the first time since this had begun, his captors had left him alone. There were only two of them now. Seymour and the others had left to continue their mission.

Those two were downstairs, probably making coffee or getting something to eat.

Ali listened carefully for signs of movement somewhere in the two-story safe house. He heard nothing. He knew the house and the location. He had used it once before. He was in a remote farmhouse in West Virginia, not too far away from where Brett and his team called home. It was likely Seymour and his group of criminals had used this place because of its strategic location near the people they intended to mislead.

They had flown here in a couple of Bell 505 helicopters. One had left long ago. It had ferried Seymour and the others out of here. If Ali's escape attempt worked, he would commandeer the other and begin his pursuit of his former friend.

The chair he was tied to was a simple wooden one confiscated from a kitchen table. His hands were bound behind his back with a piece of rope. His ankles were strapped to the front legs of the chair with more of the same. He could move a little, but not much. It would have to do. And he only had one chance to get it right. He rocked forward until he was hunched over, balanced on his feet, the chair suspended in the air below him. He used the little bit of flexibility he had to straighten as much as he could, gritted his teeth, then slammed himself down onto the floor as hard as he could. Nothing happened. There wasn't even the slightest crack heard in the wooden frame. He cursed silently and rocked forward again, repeating the process. This time there was a slight snap heard as the chair gave against his weight and the sudden impact. He also heard the scurrying of feet on the stairs. He rocked forward a third time, balanced himself upright, and slammed himself down. This time the chair gave in two places. One of the front legs snapped, allowing him even more movement with his feet. He stood and slammed down a fourth time, this time shattering the chair. He made it to his feet as quickly as he could and charged the door to his room, his hands still behind his back. He made it there just as the door crashed open, a once fellow agent filling the space with his muscled body.

Ali crashed into him at full speed, leading with his left shoulder, his legs pumping for all they were worth. The man was driven backward, unprepared for the full weight of Ali to ram into him. The man grunted and stumbled with Ali pressed into him and shoving. They hit the railing of the staircase. It buckled instantly and the sound of splintering wood filled the air. Over they went, falling a few feet before slamming onto the steps halfway down. With a crunch of bone, the man below him stopped moving and did a slow, wheezing exhale. Ali rolled off and came to a knee on the step below, looking at his adversary. The agent's neck was broken, his head shoved against the stairwell wall at an unnatural and gruesome angle.

Where was the other agent, he wondered? Maybe outside smoking? The man reeked of cigarettes when he had been punching Ali into submission. Ali looked around and found the man's gun a few steps further down. He sat in front of it and grabbed the butt awkwardly from behind. He didn't know how he would use it with his hands still tied behind him, but he felt better with it than without.

He finished the descent of the stairs and listened. Hearing nothing, he ventured into the living room and peeked through the windows. On the far side, he spotted the helicopter and two men walking back this way. *Crap*, he thought. *I thought there were only two*. If he was wrong about the number of people still here with him once, might he also be wrong a second time? How many other people were here? He needed to get these ropes off his hands if he was going to stand a chance.

Ali went to the kitchen next and found what he had hoped for. Sitting on the counter like a golden prize was a set of kitchen knives in a worn, wooden holder. He raced for them, snatched the paring knife from its slot with his teeth, and dropped it on the counter. He spun about, set the gun aside, and fumbled around for a second before his fingers closed around the plastic handle. He reversed the blade and carefully inserted it between the strands of rope around his wrists like he had been taught so long ago.

He heard the front door open and steps heading this way. Someone mumbled, asking how much longer the other thought they would have to be here. Ali's jaw tightened and he tried to put as much leverage onto the blade as he could, sawing at his bindings. Closer, the footsteps came. Harder, Ali sawed. And then, he was out of time. First, one agent stepped around the corner. Then, the other. For a moment, neither really noticed he was there standing off to one side. Perhaps, from their peripheral, they assumed him to be their friend. The one who was dead on the staircase. But then, nearly as one, they both saw him and went for their guns. Ali turned sideways, his hands back around the stolen pistol, and began firing from behind his back. A few missed. A few landed. He kept firing, doing his best to visualize where the rounds would go, pulling the trigger over and over again.

The two agents jerked and spun, doing a weird death dance that people do sometimes when they are shot in multiple locations. Their belly, their feet, their legs, their waist, their chest, his bullets tore into them repeatedly. With every round fired, Ali felt burning gunpowder pepper his back, searing through the thin fabric of his once nice dress shirt. He ignored the pain and kept firing. Seventeen times, Ali pulled the trigger on the Glock behind his back until the slide locked, indicating it was empty. When it was over, the two agents lay on the floor, ruined. Ali wasn't done with them. Not by a long shot. He stepped up to the closest and stomped down hard on the man's throat, twice, crushing the windpipe. He repeated the process on the second man, and then stood over them, breathing hard, seething in anger. For a long moment, he stared at them, silently daring them to move again.

Satisfied they were no longer a threat, he moved back to the counter to finish the task of freeing himself of the rope. It took a few more minutes to slice his way through, then he rifled through the dead men's clothes, confiscating a new firearm and a handful of mags. He also found his phone lying on the kitchen table. He walked out the front door, heading to the helicopter, dialing a number from memory. Before he could complete the dial, he was shot from behind. The bullet clipped his left ear and Ali pitched into a roll to the right. He came back to his knee and brought the gun up, looking for a target. Coming around the side of the house was a fourth traitor. The man got off a second shot before Ali could draw aim. The bullet took a chunk out of his right shoulder and Ali fell onto his left side. A third round just missed. Ali's answering gunfire did not, and his enemy toppled into a bush.

For a while, Ali just lay there in the summer sun, gasping for breath and thankful he was still alive. Rolling over onto his back, he looked up into the blue sky, wishing he could just lay here for a while. Maybe take a nap. But he couldn't. There was still work to do. Besides, Ali was practically boiling with anger. There was only one way to put that fire out. He had heard said that revenge was a dish best served cold. He wasn't sure where the statement came from, but he was sure they were dead wrong.

Abbi was shoved through the front door of the barn and into the bright sunlight of a summer afternoon. It would have been a nice day had not everything in her life gone tragically wrong. Behind her, Bill kept prodding her forward with the toe of his shoe. Even with her hands zip-tied behind her back, she was sure she could pound him into poo. Except, of course, Ted, who was at the rear of the procession, might shoot Cassie.

They had allowed her to place the baby into a carrier, the kind meant for clipping into a base and seat belting into a car, as well as packing up a diaper bag. She wasn't sure where they were going, but she knew their intent. DJ and the rest of the team were supposed to have died. Things didn't go according to plan, and until these idiots were sure her team had been finished off for good, she and the baby were needed as hostages.

She was instructed to head to the lead SUV, and she did so. In her heart, Abbi wanted to start issuing roundhouse kicks to her captors. But instead of dealing out pain, her legs plodded along through the dust, feeling like lead weights were attached. Halfway to the vehicle, things began to look up. She heard a man's voice shout, "Hey!" Before she could turn around, there was a single gunshot. When she finished her turn, she saw Ted had dropped the baby carrier and was in the process of falling like a felled tree, the left side of his head a bloody mess. She wasn't sure where the shot came from, but she wasn't wasting her opportunity.

Abbi was a person accustomed to getting things done. She never waited around to be told what to do or hoped someone else would do it. So, when she saw Bill frantically looking for the shooter, she placed the toe of her running shoe under his chin with as much force as she could bring to bear. And since she was always thorough with everything she did, she didn't assume the man was out of the fight, even though Bill was flat on his back, his eyes rolled back in his head indicating he was unconscious. She threw herself high into the air, rolled to her right in midflight, pointed her elbow as best she could due to her restraints, and collapsed on the man, her elbow coming down on the bridge of his nose. The resulting crunching sound warmed her heart to no end. The act also snapped her plastic restraints.

"Wow," a familiar voice spoke behind her. "Hell hath no fury, right?" She turned her head, looking for the speaker, her savior, and found a man she almost didn't recognize. His face was bloody. His shirt was bloody. His whole body was a bloody mess. Agent Ali stood there, gun in hand, looking down on her with a fondness in his swollen eyes.

She rolled to her knees and crawled to Cassie, inspecting the child for injury. Other than a few specks of someone else's blood on her face and clothing, she was fine. Cassie grinned up at her as a snot bubble formed under her nose. She wiped it free with a bit of blanket that had been tucked to one side of the carrier. Abbi didn't look up at Ali when she spoke. "Half of my team is either dead or injured." Then she pointed at the open door of the barn. "And they shot Brett."

Ali was running then, streaking for the barn. She didn't have the heart to tell him there was no use. The man who had been like a second father to her was gone. Alive and well one minute, seemingly far from harm's way, and dead the next, still sitting slumped in the chair he loathed so much.

And then, all at once, as if God had breathed hope into her, things began to look up even more. From the open doorway, the muffled voice of Ali called out to her, hope and panic twisted together in his voice. "I have a pulse!"

Chapter 9: The Big Reveal

DJ and the remaining members of his team floated at the rendezvous location for the Vermont. The wait served only to strengthen his foul mood. Cash had been steadily dialing the farm on their satellite phone, attempting to communicate with Abbi and Brett. So far, there had been no answer. This fact wasn't helping DJ's mindset either. He was certain failed communication with his wife was a portent of more bad news about to befall his group. He cast his eyes about their Zodiac and considered what he did know, trying to take his mind off what he didn't.

Bounder was dead, shot in the back of the head. The young fighter never even had the chance to defend herself. She had never seen it coming. She never had the opportunity to know she had been betrayed by a member of their team.

Cash was wounded, but not severely. A pressure bandage stopped the bleeding from the bullet hole through a meaty part of his right bicep. DJ had examined it and determined the bullet missed the bone and any major arteries. He also had a grazing wound on his cheek, but it wasn't deep. DJ doubted it would even leave a scar.

Coonie had a bullet wound as well. A round had punched through the boat and nicked her left buttock. It wasn't much to write home about, and she had no problems exposing herself to her team so that DJ could clean it and check it out. It was the only brief moment of humor they had. She had done it with her eyes on the Sheriff, commenting how she had always thought Sam was a pain right where he had wounded her. She had smiled at her wounded teammates when she said the traitor could kiss her hole. She had said it to make Argo smile. It had worked.

Argo was in bad shape, and DJ was uncertain of the outcome. On examination, DJ found that both bullets tracked into the side of the abdomen running from his left side to his right. There was no exit wound, so this meant the angle had taken a deeper path through Argo's middle than DJ had hoped. There was nothing DJ could do to make it better. The man was bleeding internally and who knew what organs had been damaged. If the sub didn't surface soon, DJ wasn't certain how long the man would survive. The Sheriff needed a surgeon. For now, he was reclined in the boat resting, his eyes closed but conscious. *Hang on, buddy*, DJ thought.

It wasn't clear what Traitor Sam's play was. Why choose enemy waters to steal the data drive? There were few places he could go and his chances of escape were slim. Was there some plan that DJ didn't know about? If there was, when had the man had the time to put something in place? It didn't make sense. He needed more information.

DJ glanced at Carbon. The hacker wasn't wounded in any way, physically. Psychologically was a whole other matter. The man sat sideways on the bottom of the boat with his knees bent, leaning against the inflated side. His eyes were glassed over and his head down. While usually out of harm's way, the man had seen some hard times before. He had been nearly killed twice that DJ could remember. But this was different. Argo had saved his life and had paid a price for it. He might die for his act of self-sacrifice. This had to be weighing heavily on the man's psyche. Yet, if there would be any justice to come out of this, Carbon needed to get his head right and focus. DJ needed his skill set and his analytical way of thinking.

Cash seemed to be reading DJ's mind. He leaned forward and snapped his finger in front of Carbon's face. "Lock that crap down," Cash commanded. It was uncharacteristic of Cash to show any emotion at all. He was usually as granite-like in his personality as he was in his dependability. "He took a bullet for you. Get over it. Anyone here would do the same. You do his sacrifice an injustice by moping over it. Now, did Sam say anything about why he did this, or did he just start shooting?" Carbon just shook his head and looked at Argo.

DJ shifted his position to take the sun out of his face. "It doesn't make sense. He would have to know that every intelligence asset the U.S. has will be brought to bear looking for anyone trying to sell science fiction blueprints on the black market. They'll find him. He's a dead man walking. It's just a matter of time."

Cash offered a rebuttal. "Unless he already had an offer."

DJ disagreed. "No. There was no time. As soon as we heard about this, we had ourselves on that helicopter and on the way here."

Cash nodded in agreement. "So, then agent Seymour had to be in on it. Maybe he's a turncoat too and privately offered Sam a pile of cash to kill us and take the drive."

Carbon spoke up. "You're both right and wrong at the same time." DJ and Cash went silent and stared at the hacker. This was what DJ had been hoping for. Carbon had a talent for puzzling his way through problems, seeing things the others could not. "There's no top-secret blueprints on that drive. There never was. This was a setup from the very beginning. So, yes, Seymour is in on it. He inserted Sam into the team a month ago when he planned this whole thing. Sam was never looking for a job. He was just playing the game to get to this point."

DJ shook his head, trying to follow along but failing. "Wait, how do you know there are no blueprints on that drive?"

Carbon looked at him, sadness still lingering in his eyes. "Because I managed to break the code and had a peek before Sam ambushed us."

It was Cash's turn to be confused. "But I thought you needed the active brainwaves of that doctor to get inside."

Carbon's voice took a harder edge, anger growing in his voice. "It was all a lie! That's how I know Agent Seymour, and *probably* Agent Ali planned this whole thing and put a wolf onto our team. We were never supposed to make it out of this alive. You want to know what was on that drive? I'll tell you. But I warn you, you're going to be a lot madder than you are right now. You have any duct tape in that bag of yours? You might want to wrap your head with some. Because when I tell you what it is, your head is going to explode. The tape won't stop it from blowing up, but you'll at least have all the pieces stuck to the tape for the doctor to try and put your skull back together."

DJ's voice rose to a shout, snapping at the man. "Enough! What's on the drive?"

Carbon smiled, but it wasn't genuine. "Cryptocurrency. A lot of it. Mountains and mountains of it. All of it sitting in wallets with a text file containing everything needed to use them."

DJ blinked. "Crypto what?"

Carbon shook his head, exasperated at DJ's inability to climb out of the technological Dark Ages. "Cryptocurrency. Digital money. There are all kinds now, but in the beginning, there was only one. You can use it to buy stuff or exchange it for cash. There is a finite amount of it which has made its value climb. The only way to get it is to buy it or mine it."

DJ had heard of the stuff but truthfully didn't know anything about it. "Mine it?" he asked.

Carbon nodded. "Yeah. You mine it with software on the internet. That is a really simple explanation, but, yeah. Didn't you say these contractors you killed were Asian?" DJ nodded. "Well, then this all makes sense. Think back to when North Korea was making all kinds of trouble, threatening nuclear annihilation of the U.S. if we didn't lift sanctions. The dictator had no real way to make money. Not legally, anyway. He was starving for cash. The country was on the verge of economic collapse. He wasn't too concerned with his people starving. He was worried about how he was going to get his next sports car.

"Hackers caught wind of one of his plans to make money. He put a bunch of his tech geeks in a room and had them start mining cryptocurrency as fast as they could. A whole army of them in a room working twenty-four hours a day, seven days a week, generating the stuff. He used it to build giant resort-styled mansions and fund his nuclear ambitions. It was rumored that he stashed a bunch of it for his retirement one day. Supposedly, he planned to sneak out of the country and disappear, set up a new identity for himself, and live out the rest of his life in luxury somewhere. Now, I'm not one hundred percent certain it was *his* stolen cryptocurrency on that drive, but it makes sense based on how much of it there was, where the meet point was located, and the fact that those contractors were probably North Korean. I'll bet you anything that a few of his own people stole the drive, figured they would never be able to break the encryption, and offered it to that Russian general in exchange for three bags of money."

Carbon looked around at them, his anger and frustration causing him to repeatedly clench his fists. "Agent Seymour learned about the exchange and set up a plan to steal it all for himself. This was never about securing the secrets of the American military. This was nothing more than a good old-fashioned heist. This was about money and a lot of it."

Coonie spoke up from the front of the boat. "How much are we talking?"

Carbon shrugged. "No way of knowing for sure, but based on current prices, somewhere north of a billion dollars."

Coonie's mouth fell open in shock. "Well, there you have it. A billion reasons to kill us." She snorted as another thought hit her. "I would have killed all of you for far less. Kidding. Maybe."

DJ ignored the joke. "Just one flaw in their plan. They *didn't* kill us."

The satellite phone suddenly rang in Cash's hand. He glanced down and then up at DJ. "It's Abbi."

Chapter 10: When Things Go Boom

Sam Kenny pulled alongside the aging fishing trawler and grabbed the rope that was tossed to him. First, he secured the box with the data drive in his small pack. Next, he shouldered his rifle, disconnected the compressed canister for keeping the raft filled with air, and punctured the sides with his knife. It wouldn't take long for the inflatable to lose its buoyancy and the weight of the outboard to carry it to the bottom of the ocean. Finally, he hauled himself on board the trawler for the next leg of his journey.

From here he was to travel due north. The extra fuel onboard would take him to a small Russian fishing village called Nel'ma. It was remote and isolated, well off the beaten path. He would meet his next contact there, a former deep undercover operative who had functioned as a mole within the Russian intelligence community for nearly two decades. He had since been labeled as dead after vanishing over ten years ago. The reality was he had simply decided to retire from his life as a double agent. He had met someone, a young Russian woman, who had captured his heart. The former secret agent had decided to settle down and live out the rest of his life with her. Agent Seymour had helped arrange the disappearance and divert any questions the CIA might have. The double agent's happiness in retirement was short-lived. His bride was gone now due to cancer. Even though the former agent was older, out of shape, his best years behind him, Agent Seymour found a use for him once more. He would get paid a handsome fee for transporting Sam from one side of Russia to the other, all the way to Finland. Sam had only to sit and wait for the man to show up.

It would have been risky to hop on a plane and make the trip. As connected as the security cameras were at all airports, and as cooperative as the Russians were being on the hunt for global terrorists, he would certainly be spotted by facial recognition software. No doubt the CIA would have him uploaded to a database as soon as DJ Slaughter made it back on that sub.

Every mission has complications. It was a fact of life for an operator, but not killing DJ Slaughter was a big one. Sam's original plan was to wait until they got to the coordinates for meeting the Vermont. They would shut down the engines, lash the two boats together, and wait for the sub. With everyone within spitting distance and suspecting nothing, Sam could have picked off the entire team with headshots and then headed to meet the trawler.

Carbon threw the plan into the trashcan. He wasn't supposed to try and hack the drive. With him successfully breaking in, the entire ruse was just a phone call away from being blown up. It wouldn't even need a call. All Carbon would have had to do was send a message from his tablet computer explaining what was really on the drive, or worse, email the entire contents. Agent Seymour and his team would have been placed on every watch list there was, with every intel organization alerted to be on the lookout. The longer it took for people to become aware of what was going on, the easier it was going to be to escape.

Sam called an audible and attempted to kill the team while they were in motion. He was certain he had wounded a few of them, he had shot Latricia through the head, and it was unlikely Argo had survived the ambush. Still, Sam had failed. He was lucky to have escaped with the drive at all. By now, a call had been placed to the CIA. Agent Seymour, Sam, and the others were going to have to move slow and careful if they were all going to get away. Especially Seymour, who was still in the U.S. supervising things on that end.

Sam lived by a few rules as an operator. The first: early and often. This meant that at the first sign of something going south, notify your supervisors. Sam had followed this rule to the letter. As soon as bullets stopped being hurled in his direction, he used his satellite phone to contact Agent Seymour and inform him of what went down. He also called the farm, the place DJ called his base of operations, and notified the agents on-site to not kill Abbi but take her and the baby prisoner. They might need her for leverage in subduing DJ and whoever remained operation of his tea.

To say Seymour wasn't happy was an understatement. Still. Sam still got away with the drive intact, so the man wasn't furious. The nearly 2.9 billion dollars in cryptocurrency was safe and secure. All would be forgiven once Sam delivered the small case and its contents.

The second rule was a statement ground into his head while serving as an elite warrior for the military: don't see the problem, see the solution. The solution was simple.

Slaughter was going to come after them. It didn't matter if the CIA sanctioned it or not. It didn't matter if they gave the team access to intel or not. DJ would harness that big brain of Carbon's to hunt down both Agent Seymour and Sam. According to the profile written about Slaughter, the man was worse than a starving street dog with a bone when he decided something needed to be done. He couldn't let go. He would use every resource and spend any amount of money required to hunt down the agent who set them up and the team member who betrayed them.

See the solution, not the problem. DJ Slaughter and his team needed to die. The sooner, the better. This meant that Sam needed to call another audible.

As soon as he was on board, he killed every crew member of the trawler, tied them all to a spare boat anchor, and threw them overboard. He wasn't going to that small fishing village on the shores of eastern Russia as ordered. He turned the boat south and began plotting a route that would take him into the Philippines. He had twenty-grand in cash stashed in the bottom of his bag that would help him along the way. He wasn't planning on stealing the drive and keeping the contents for himself. Sam was sure Agent Seymour had enough seedy contacts throughout the world to find Sam if he tried to run. Instead, he was only taking a detour. He would still rendezvous with Agent Seymour as planned. Besides, it would have taken nearly two weeks waiting for his contact and negotiating his way across Russia. There was plenty of time to kill Slaughter. Sam knew Agent Seymour would use Abbi as planned, but he also knew how good DJ Slaughter and his team were, even on a bad day. How much more effective would they be when motivated by revenge?

No, let Seymour do what he was going to do, but Sam had already screwed up once. He needed to make sure for his own safety that the job was finished exactly as originally planned.

Sam dialed Agent Seymour to tell him of the change. He was sure the agent would insist Sam stick to his orders, but that was too bad. When it came to self-preservation, Sam followed no one's orders but his own.

Sara Anderson had a problem. She loved blowing crap up. This, of course, was often considered illegal. Getting your hands on the chemicals and equipment for making things go boom could be challenging at times, and it was easy for accidents to occur. Make no mistake, by now she had acquired enough knowledge and experience to overcome such challenges, but in the beginning, when she was just finding her way, just a raw acolyte with a fetish for the rapid expansion of gasses, she often got herself into trouble. Thankfully, none of it resulted in jail time or missing appendages. She should have sought counseling for her problem. Instead, she sought training and permission. She found the one place she could receive tutelage in her craft and be sanctioned to indulge herself.

The United States Marine Corps gave her a great start. It taught her many fundamentals and gave her the discipline she desperately needed. Still, it wasn't enough. She needed more. After eight years swaddled in digital camouflaged clothing, she applied for the Central Intelligence Agency. She had all the traits they sought, so they scooped her up.

Now, don't get her wrong, the CIA was great. It gave her even more access to specialized materials and pointed her at bad guys who needed extermination by more thorough and less secretive means. After all, what was the use in blowing crap up if there wasn't a little blood involved? More importantly, she began to make contacts outside of the agency who made her realize that she could become very wealthy doing what she loved. As an assassin, she could focus on improving her craft, exercise her creative side, bank a lot of cash, and for the most part, obliterate people who largely deserved eradication. In short, she got paid a lot of money to have fun. How awesome was that? If you're doing what you love, it ain't work, right?

Yesterday, an old friend she had met in the CIA reached out to her with a lucrative offer. Agent Seymour needed her to erase a guy who was currently hospitalized. This was a challenge, and it was what compelled her most to take the contract. It wasn't challenging because she had to infiltrate a hospital, no, of course not. It was challenging because it was maybe the most secure hospital in the world. One would think, anyway. After all, Walter Reed sat on an Army base.

Now, one might think you would have to breach two layers of security to gain access to the hospital. This wasn't true. The hospital needed rapid access for ambulances and easy access for visitors, there was a gate located off Rockville Pike Road that ran right in front of the storied building. Across the street was a visitor's parking lot. She could park a stolen vehicle there, take the visitor's tunnel under the street, flash an ID provided by Agent Seymour, and waltz right in like she owned the place. Wearing a disguise, of course. The place was covered in cameras that recorded everything.

When she first was presented with the offer, she got nervous. Walter Reed is where Presidents and members of Congress were treated. She didn't need that kind of heat, but Agent Seymour assured her the target was a vet. She asked, why a vet needed killing. None of your business, she was told. Just kill the target and anyone who might be visiting him.

Challenge accepted.

Here's the deal when killing a target in a hospital: unless you are a visitor, almost all the medical staff know each other. Regardless of the size of the facility, doctors know doctors, nurses know nurses, phlebotomists know phlebotomists. You get the picture. So, you can't pretend to be one of those. Somebody is liable to notice you and either call you out or point security in your direction. It can get real messy when that happens. Can't pretend to be a visitor either. The staff tends to pay attention to them more to ensure they don't go where they aren't supposed to. No ma'am. No sir. To pull off a job in a hospital, one needs to be invisible. And no one is more invisible than a janitor with a cart full of cleaning supplies. If anyone asks a question, you just mumble about being on your way to clean up vomit and people will steer clear. Wouldn't you?

Agent Seymour even provided the room number the target was located in. John Argo was on the second floor with a view of the front lawn. Easy sneezy.

She entered the hospital with no problem, pretending to be a visitor, crying and carrying on about the condition of her brother, flashing a fake driver's license that would have fooled anyone, and signing with her borrowed name of Joyce Smith. Bags were screened at the entrance, and she had to step through a metal detector. She left any weapons behind, and the X-ray machine thought the lunch in her bag was legit. It looked just like a sandwich, two juice boxes, peanut butter with celery sticks for dipping. All a lie, of course. This wasn't her first attempt at fooling bomb-sniffing dogs or X-ray machines.

Inside, Sara flagged down an orderly, explained she was a new employee, flashed her baby blues at him, and learned where the janitorial closet was on the second floor. He was so enamored with her flirtations, he never noticed she had swiped the bundle of keys from his waist or bothered to ask why she wasn't in scrubs. Orderlies always had keys to the janitorial closets. They had to clean up all sorts of vile messes. For this reason, many of them were quite invisible themselves.

From there, she found a bathroom, removed her first layer of clothes, exposing her pale green hospital scrubs, and clipped on her fake badge. She also tucked her first layer of clothing, along with her purse, into a red plastic hazardous waste bag. She wore gloves as she did to not leave fingerprints on the bag. She dumped the contents of the juice boxes on top and tied the bag closed. The fluid would begin to create fumes that would permeate the clothing and destroy any DNA evidence found inside. Sara then crushed the boxes flat and dropped them into a pocket of her scrubs. She carried the bag through the hallway with no one batting an eye and dropped it into the first trash can she saw.

On the second floor of building A, she found the janitorial closet and used her pilfered keys to gain access. Inside, she found exactly what she wanted. Three janitor's carts stood in the middle of the small room. She scanned the bottles on the shelf looking for cleaners and floor strippers. It didn't take long to find one that fit the bill. According to the chemicals listed on the bottle, it contained an ingredient that would do nicely. Next, she scooped her peanut butter with one gloved finger into the bottle, resealed it, and shook it vigorously. The compound that resembled peanut butter quickly broke apart and began to dissolve. In a few minutes, the mixture would become a powerful explosive. While she waited, she ate her sandwich and munched on the celery sticks. If anyone interrupted her, she would turn on her charm and beg to not be reported for eating in a cleaning closet. If that failed, she could always kill them. The Marines and CIA had taught her all the skills needed to metaphorically flip off someone's light switch.

When she was done eating, Sara tucked the remainder of her lunch, the sandwich bags and small plastic container she had kept her peanut butter in, into the deep pockets of her scrubs. Finally, she placed the modified floor stripper bottle onto a cart, pulled her latex gloves tighter, and pushed it out into the hallway.

Time to make things go boom.

It took her only a few minutes to locate John Argo's room. She hadn't expected security outside the room, and there wasn't. It wouldn't have mattered of course. The explosive on her cart would take out everything in a twenty-five-meter radius. She could have simply parked the cart along the wall outside, and let her little friend take care of the rest. Still, with no security, she could push the cart inside and verify the target was there.

He was.

Sara had been provided a picture of the man she was to kill. She found him slightly reclined in a hospital bed attempting to watch the TV. Poor guy was having a hard time of it. There was only one other person inside: a short, overweight woman, chattering on about how real gumbo didn't have tomatoes in it. Her recipe was the best, the woman promised. She would make him some just as soon as he got out of here to prove it. John Argo nodded and grumbled, flipping the channel on the TV.

Sara smiled politely and pushed her cart off to one side. She stepped in front, keeping her body between the cart and the other occupants to shield her next activity from view.

She opened the bottle and set the cap aside. Next, she pulled out an ink pen from her scrubs and hit the plunger three times fast. Just like it was supposed to, a tiny LED began blinking red. She grinned to herself and dropped it inside, resealing the bottle. The pen was a sophisticated detonator on a seven-minute timer. Through the opaque bottle, she could see the pen softly winking. This was going to be so cool, she thought to herself. She lifted a white cloth towel from her cart and draped it over the bottle to hide the flashing light of the detonator. She would have liked the bottle to have not been translucent, but this would work fine.

Turning to the doomed man and his girlfriend, she said she would be right back. She was missing cleaner for the toilet, she explained. Sara headed out the door whistling the tune to a popular pop song on the radio. She checked her watch as she walked, picking up the pace. She needed to be on the other side of the front gate when this thing went up. They would lock the place down quickly, and she would prefer to not be here when that happened.

Sara Anderson dropped her hands into her pockets and strode towards freedom. She couldn't wait to be out front when things went boom. As John Argo's room was facing the front lawn, she would get a great view of the explosion through the fence. She should have brought popcorn. Yep, do what you love and it ain't work.

———————

Bettie Walden, aka Coonie, sat chattering away in her chair wishing she had more control over her mouth. She just couldn't seem to help herself. When she was on a mission, it was different. Put a gun in her hand and she was focused, poised, and silent. Any other time, she flapped her gums like she might die if she didn't get the next word out. She was sure it had to do with her having low self-esteem. She ran her mouth to stay relevant, desperately searching for something witty or pithy to say so others might see her as the life of the party, or smarter than her red-neck, mud-hole-stomping, crawfish-boiling self appeared to be. She knew she could be funny, even it was only a blanket to cover her insecurities. She knew she was smart, even if she only went to college for about five minutes. But she was convinced everyone else saw her as toothless trailer trash. Even if she did grow up living in a trailer that had a hole in the living room floor. Sometimes the cat used it to come and go. It was sad.

She had eagerly volunteered to stay with Argo while DJ and Cash had gone to see Brett. Their fearless leader had been shot through the heart and had been on the table for nearly six hours while the surgical team at a hospital in West Virginia worked to fix the damage. He had made it, of course, Brett Foster was too stubborn to die, and since DJ and Cash were so close to him, and they knew Argo was going to make it, they had gone to be there when their friend when finally opened his eyes from his medically induced coma.

Abbi and Carbon had gone back to the farm to see if they could track down Seymour and Sam. The place was well secure now that Agent Ali was back involved. The angry Agent had turned their headquarters into a Fort Knox. He had even put a detail on the hospital where Brett was recovering. None was needed here. The place was secure as it was. After all, the President of the United States even had his own building here.

She heard herself go on and on about the various ways you could tweak gumbo to make yours unique and all your own. She explained how there was an imaginary dividing line through the middle of Louisiana right around Lafayette where the food changed. Everything east had a more commercialized/gourmet flare to Cajun cuisine. Everything west was more homestyle and comfort oriented. The whole time she talked, she could see the look in Argo's eyes. He was wishing she would shut her cakehole, or just go away altogether. Even though she could see it as plain as the wart on her big toe, she couldn't stop herself.

You might think that when the janitor showed up to do some cleaning and take out the trash, this would become a distraction for her. Not even a little bit. Coonie just yammered on without pause. She was even convinced the only reason the poor girl left for toilet bowl cleaner was to avoid hearing the finer points of Cajun cooking. It was obvious. Coonie could see a bottle of the stuff on the bottom shelf of the cart. It was possible the girl missed it. Nah, the janitor left to avoid hearing a nonsensical monologue. Had to be it. Maybe doing some cleaning herself might make Coonie shut her yap.

She stood and walked to the cart, promising Argo she would cook them all a gumbo that would make them weep with joy once this was all over. She was a great cook, didn't he know? As she talked, she surveyed the cart to see what she had to work with. She was sure the janitor would be pleased the job had been done when she returned.

It was taking the girl longer than Coonie had expected. She had spotted the janitor's closet just down the hallway. Paying attention to details was what she was trained to do. The conclusion was easy. Bettie Walden, aka Coonie, was annoying. It was just that no one had the heart to tell her.

It was only when she removed the towel from a gallon jug sitting on top that her intelligence was proven. She guessed most people would have looked at the strobing light inside the bottle as only a curiosity, but Coonie connected a lot of dots in a short amount of time. Someone tried to kill them all. That someone failed. DJ had a nasty reputation for not letting something go. With one of his team members dead and two more gravely injured, it was logical to believe DJ would hunt Sam and Seymour down no matter how long it took. It would be job one. The janitor had not returned even though the errand should have only taken two minutes for a round trip. This was some sort of bomb she was looking at. A weird one, for sure, but a bomb, nonetheless.

She lifted the jug and turned to Argo. "I've got a bomb."

He seemed to shake himself out of whatever thought he was having; she was sure it had nothing to do with gumbo. "I'm sorry, what?"

She held the jug up. "That chick left a bomb in here!"

Argo tried to shift himself out of the bed. "We got to get out of here."

She shook her head, looking around. "We don't know how much time is left before this thing goes. Won't be enough time to clear the building. I got to get it out of here." Coonie began doing math in her head, trying to deduce how long the janitor had been gone. The girl would need enough time to not only get out of the building but outside the gate. Coonie turned her head and looked through the window. There were a fence and gate right there. It would only take maybe five minutes or so if the bomber took the stairs. Coonie was running out of time.

She set the jug down, picked up the plastic chair she had been sitting in, and used it like a baseball bat to shatter the window.

Argo recoiled in the bed. He looked at her, worry covering his whole body. "You think you can throw that far enough? We don't know how big of an explosion that's going to make."

She used the chair to knock off the remaining shards of glass, then dropped the chair and snatched the jug from the floor. "Don't plan on throwing it," she said. It took Argo a second to figure out her plan, but before he could begin to argue, Coonie stepped up on the windowsill and dropped down. It was only the second floor, but it was still high up. She made sure to hit the ground at an angle and roll to keep from injuring herself.

To one side of the lawn in front of the hospital was a small pond. If she could manage to get the bomb into the water, a lot of the explosion could be contained. She took off at a sprint, pumping her short legs as fast as she could. To her left, two armed guards stationed at the front entrance started running in her direction, drawing their sidearms as they did. *Crap*, she thought to herself. They had seen her jump from the window and could only assume the worst.

Coonie put her head down and focused on her goal. She had a good lead on the guards, but they had an intercepting route, running diagonally to her. They were closing the gap. She heard them shouting at her to stop. She refused, stretching out her stubby legs as best she could. Why had God built her so close to the ground?

Gunfire came next and Coonie began cussing as she ran, almost laughing at what DJ's face would look like if he could hear her. The first few rounds missed, flying past her towards the street that ran in front of the place. That's not very good weapon discipline, she thought to herself. Finally, she took one in the thigh and Coonie went flat, sliding across the grass like a soccer player who just scored the winning goal.

She clambered to her feet as fast as she could, holding the jug in front of her as she did, ignoring the pain in her leg. "Stop!" she screamed. "I've got a bo-." She never completed the sentence. Not that it mattered. The guards got the message soon enough when the explosion tore her to pieces, leaving a small crater in the grass and sending the guards flying from the blast. She would have thought it all hilarious if she were still alive to have witnessed it. But she wasn't. Bettie Walden, aka Coonie, was nothing more than tiny pieces scattered in a giant circle. The forensics team would be gathering remnants of her over the next two days.

Sara Anderson stood outside the fence of Walter Reed Memorial Hospital and watched in open mouth amusement as the squatty girlfriend of John Argo raced across the front lawn. She couldn't believe what she was watching. The poor thing didn't have a prayer of escaping. According to Sara's watch, there were only seconds remaining on the timer. She began to giggle when the guards gave chase. She was openly laughing when they started shooting. She was laughing so hard; Sara nearly didn't make it around the brick column in the fence before the bomb went off. The concussion nearly caught as she stepped behind for protection.

She staggered away from the scene wiping tears from her face. At a distance, she was sure others would have thought her distraught. She should have been. Sara should have been upset that John Argo was still alive, but she couldn't help herself. It had all been too funny. She doubted Agent Seymour was going to be as amused as she, but that was too bad. Things happen. It was why she got paid upfront.

Even when things don't go according to plan, if you love what you do, it ain't work.

Chapter 11: Tiger, Tiger

The CIA was comprised of multiple divisions. The one where DJ and his team got their contracts was called the National Clandestine Service, or NCS. The person who ran this division was Deputy Director Sharlette Hartley. She was a career veteran of the CIA, serving for over thirty years. DJ had never met the woman but had heard stories. Supposedly, being a woman, a black woman, a gay, black woman who had fought stereotypes and misogyny by her peers for nearly three decades, yet still managing to acquire such a high-ranking level despite those adversities, had conditioned the woman to be a real punch in the gut to work for. But as he stood next to the still unconscious form of Brett Foster lying in a hospital room, talking to her on the phone, DJ found her to be quite charming. Since she worked for an entity whose entire existence focused on keeping secrets, stealing secrets, and killing people because of those secrets, DJ was certain it was all an act. She was very good at it.

Her apology at what had happened to his team sounded sincere and heartfelt. She assured DJ that anything required to get Brett and Argo back on their feet would be done. She promised a burial at Arlington with full military honors for Latricia. She even pointed out that new treatment and techniques for Brett's back injury had been developed. As soon as the man was better, and as soon as he felt up to it, she would arrange for Brett to be placed on the list. With a little bit of luck and a lot of physical therapy, he might regain the full use of his legs.

DJ thanked her, telling her that he did not blame her or her department for what had happened. He knew that Agent Seymour going rogue had come as a complete surprise to everyone. DJ did, however, expect full cooperation from her when it came to sharing any intelligence she discovered on Seymour and Sam Kenny's whereabouts. He all but demanded it. DJ had a score to settle. He would appreciate it if they just passed any information along and then stepped out of his way. He would clean up their little mess, free of charge.

There was a moment of silence after his request, as she seemed to be struggling for the right words to say. Then, "Mr. Slaughter, you and your team have been very effective at what you do for us, so don't misread me here, but this is an internal matter that *we* need to rectify."

DJ wasn't backing down. "I have a member of my team dead and others with injuries. Two of them very nearly didn't make it. One was shot through the heart at point-blank range. Again, I expect full cooperation."

She sighed before replying. "I could make this an order."

DJ's voice took a harder edge. "I don't work for the CIA."

Her own voice was instantly sharper in tone. "Don't call it an order. Consider it a threat against future employment. Get in our way and you'll never get another contract from us."

DJ chuckled. "Get in *my* way and your people might just suffer collateral damage."

Her voice was incredulous. "Did you just threaten me?"

DJ rubbed his forehead, closing his eyes as he did. He hated politics. He hated politicians. He hated bureaucracy. He had tried to muddle his way through this conversation diplomatically but had failed. He just wasn't cut out for it. "No ma'am, it was not a threat. Let me try this again. I will put former CIA Agent Seymour in the ground and any with him when I do. It's going to happen. No law is going to stop it from happening. No polite request is going to stop it from happening. Your failure to cooperate with me isn't going to change that reality. He's a traitor to this country and he killed a member of my team. There is no intel you can extract from him that will matter. He's nothing more than a low-life bank robber and murderer, and he will die for making that life choice. It's as simple as that. I would appreciate your help in this matter, but it won't change a thing if I don't get it, future contracts or not."

Deputy Director Hartley was silent again. Finally, she sighed, her voice becoming more conciliatory. "I suppose I could send in a team to apprehend you, but that would just get good people hurt, wouldn't it?"

Though she couldn't see it, DJ nodded. "You're probably right."

She continued. "Fine, Mr. Slaughter, we'll do this your way. You go ahead and do what you do. I'll have my guys sit on the sidelines and run support. You need something, let Ali know and he'll make it happen."

DJ was surprised at the sudden reversal and it showed in his voice. "I... Thank you, ma'am. I appreciate that."

Her voice returned to being hard. "Oh, don't think I'm doing you any favors. When two dogs are going for each other's throat, you don't step in and try to break it up. You wait until they tire out or kill each other first. Oh, and one other thing, Mr. Slaughter. Any of your team gets any ideas about keeping that drive for yourselves, I'll bring the full weight of this agency down on your heads. Make sure you let Carbon know. I know how his little weasel-like mind works."

DJ didn't get the chance to respond. Deputy Director of NCS, Sharlette Hartley, hung up on him.

DJ didn't have long to ponder the exchange. His phone rang again. The display said it was Sheriff. DJ answered, thankful to hear from the man. What his friend told him had DJ slumping into the floor with his head buried in his hands. DJ had lost yet another team member. His anger and grief were overwhelming.

Sam Kenny crossed the Mexican border into Texas with no issues. He did it under the cover of night, trailing a group of illegals on their way to try and make a better life for themselves. He figured they might either have inside information or were following a coyote: a Mexican cartel member who charged to smuggle people over the border. On the outskirts of El Indio, he stole a car and swapped the plates out with a similar model in a grocery store parking lot. From there, he made his way north to Dallas. In Dallas, he did two things.

First, he bought a ticket to a major water park. Inside, he made his way to the building where patrons changed out of street clothes and into a bathing suit. Underneath a large canopy were several rows of rentable lockers. They were meant for patrons to lock up their clothes and small valuables. He dropped four quarters into an available locker, allowing him to take the key. He removed the data drive from the boobytrapped storage box and placed it inside the locker, pocketing the key and closing the metal door. There was no marking on the key other than a number. Without knowing where the locker was, nobody would be able to find the drive.

He elected to keep the storage box. The inside was lined with plastic explosives. It could come in handy. He didn't have the detonator, but he could rig something up in a pinch. One never knew when a pound of C4 might come in handy.

Next, he used a fake ID and credit card to rent an airplane from a smaller public airfield. No one knew of the ID, so he was sure it would be safe. He could have used it to cross the border at a checkpoint, but he knew Carbon was probably screening every available feed with facial recognition. So he went old school, staying off the grid as much as possible. He made an exception for the twin-engine Cessna. It would make getting across the country far easier. The credit card was fake and tied to accounts covert agents used when abroad. Those accounts were never audited. They were just paid.

He had no real plan other than getting close to Slaughter and the remaining members of his team. He would figure out what to do after he got a lay of the land.

When he told Seymour of his plan to go after Slaughter, Sam was instructed to proceed with his original orders and deliver the drive. Sam politely refused, told Seymour to relax, and promised he would never consider double-crossing a man with so many resources. Sam said he would see Seymour soon, and turned off his satellite phone. He wouldn't use it again until the job was done.

But it *would* get done. DJ Slaughter needed to die. There was no other choice.

Cash watched DJ pace around the upper floor of the barn. He knew the man well enough to know the pacing was akin to a tiger in a zoo. He just wanted out so he could do what tigers do. Still, DJ hid it as best he could, his baby girl bouncing on his hip, telling Cassie he had her nose. DJ did his best to always compartmentalize the hurt from his past and shove it into a shadowy corner in his mind. This was a dangerous practice, Cash knew. If left undealt with for too long, those feelings could manifest themselves into vicious creatures to torment you. Cash had seen that happen to the man before, suffering from a severe case of PTSD. Since then, DJ had learned to talk about issues with a pastor from town. Still, it was concerning. DJ Slaughter had a lot of bad memories to deal with. These new events were just more logs to add to that fire. One day, the man would either snap or have a heart attack.

Carbon distracted Cash from his thinking, standing from his desk chair and proclaiming to the room, "I got intel!" Agent Ali, Abbi, DJ, and Cash all converged on the man, demanding to know more. Carbon pointed to his computer screen. "That Deputy Director chick came through. The person you see on the screen is our bomber from Walter Reed. Facial recognition picked her up on a camera at a gas station three blocks away, thirty-eight minutes after the explosion. According to the CIA, none of the cameras at the hospital picked her up, but they did spot an unidentified female entering Argo's room a few minutes before it went off."

DJ responded first, switching Cassie to the opposite hip. "But how do we know it's her?"

Carbon nodded, seeming to anticipate the question. "The girl on the screen is Sara Anderson. She worked for the CIA for a while before going independent. Her specialty was explosives. The CIA allowed her to hire out her skills, choosing to use her as an asset from time to time."

It was Cash's turn. "Wait, you mean the CIA knew she was out there blowing people up and didn't do anything about it?"

Agent Ali answered. "We do this all the time. If we think we can use the person for our own purposes at some point, either for intel, or using them to get close to a target, then we'll just keep tabs on them. The only time we'll step in is if they use their criminal ways against us. From what I am reading, most of her targets were all overseas bad guys. One guy hiring her to kill another bad guy. We wouldn't have cared about that at all."

Cash didn't like the answer, focusing on Agent Ali. "So, we wait until she kills one of our own before we decide to do anything? She had to get away with murdering one of us before you step in? That sounds like a perfectly ethical way to handle things."

Agent Ali shrugged. "I'm not endorsing it. I'm just telling you how it's done."

Carbon interrupted. "Guys, you're missing the point. The CIA hired her from time to time. Guess who her contact was."

DJ's voice sounded like sandpaper on steel. "Let me guess, Agent Seymour."

Carbon nodded. "You got it. And even while we don't have her on camera at the hospital, we do know a woman went into that room, probably wearing a disguise. Since Sara, the mad bomber, was only three blocks away just minutes afterward, we can assume she had something to do with it. And here's the thing: according to this report, the CIA has been reaching out to her through her standard channels, but she isn't responding."

Ali nodded. "So, she gets contacted by Seymour for a hit. She thinks it's a CIA-sanctioned job. Afterward, she learns she's been set up just like you guys were and goes into hiding."

Abbi offered up her own question, taking the baby from DJ. "Great. We're sure she did it, but she's in hiding now. How does that help us?"

Carbon smiled. "Because, since the CIA always keeps a close watch on these types of people, we have a list of places she likes to use as safe houses. I did some snooping online, and there's one in Alabama that just saw an increase in electricity consumption. Deputy Director what's-her-face just passed over the list, and I figured it out from there."

DJ shook his head, still confused. "So what? That doesn't really help us. Sure, we can go take her out, maybe get some payback for killing Coonie, but that doesn't get us any closer to Seymour."

Carbon crossed his arms, obviously pleased with himself. "Sure, it does. We know she has a way to contact Seymour. We know she failed at killing both Argo and Coonie. She only got one of them. Stands to reason he's mad about her failure. He would probably want her to finish the job. All we have to do is persuade her to make contact with him and agree to give it another shot. When she does, we'll know right where Seymour is, and you can go pick him up."

Agent Ali slapped Carbon on the back, causing the hacker to wince. "I like this one, DJ. You said he was only good at pushing buttons. Turns out he's smart in other ways too." The agent smiled at the room. "Let's go pay Sara Anderson a visit, shall we?"

Cash looked at DJ. He could see his friend was already concentrating on his next mission, his eyes focused and his face hard. A glance down showed DJ was clenching his fists. The tiger just got let out of his cage, Cash thought.

Chapter 12: Volcanus Eruptus

Sara Anderson looked at her computer screens, scrolling through personnel records, reading highlights of individuals she should have become more acquainted with before blindly accepting Agent Seymour's contract. She should probably stop calling the man an agent. He was a traitor. He had been blacklisted from the CIA with a standing kill order in place if found. She wasn't sure what transgressions the former agent had done to be placed on a blacklist. Sara was only sure of what he had done to her.

The people on her screens were patriots to America. They had files that were extensive in accomplishments, and diverse on their background. Some were former military. A few served as combat veterans, one as a Navy corpsman. Some had even spent time in the FBI, working on a project that involved the Pentagon. During that stint, they had even saved New York City from a terrorist plot involving a nuclear weapon. John Argo, the man she had been contracted to kill in Bethesda, Maryland, had a complete career as a Sheriff's Deputy before joining the FBI for a short run. All of them eventually found themselves as a part of a private combat unit with exclusive contracts with the government, primarily the CIA. They were heroes, every single one.

She wished she had used her connections to access Argo's files and learned who the man was before attempting to kill him. At the time of the offer by Seymour, she simply didn't care. She only assumed he had done something egregious enough for the CIA to want him gone. She had been set up, used by someone she thought she could trust. Because she had failed to do a thorough background check on her target, Sara Anderson now had a standing kill order on her as well. She wasn't sure how she was going to get out of this one.

The CIA wasn't infallible, incapable of making mistakes, but they did have long arms, and more importantly, lots of money to use in acquiring intelligence. Sooner or later they would find her. Unfortunately, she wouldn't realize they had zeroed in on her location until they were shooting at her.

This was bad. This was *very* bad. As far as she could tell, there was only one way that might, emphasis on might, get her back into the good graces of the CIA. She needed to serve former Agent Seymour's head up on a platter and beg forgiveness.

This presented a new problem: where, in the ever-lovin' world, had the slimy snake slithered off to?

While she still had backdoor access to some of the CIA computers, she was confident any contacts she once had with the agency were burned. If she reached out for assistance, she was sure she would end up dead.

Any other person in her position might consider going into hiding and never working in the occupation of contract killing again. Drop off the radar, get some plastic surgery done, retire somewhere nice. Those people didn't have the mental condition Sara Anderson had. While she was reasonably sure she could stop doing what she loved for a while, she knew that nagging need to blow the crap out of something would eventually press her into service again. A vacation, she could manage. Retirement, she couldn't. Sara needed to light a fuse to something or she would die from boredom. So, catching Seymour was the only thing left for her to try.

Maybe she could dig through the man's contacts to see if she could find a clue on where he had vanished. Even though Sara had no idea what line the man had crossed with the agency, she was certain it had to be big enough to involve accomplices. She should broaden her search to look for one of them. Maybe, just maybe, they would lead her to the prize. She had to be quick about it too. The CIA would likely be following the same line of thought and she needed to get to him before they did. She minimized the service records into the background and keyed up a new search.

She had not been at it long before an incursion alarm flashed onto her screens. Someone had entered the grounds to her safehouse. She quickly pulled up her camera feeds. Crouching by the southern wall of her make-shift compound, a single individual, dressed all in black, was looking over the area, trying to decide if they were truly alone. She shouldn't panic just yet, she thought. There was only one of them. The person might be just a common burglar looking for something to steal and sell at a pawnshop.

She quickly changed her mind. Whoever it was, draped in shadows under the concealment of night, was attaching a suppressor to a pistol. Burglars didn't usually have suppressed weapons. Was it possible Seymour had made the decision to come for her? She couldn't identify who it was due to the grainy video, but Sara was hopeful. If the idiot came to take her out, it would make her task so much easier. Whoever it was, she had a few surprises for them. She couldn't help but giggle out loud. Time to have some fun. God, how she loved this stuff!

Before she could move from her makeshift desk of planks on milk crates, she saw one more figure drop over the wall. *Would you looky there*, she mused. Seymour chose to bring backup. Without warning, the lights went off, plunging her hideaway into darkness. The extra screens shut off. Even the laptop shut down. Which was odd because it had a battery. Things just got more exciting. Seymour must think he had the advantage. What an idiot, she thought. What had they done to kill even the laptop battery? A localized EMP of some kind? Of course. It's what she would do if she was going to sneak into a place that might be wired with explosives using lasers and motion detectors for triggering. Things just got more interesting. Still, there was plenty in this building that didn't require electricity to be deadly.

Sara fumbled around in the dark until she found a cigarette lighter. Sparking it to life, she found her next goal. She tucked the nearby Glock G17 into her belt and grabbed the silenced Scorpion Evo submachine gun. It only had the one mag, but that was in the form of a fifty-round drum. If called on to fire it, she would have to use short bursts and carefully choose when to shoot. She tucked two more mags for the G17 into her back pocket and eased to the center of the room. She would have liked to use her night-vision goggles, but an EMP would have rendered them useless. Still, below her feet, past the steel hatchway, there was a flashlight in the steam tunnels waiting for her. She had left one hanging on a lanyard wrapped around a ladder rung in case she had to try and escape. Escape was not her plan. She had no need to run. She just needed to get into the tunnels of the old building for safety. Things were going to start exploding any minute. One of the idiots would hit a tripwire, a claymore antipersonnel mine would go off, and hundreds of ball bearings would begin punching through walls. She preferred to be below all the action when that happened.

She fixed her eyes on the latch, let the lighter go out, and dropped it into her pocket. Crouching, completely blind now and functioning off feel alone, she pulled on the hatch, carefully making her way down and closing the steel door behind her. At the bottom of the ladder, she felt around, looking for the flashlight.

Her hand closed around it at nearly the same time as a gun barrel was placed against her head. She froze, suddenly terrified. She had been outsmarted. The invasion from above had all been a ruse. Seymour would have known the place was wired. He would have figured out where the escape path would have been, and then tricked her into entering the tunnels. He had been patiently waiting for her to retreat. Surprisingly, it was not the blacklisted agent who spoke. It was someone else. The voice was male, with controlled anger barely detectable in his voice. "I would like to shoot you right now, but I have a few questions first."

Sara blinked in the darkness, wishing she could see something. With a hesitant voice, she asked, "Who are you?"

The man didn't answer. Something struck her with tremendous force at the base of her skull, a bit harder than required to knock her out. Stars shot across her vision: tiny, dancing blue fireflies twisting in an imaginary wind. Then she was gone.

DJ, Cash, Ali, and Carbon stood inside a room of what used to be a recycling depot for the county. Before that, according to the paperwork, it was some sort of small manufacturing facility. Sara Anderson had acquired the run-down place under an alias and used it for one of her safe houses. Currently, she sat slumped against a wall in what appeared to be the headquarters of the place. A lifeless laptop sat on top of a desk that had been created from laying old boards across stacked up plastic milk crates. There was a bed against one wall, a few wall lockers, and shelves with all kinds of small circuitry and wiring used for building her weapons of destruction. There was even a couple of free-standing in-room air conditioners to cool the large room. It was dusty, rusty, and grim living conditions for a woman to live in. DJ supposed it wasn't meant for long-term occupation. Sara merely used it from time to time when she was hiding. According to the list acquired from Deputy Director Hartley, most of the other safe houses were small homes or apartments. Some of them quite nice.

The space was lit by a trio of flashlights pointed at the ceiling, the light spilling into the room and allowing all parts to be seen, albeit dimly. Carbon was sitting at the desk studying his coveted tablet computer, watching live footage from the surveillance drone he had circling overhead while disassembling Sara's laptop. His goal was to connect her hard drive to his computer and see what he could learn. DJ and the others were lined up, prepared for the unconscious bomber to wake. At DJ's nod, Ali tossed a bucket of cold water on the murderer against the wall.

Sara awoke with a start, jerking and sputtering, eyes suddenly wide and blinking around at the flashlight-lit room. She zeroed in on DJ quickly, shoving herself up against the wall and sitting straighter. With one hand, she rubbed the back of her head, with the other, she held up a finger. "Wait just one minute," she pleaded. "This was not my fault. I was set up. I was tricked into killing your friend. Please, just let me explain."

DJ took a step forward, drawing his pistol from his low-slung holster and crouching down. "You know who I am?"

Sara nodded. "I know who all of you are. I do now, at least. The one breaking into my computer is the hacker known as Carbon. The man to your right is Bradford Cashin. You served in the FBI with him for a while. The one on your left is your CIA Handler, Agent Alimayu Salana. Once I figured out Agent Seymour had set me up to kill someone for his own personal gain, I started doing research on all of you."

Agent Ali tossed the bucket aside and stepped quickly forward. "Why didn't you do that before taking the job?"

Sara's face was desperate. She knew an unbearable amount of torture and questioning, followed by a quick death, was headed her way at break-neck speed. "I should have. I really should have. I made the mistake of trusting a person paid to lie. I had no reason to doubt his sincerity. He used me. He double-crossed me. Trust me, I want him just as bad as you do."

DJ stood. "If your bomb would have gone off as planned, you would have killed a lot of innocent bystanders. What about them?"

Sara blinked, honestly confused. "But that's what we do. You should know that better than anyone. Surely innocent people have had to pay the price when *you* went to war with the enemy. Collateral damage is always a possibility in our line of work. You know this. You can't possibly *not* know this."

DJ shot her. It was a carefully placed round through the outside of her calf, but he shot her all the same. She screamed a string of profanity and clutched the wound in both hands, rolling to her side in pain. "Sorry about that," DJ deadpanned. "Just write it off to collateral damage."

He wanted to do more; was compelled to do more. She deserved far more than a flesh wound. She deserved death. Even though she may have focused her destructive, psychopathic tendencies on those who largely deserved it, she was reckless, careless, with no regard for any human life other than her own. She got off on killing, on blowing people into little pieces. It brought joy to her. There was no making amends for her past or her very nature. She would never be rehabilitated for her condition. She needed to be exterminated by the most expedient means possible. Still, it was Carbon's idea to see if she could contact Seymour and lead them to the traitor. DJ would see it through until he was certain she had outlived her usefulness. Then, he would shoot her one more time.

Agent Ali spoke next, taking over. "The only way you walk out of this is to help us catch Seymour. We know you have a back channel to him. So, you're going to reach out, make him think you want to finish the job you started. You're going to lure him in for us."

Gritting her teeth through her pain, Sara nodded. "Absolutely, of course, I will. There's... there's just one problem. He's gone dark since the news broke the story of the bombing. To be honest, I'm not sure he'll ever reply now. Isn't he wanted by the CIA? Still, I know some people he routinely does business with. I'm sure we can figure out a way to get to him through one of those. I'll help in any way I can. Like I said, I want him just as bad as you."

Cash had remained silent up until now, stoic as always. But on hearing this claim, he corrected her. "I assure you; you don't want him as bad as we do."

Before any other questioning could take place, Carbon called out from the other side of the room, his voice filled with dread. "Um, guys? We've got a problem."

Ali stepped over and looked over Carbon's shoulder. "That's a lot of bad guys. We've got fifty or so closing in on the compound from all directions."

DJ stepped over to look. Sure enough, the drone feed had several thermal signatures: all of them little, white cartoon-looking figures advancing in teams of four from different angles. He glanced at Ali. "Any chance those are friendlies?"

Ali shook his head, his thick African accent coloring his words. "None. The Director said she was leaving this to us. This has to be Seymour's work. He either is tying up loose ends with Sara, taking her out of the picture lest she give up anything on him, or he found out we were coming. Either way, we cannot hold back an assault of that size."

DJ nodded. "Fine. We take the tunnels out of here and live to fight another day."

Carbon disagreed, worry causing his voice to waver. "Can't. Whoever it is, they must know about the back way out of this place. I count four people watching the manway at the exit. Anyone popping out of the tunnels won't have a chance."

Cash voiced the only other option available. "We can stay here, make this room our last stand."

DJ shook his head. "We wouldn't last long. These walls are sheet rock. They wouldn't even have to breach. They could just lay down sweeping fire at knee level and kill us all from a distance."

Ali checked Sara's confiscated Scorpion, slinging his own AR rifle over his shoulder. Liking what he felt. "So, then what's the plan?"

DJ smiled. "Do you really have to ask?"

Sara spoke from her position by the wall. "I might have a few toys to help even the odds." She pointed to a wooden crate under her desk. "Check that."

DJ did. He liked what he saw. He liked what he saw indeed.

————————

Jeremy Crowder led his team of four to the door located on the northern edge of the compound. There was no way DJ Slaughter and his tiny group could withstand the attack headed his way, no matter how amazing he was supposed to be as a gunfighter. Still, Jeremy was cautious. No need to go into this cocky. Cocky got you killed. He would normally check the door for explosives, but this was the same door DJ's group had used for entry. He had spotted them from the roof of an abandoned supermarket two hundred meters away. He had a sniper stationed nearby and lobbied for a quick change in plans. They could have ended this right then and there. He had been overruled, of course. Sara Anderson was supposed to be inside. He was told to let them enter and engage her. There was a good chance she would blow them all to pieces and they could call it day, slipping away before the cops showed up to this decrepit section of town.

No explosions had gone off. This meant DJ and his crew had successfully navigated any booby traps the girl had set. They probably were inside questioning her right then. So much for them all killing each other.

Inside revealed a large room that might have been used as a reception area, and two hallways led off in different directions. They chose the one leading into the heart of the complex. At the entrance to the hall, Jeremy found the remnants of the first trap. A snipped wire at ankle high indicated DJ and his group had disarmed the device. Tracing the wire led to a claymore mounted in the ceiling. Nasty, Jeremy thought. Scanning the length of the hallway with his thermal goggles showed nothing moving. He motioned to the three others to watch for traps and began moving forward carefully, scanning for threats as he went.

The coms tucked into his ear announced similar breaches around the building, more armed men slithering their way inside, all of them focused on one target. DJ Slaughter stood no chance. No chance at all.

They checked each room branching off the hall as they moved, wary of an ambush. Suddenly, a flash of movement at the end of the hall. A figure sprinted past, visible for only a second. Whoever it was had not seen them, and Jeremy launched into a pursuit. He would put a couple through the shoulder blades of whoever it was fleeing. His men followed, running hard and right on his heels. All four rounded the corner, sliding on the ancient dusty floor, guns up and ready to destroy their first victim. The hallway was empty. They must have ducked into one of the three rooms just ahead.

Jeremy's heart sank. He had been played. He had fallen for a trap. Maybe he heard something that tipped him off. Maybe it was his sixth sense kicking in to alert him of trouble. Whatever it was, Jeremy dropped to a knee and spun about, looking for the threat he knew was behind him. He didn't even complete the spin before a bullet tore through his jaw, the sound of shattering bone and mutilating flesh filling his ears.

Jeremy was falling then, right alongside his men. Each one of them collapsing without firing a single round; each one stepping into death as easily as breathing. Jeremy spotted him then, DJ Slaughter, standing flatfooted in the hallway, feet shoulder-width apart, rifle slung over his back, a silenced pistol held loosely in one hand like a scene from an old western. If it weren't for the thermal goggles strapped to the man's head, Jeremy might have thought he had been teleported into a Zane Grey novel his great grandfather used to read. Jeremy was still alive, though. DJ's reputed tendency for hip shooting people through the head had just then been proven more than legendary. Still, Jeremy was alive. He had to kill Slaughter. Jeremy wasn't sure if he could live with the injuries he had sustained; he had no idea how much damage the projectile had done, but it didn't matter. He had to try. He moved with as much speed as he could muster. DJ moved faster, the pistol held at his waist, flicking just slightly as the barrel refocused on a new target. Jeremy wasn't sure what happened next. Jeremy wasn't sure of anything anymore.

Agent Ali stood over the bodies in the hallway. He was impressed. He had seen DJ at his best more than once, still, it was always astonishing to witness someone as gifted as they were up close. The man was good at any distance, but within seventy-five feet, DJ fired the pistol he named MP as easily as pointing his finger and wishing his targets gone. "Nice job, DJ. Next time, you be the rabbit. By intercepting these when we did, we can get the others and escape while they think we're still here."

DJ nodded. "It's a good idea." He unslung his AR and held it out to Ali. "Give me that Scorpion. It's smaller and more maneuverable." Ali did as asked and spoke over the radio, telling the others it was safe. DJ inspected the new weapon before slinging it over his back and heading further into the building.

Ali blinked. "What are you doing? This is our break. Let's get out of here."

DJ called over his shoulder. "You take the others and leave. I'll meet up with you later."

Ali snapped at his friend, frustration coloring his words. "Get back here! There's no need to prove anything."

DJ paused, turning to look at Ali. "It's not about proving anything. It's about sending a message." With that, DJ rounded a corner and was gone. Ali punched the wall in response. What was the man thinking? He was good at close combat, sure, but this was foolish. He would never make it out of here alive by taking on that many combatants.

A shuffling noise from behind him had Ali spinning with his gun raised, ready to kill whoever it was. Instead of more bad guys, Cash was leading Carbon and a limping Sara through a doorway. Cash stopped, seeing the look on Ali's face. "Where's DJ?" he leerily asked.

Ali's disgust was apparent. "Where do you think?"

DJ pushed into the building carefully, on the lookout for the enemy within, doing math. Four dead guys and five rounds spent, meant he had sixteen left in MP. He had three spare mags with a total of sixty-three rounds between them. Plus, there was the newly acquired Scorpion Evo with its fifty-round mag. It wouldn't be sighted for his eye, but the distances would be close enough that it wouldn't matter. It had open sights, and his state-of-the-art goggles would see them perfectly. Even if Sara had never bothered to zero the weapon, it would be close enough from the factory. It might only be two inches off. Still enough for a headshot for the closeup work he was doing. Ali had guessed there were maybe fifty shooters closing in. It was likely less. He had more than enough ammunition to get the job done. He tended to only shoot when he was sure of a hit.

He was impressed by the number of shooters that had been sent. Since the CIA had disavowed Seymour, the man would have had to reach deep into a hidden reservoir of cash to finance this hit. It would have been expensive to hire so many men. Another thought hit him. Traitor Sam might have already handed off the drive and Seymour cashed in some of the cryptocurrency to pay for this. If that were so, once DJ caught up to him, Carbon would have to recover what was left. And there would be a lot left. Enough to satisfy Deputy Director Hartley.

He eased up to another intersection and listened. Sure enough, he could hear the soft approach of footsteps coming down the hallway. If he waited until they reached the corner, they would be even more on guard than they probably were. He would have liked to get further in, maybe come up behind them and catch the whole group of them together. Engaging this group now meant they might radio in his position before he could kill them all. So be it, he thought. One never got to choose the cards that were dealt. You simply played the hand you had.

DJ stepped out, picking out glowing targets with his thermal goggles quickly and firing from the hip with ease. It was another four-man team. They never got a chance to radio his position as he feared. They just died as they were supposed to.

Twelve rounds in MP. Sixty-three in his spare mags.

Further in, DJ approached another doorway. For a moment, he thought he heard something. He paused and listened carefully. Hearing nothing more, he edged in closer to the doorframe and peeked in, ready to retreat from gunfire. Nothing. He had been mistaken. He stepped into the doorway, seeing another open door on the opposite side of the room, intending to follow it.

The room was a thirty-foot square. It looked to have at one time been a break room for employees. There was cabinetry on the far side room. Some of the doors were missing, others hanging askew by ruined hinges. Graffiti decorated every portion, and trash littered the place. There were still tables and chairs, flipped, scattered, and on their sides. He stepped into the room, heading for the other side, and realized his mistake. The tables all had their tops pointed in his general direction. They had been set up as cover for people to hide behind. As one, guns began peeking over the tops and rounds started to fly. They had known he was coming. While no one had said anything over a radio, this group must have heard him. Silenced gunfire wasn't silent, after all.

He reversed and drove right along the hallway, narrowly avoiding the gunfire intended for him. He kept going, knowing the sheet rock walls would offer only concealment and no protection. Bullets ripped through, walking their way from the door and in the direction he had gone. He had a choice. He could continue running, or he could wait for the pause in gunfire and attack. He liked the latter option the best. It was time to use the equalizers picked up in Sara's office.

Stashed in a box under her desk were eight hand grenades. They were NATO issue and ones he was familiar with. This meant he knew they had a five-second fuse. He pulled the first one from his vest and removed the pin. DJ waited for the hail of bullets to pause, released the spoon, counted off two seconds, and raced back across the opening, hurling the grenade into the room as he went. Inside, men were coming out of concealment and heading for the door with weapons raised. His reversal in direction caught them off guard. There was gunfire, but nothing that came close.

Only a second passed from his throw before the explosive went off. The sound was deafening, a mighty thunderclap that would have rendered him deaf if not for the high-tech earpieces he wore. They served to not only communicate with his team but to save his hearing from the noises of battle and training. Even with hearing protection, the blast was loud. Shrapnel ripped through the walls, some of it peppering him. He felt a burning in his right leg and the back of his neck. It was nothing to slow him down, however, as he reversed course once more and charged into the room.

Three were clearly dead, the remaining five injured, some gravely. He finished them off with little fight, a single bullet ending them all. The last managed to get off a shot, hitting DJ square in the chest, causing him to stagger as the projectile impacted his plate carrier. Shame, DJ thought, the man should have gone for the head. DJ put his answering round just below the idiot's left eye.

Four rounds left in MP. Sixty-three in his spare mags.

DJ performed a hot mag swap, leaving twenty-two rounds in his pistol and two full spare mags. He positioned the next grenade for easy access and moved through the far door as intended.

He was met instantly with four more adversaries. The first was practically in his face, the man's weapon inches from DJ's cheek. He reacted instantly, moving his head to the right and pushing the man's barrel to the left. It let out a short string of gunfire through its silenced front end and they flew harmlessly to the side. DJ placed MP under the man's chin and squeezed the trigger, the dead man falling to DJ's left. The next man received nearly the same punishment. DJ extended his arm, placing his pistol against the man's lips, and fired again. The last two men were shooting back then, through the body of the dead man in front of them but DJ retreated into the breakroom. He was there for a moment, putting six rounds through the wall, walking them sideways, hoping to at least injure them. He stepped forward once more and into the hallway beyond. His enemies were retreating. They saw him and fired at nearly the same time as DJ. It did little good. DJ dropped both with two more quick shots.

Twelve rounds left in MP. Forty-two in his spare mags, plus the four in his nearly depleted mag. Still plenty enough ammo to make them wish they never took this job.

At the end of the hallway, more people appeared. He ducked into the room and pulled the pin on a grenade. Leaning into the hallway briefly, DJ chucked the thing as far forward as he could. Ducking back into the room once more, he imagined the combatants at the end of the hallway were scrambling like pigs at a bacon convention. He performed another hot mag swap before the grenade went off, then charged down the hallway as fast as he could, hoping to catch them off guard.

The room was two stories tall and looked to be part of the manufacturing floor during the original construction. Rusting walkways stretched overhead, dividing the space into large cubes. Remnants of machinery, some of it still bolted to the floor, others laying scattered about like refuse, filled the place. Large steel tanks, chains, pulleys, and other things DJ couldn't identify, made the place feel creepy and ominous. The ceiling was comprised of peaked skylights, many of them broken or missing. Light from a nearly full moon cascaded from above like many fingers, poking through the thin dust that hung in the air like light fog. Even though he was wearing thermal goggles, it was still visible, casting an ethereal, otherworldly gloom over the space.

Immediately in front was one dead soldier and another who had been downed but was reaching for a fallen weapon. DJ took him out with a pull of the trigger, blood spraying from behind his head as the round passed through. Spotting no one else, DJ raced for the side of a concrete pedestal off to one side, the base for a piece of missing machinery that had once perched on top. A blast of full-auto gunfire came from somewhere to his left as he slid in behind, bullets ricocheting off the corner of the concrete. He peeked once to see where it was coming from and nearly took one through the face for his efforts.

"Be more careful," DJ mumbled to himself.

His peek had verified at least four shooters hiding behind a concrete retaining wall, all lined up in a row about fifty feet away. He would have trouble picking them off one at a time. So, DJ pulled another grenade, yanked out the pin, and tossed it overhead as high and as far as he could.

The thing always overlooked in the movies was just how heavy a grenade was. On-screen depiction showed the heroes hurling them great distances like baseballs. That was a farce. A baseball is just over five ounces. A grenade is three times as much, coming in at about a pound. It's like a small shotput. One did not fire it in like a baseball, you could injure yourself that way. You lobbed it in a long arc when distance was required.

Luckily, DJ worked out. The distance wasn't an issue here. The overhead catwalks were. The grenade landed on a steel-grated walkway halfway to his target. "Crap," DJ muttered, and tucked in as close to the concrete pedestal as he could get.

The grenade went off with its standard clap of thunder, sending shards of metal in all directions, including DJ's. One of them dented the top of his steel-toed boots, pinching his toes. For a split second, he panicked, thinking he had blown part of his foot off. Seeing the damage was only superficial, DJ popped up, caught another person in the face with a well-placed shot, and dropped back down before the dead man's friends had a chance at payback. The answering gunfire skipped across the top of the pedestal, causing one of the soldiers to swear and call DJ a quite inventive combination of swear words. At least his adversaries were creative with colorful metaphors.

Crouching next to the concrete base, DJ caught a flash of movement from the doorway he had come through. A person peeked in, darting his head out and back again. Then he leaned out once more, swinging a rifle up. DJ drilled him in the forehead before the man had a chance to fire.

Nineteen rounds left in MP. One full spare. Two partials. Four rounds in one, twelve in the other.

Knowing the man at the door wasn't alone, they seemed to be traveling in groups of four, DJ pulled another grenade, let the spoon fly, and tossed it through the opening. Before it had a chance to go off, he readied the Scorpion: pulling the strap over his head and resting the weapon on the floor.

DJ did some math in his head while he freed himself from the submachinegun, waiting for the grenade to do its thing. When he entered the room, there was one dead guy, another DJ killed, and four hiding behind the retaining wall. That was six. If they traveled in groups of four, where were the other two? DJ felt the hair stand on the back of his neck. They must be trying to flank him. But from where?

There was a shouted curse from the hallway and the grenade blew. Five seconds was a long time in the world of combat.

He couldn't stay here any longer. He was pinned down. It was only a matter of time before the missing men flanked him and ended his vigilante vendetta. He had to move. He closed his eyes, took a deep breath, and stood.

As often happened in times like this, time slowed down. Not really, of course. No one could change the passage of time. Instead, sometimes, in high-pressure situations, his brain processed things more quickly. Maybe it was due to more neurons firing than normal. Maybe it was due to a sudden flood of adrenaline. DJ wasn't sure. While he seemed to have no control over when this happened, he was thankful for the moments it appeared. Right then, it was showing up just in time.

Distance demanded he take out the three remaining men behind the retaining wall without missing. So, as he stood, he was already pointing, looking through the sights, hyper-focusing on accuracy. The first man died instantly. The target taking too long to draw a bead on DJ. The second one got off a shot a fraction after DJ, the impact of DJ's 9mm round tearing into the man's left nostril and causing him to pull his own shot just enough to miss. DJ felt the whiff of the bullet past his ear, so much so, he flinched. The third, perhaps, concluding he had bitten off more than he could chew, ducked out of view.

He did a one-eighty and focused on the door, waiting for wounded men to come out. He paused for only a second, considering the remaining man behind him, but none from the hallway emerged. He spun again, snatched the Scorpion with his left hand, and charged toward the retaining wall, maneuvering through the steel debris littering his path, searching for the two missing men and waiting for the last one behind the retaining wall to peek again. One of the two missing team members found him first. A bullet impacted the rear of his plate carrier low on his back. He grunted and hunched from the blow, turning and diving left onto his side, dropping the submachine gun to the floor and aiming back the direction he had come. On an elevated walkway, a solitary figure was shooting down at him. Before DJ could get off a shot, a second round impacted the cement floor near his head, sending shards of debris into his face. DJ involuntarily blinked and sputtered from the bits of concrete in his mouth and fired from instinct alone. The round took the man in the hip, and the soldier stumbled. It was enough of a pause for DJ to take a more precise shot, his bullet smashing through the man's face. He rolled quickly and refocused on the retaining wall just in time to see a face appear. DJ put one between the eyes and scrambled to his feet, gathering up the Scorpion and sprinting for the concrete barrier the others had hidden behind. He hoped to use it for cover as well. He was certain those in the hallway had not all died from his grenade.

Fourteen rounds in his pistol. One full spare and two partials at his side.

Hurdling the short wall, DJ was surprised to see the last missing team member laying wounded on the ground beyond. DJ had assumed he was trying to flank. Instead, the man had been wounded by the grenade and was laying bleeding, hoping his friends would take care of the threat. As DJ cleared the wall, the wounded man let loose with a blast of automatic fire. The first two drilled DJ in the chest at point-blank range with all the impact of a mule kick, pushing the breath from his lungs. The third ripped through the top of his left shoulder, sending searing heat and stabbing pain through his arm. The rest of the burst flew past DJ's head.

Despite the close range, the shock of being shot threw him off and DJ's returning shot missed by a mile. He hit the ground awkwardly and racked his elbow on the hard flooring of the facility. MP fell from his tingling fingers. The Scorpion wasn't an option either, holding it just forward of the ejection port in his left hand. The other man was flat on his back and bringing his rifle over across his chest to have another go. DJ could now see it looked to be the newer Sig Sauer NGSW-R. This spoke to just how well-financed these guys were. It was weird just how much one could process in so short a time.

Desperate, DJ didn't scramble for his modified X5 pistol, nor did he try to get a better grip on the Scorpion. There was no time. He dove for the man, locking his left hand around the suppressor, thankful for his gloves shielding him from the heat. He pushed it wide and scrambled on top of the man, smashing down with his right fist like a carpenter with a hammer. Once, twice, three times, four. Stunned, his adversary released the weapon. DJ yanked it free, slammed the butt into the man's face once more for good measure, got to one knee, reversed the rifle, and shot him through the eye. The impact of such a large caliber round from so close made a bloody mess. Some of it splattering into DJ's face.

Grimacing in pain and anger, DJ stood and looked around, daring any others to show their face. He spotted a form coming through the door he had entered, and out of sheer rage, he shouldered the commandeered rifle and let loose with a full-auto blast, emptying the remainder of the mag into the poor man.

Up till then, DJ had done his best to reign in the fury that bubbled just below the surface, but he could hold it back no more. He had been lied to by someone who was supposed to represent the good of his country. He had been infiltrated by a two-faced traitor who had murdered a member of his team and nearly killed another. Brett, his best friend, had suffered so much in such a short few years because he had chosen to follow DJ into this life. Divorce had ripped his friend in two. He lost the use of his legs simply because he was DJ's friend. He had nearly been killed in a Saudi Arabian prison in an ambush. Right then, the only person besides Abbi who seemed to understand him and accept DJ's brokenness was clinging to life from a bullet hole in his heart. DJ knew that giving himself over to emotion was a sure-fire way to get yourself killed, but he had had enough. It was all too much. The dam burst. His rage erupted in a volcano of hate.

DJ threw the empty rifle as far as he could, and shouted at the top of his lungs, straining his vocal cords. *"Who's next? Come on! I'll take you all!"*

As if in answer to his challenge, a new group slithered through the black, ducking and advancing across the assembly floor. DJ crouched, hot-swapped the mag in MP, holstered it, grabbed the dropped Scorpion, and ran at them. Teeth gritted, snarl on his lips, he went after them. With complete disregard for tactics or safety, he went after them. "Kill you all!" DJ growled.

DJ waded into battle, a grim visage of a modern-day gladiator. There was no drumbeat or theme song playing in the background. There was only death and rage.

Agent Ali moved as fast as he could, maneuvering his way through the building on his way back to DJ. He had secured Sara in the van they arrived in, leaving Cash to watch her and protect Carbon. They had almost come to blows over who would go back after their lunatic friend. In the end, Ali had pulled a gun on the determined Cash and threatened him. Ali was sure he would suffer for that later.

He followed the sound of explosions and muffled gunfire, looking for bad guys and DJ, hoping his friend wouldn't accidentally shoot him in the process. He had once before fought with the man in the middle of a Russian wilderness. He knew of DJ's skill and drive. It had been no use to try and stop the man, pleading wisdom at falling back and escaping with their witness. The look in DJ's eye had said it would have been a wasted effort.

He followed the noises of battle and dead bodies through the complex like a morbid series of connect the dots. After a few minutes, he noticed only silence, and Ali grew even more cautious. The fight was over, but what did that mean? DJ was either dead or captured. But which one was more likely? A dead DJ Slaughter, for sure, he concluded.

Stepping over a pile of ruined bodies, Ali entered a large two-story room. It looked to be the manufacturing floor of what was left of the building. The smell of burned gunpowder and an eerie silence hung in the air. He caught a whiff of movement to his left. Ali swung his rifle around, a borrowed .300 blackout AR from the arsenal at the farm and crouched. The move was blocked, and a fist hammered him in the side of the head, sending him staggering. "Stand down!" the familiar voice of DJ ordered.

Ali recovered and stood, staring at his friend. "Did you need to hit me?"

DJ shrugged. "Seemed the thing to do. Thought you might counter by shooting me with your pistol. I've been shot enough for one day. Let's go. They're all dead."

Ali was silent for a moment and glanced around, not sure if he believed DJ. "Seriously?"

DJ entered the hallway, heading back the way they had come. "I said, let's go."

Ali stared after him a moment before proceeding, wondering if he should tell DJ his new information now, or wait until the man had time to calm down. He elected for the latter. It wouldn't make a difference right then anyway. They would get clear of here before he told DJ he recognized some of the dead as active members of the CIA. He wondered what DJ's reaction would be when the man learned these dead bodies didn't belong to hired guns, but rather the CIA's own private army. Probably not too good, he mused.

Before coming here, Ali considered all of this a challenge. Right then, Ali knew they were well past that. They were neck-deep in trouble.

Chapter 13: Sam Kenny

Sam Kenny disembarked from the twin-engine Cessna, his hand on the weapon hidden under his shirt, and his pack over one shoulder. He had already tossed the AR he had carried with him. It was big, bulky, and hard to conceal.

He didn't trust the two men waiting for him in front of the lifted truck with knobby tires. They didn't appear to be armed, but of course, they were. He paused by the doorway and took a careful look around. There were several hangars around the public airstrip. Parked planes and shadowy corners provided plenty of avenues for a sniper to set up shop. The truth was, if the men in front of him wanted Sam dead, there was little he could do to stop it. Still, the order he received while flying to the east coast said these two would have everything he needed to kill Slaughter. And since the person on the other end of that call wanted the money on the hard drive that Sam had hidden, they were obligated to give in to his demands. Of course, they could always resort to tazing him until he wet himself and then torture the location out of him, but they had a vested interest in seeing Slaughter dead as well. There was more to this for them than a big payday. They had to ensure a very stubborn and resolved DJ Slaughter didn't pursue them until he had killed every last one of them.

Sam had been shocked when the voice had told him that there was far more money on that hidden drive than what Agent Seymour had promised. He had been informed of the real amount simply to ensure that Sam was aware of the great lengths that would be taken to hunt him down if he tried to run with it. In response, Sam had politely asked for a small pay increase and an assist in taking out Slaughter. The voice on the other end accepted easily and Sam turned the plane around to head back west.

Sam mentally crossed his fingers that this wasn't a setup, and approached the two by the truck. Both were dressed like average civilians for this part of the world. One wore faded jeans, the other was in cargo shorts. Both dressed in old t-shirts under long-sleeved flannel printed shirts with the cuffs rolled up a few times, likely to conceal whatever sidearm they carried. Both wore ratted-out baseball caps with frayed edges. One was emblazoned with a baseball team. The other, the brand for a popular sports clothing company. One wore shades, the cheap kind found in gas stations. The other, none at all. The untrained eye might have considered them to be the average Joe, but Sam could see the deliberate nature they had taken to blend in.

Sam walked up and the guy in the shades smiled. "You must be Sam. Got what you requested in the back seat of the truck." The truck was a four-door, late model with about a three or four-inch lift added and some beefy tires. It was dirty and looked well used but seemed to be in good condition. It was exactly what Sam had asked for.

Sam nodded, pointing to the back of the truck. "That's good. Now unload it and put it on the tailgate." Both looked at each other and back, not moving. Sam sighed. This was looking like it was going to be one of those days. "No way I'm going to turn my back on you two. So, put it on the tailgate where I can keep an eye on you both."

The one without the sunglasses spoke, his brow furrowed. "Dude, if we was gonna kill you, you'd be dead right now."

Sam smiled, his hand resting on the butt of his handgun under his shirt. "Humor me, homey." Neither one moved, their hard faces a stark defiance to his request. Sam shrugged. "I guess I could kill you both and then take a look, but it's your choice."

Shades spoke next. "You're not that good. And what makes you think we don't have a sniper pointing at you right now?"

Sam nodded. "Maybe you do. But they won't shoot, no matter what happens to you two. Your boss wants what's in my head. Besides, you'll still be dead. Unless, as you said, you don't think I'm good enough." There was a hesitation in the two. Both clearly wanted to see if Sam was just boasting. Shooters like the men in front of him never liked playing a game of chicken and losing. Sam prepared to follow up on his promise, but just before he pulled, the one with the sunglasses turned and opened the back door of the truck. He removed a large duffle with one hand, and a soft case for a rifle in the other. Sam stayed where he was until the man dropped the tailgate and rested both on top.

Sam pointed at a spot on the tarmac. "Both of you stand right there until I'm satisfied. Move funny and I'll shoot you in the knee just for fun." They begrudgingly did as ordered and Sam had a look at what was in the rifle bag first. He liked what he saw. Inside was a Savage Model 12 FTR chambered in .308 Winchester. In the world of ballistics, there were better rounds out there with flatter shooting performance. It was a veritable Howitzer shell with a deep arc, dropping thirty feet at a thousand yards. But Sam cut his teeth on this weapon. It was specifically designed for competitive shooting from the prone position at targets a thousand yards away. With this weapon, Sam could put every round within a five-inch circle at that distance all day long.

DJ Slaughter was a dead man. Sam had only to wait for the idiot to walk into position.

Sam went through the other bag to verify the contents, then backed away and pointed at Shades. "Good deal. Now load it back up." Shades wasn't happy. Sam could tell the man really wanted to shoot him. If not shoot, then punch. Certainly, the boss wouldn't be too upset if he decked Sam in the mouth. When the man turned from the truck after loading the bags, Sam thought the man was going to go for it. Surprisingly, Shades exercised some self-control and refrained from following through on the temptation. *Don't worry, Shades*, Sam said to himself. *You'll get your chance.*

Next, Sam pointed to the driver's door. "Now get in. You're driving me out of here." Shades looked at Sam like he had lost his mind. Before Shades could protest, Sam drew his weapon and stepped in, pressing the gun into the man's waist. "It wasn't a request," Sam smiled, inches from the man's nose. With his left hand, he removed the man's gun. Next, Sam reached up and removed the sunglasses, placing them on his own face instead.

There was no more hesitation from Shades. He simply turned and climbed into the driver's seat. Sam entered the back seat and instructed him to leave the airport. From there, Sam consulted his phone for navigation and relayed commands on when to turn. The whole time, he checked for a tail but spotted none. Of course, a drone could be tracking them, but he had to hope for the best. About ten miles outside of town, Sam directed Shades off the beaten path and down a winding back road. Comfortable they were isolated enough, he ordered his driver to pull over, kill the truck, and get out. Sam exited at the same time.

Shades stood next to the truck and looked at Sam with hard eyes. With venom dripping from his lips, Shades asked, "You're just gonna leave me out here to figure my way back?"

Sam smiled. "First things first. Raise your arms high and turn around. Shades sighed and did an about-face. Sam stepped in and placed the man's weapon back in the holster. He stepped back a few paces to give the guy some room, then reholstered his own, pulling the shirt back over the top. "Lower your hands and turn back around."

Sam could see understanding in his adversary's eyes. Shades knew what was coming next: a good old-fashioned showdown. He was going to be goaded into trying to outdraw Sam to see who was better. Sam confirmed the man's suspicions with a nod. "You've been wanting to shoot me since we first met. It was all over your fa-" he never got the chance to finish the sentence. Shades went for his gun.

Sam had to admit, the move caught him off guard. He lost precious time just in figuring out the man was going to try and gain as much advantage as he could, getting the jump on the draw. He also had to credit Shades for being as fast as he was. The man had certainly spent time behind his weapon of choice. Still, it wasn't enough. If shooting were considered an art form, Sam was something of a Rembrandt. Shades barely cleared his holster before Sam shot him right between his smug, condescending eyes.

Sam grinned down at the dead body. "Well, that was fun. Appreciate it, Shades. I've been needing to let off some steam for a while now. That should hold me over."

Next, Sam went into his pack and pulled out a small device. It checked for radio frequencies. He did a slow walk around the vehicle, holding the stubby antennae close to the paint. Eventually, he found what he was looking for. Sure enough, they had tagged the truck with a transponder. It took him only a moment to remove it and smash it to pieces.

Sam took over the driver's seat, turned the truck around, and headed to his ultimate destination. He hoped the voice on the other end of that phone call had been right about this. If not, Sam would have to take it out on them. He might just keep all of that money after he killed them, too. He hoped it wouldn't come to that, of course. He liked to keep every agreement. Sam had always been a man of his word.

Chapter 14: Paradise Bound

Sara Anderson was in trouble. Not because she had been shot, although that surely did really suck. But, by and large, it was a flesh wound. The maniac in charge of this group had put the bullet right through a part of her leg that meant nothing permanent or internally damaging. She would recover. She could limp around on it quite nicely as it was. No, she was in trouble because she knew what came next.

The one called Slaughter, ironic name, that would have no issue with torturing her until he had bled her for every ounce of intel she could manage to spit out. She could see it in his eyes. There was a dark desire in the man for payback over what had been done to his team, and she had played a part in the pain and frustration the man was feeling. Sara Anderson was about to suffer a very painful price for what she had done.

They had elected to take her back to their home base for questioning. They asked her very little on the chopper ride over, tending to her wounds instead. She was sure Slaughter had not chosen to begin because he preferred as few witnesses as possible.

She sat in a small room she was sure had been a broom closet just before she arrived at their headquarters. They called it "The Farm." At first, she had assumed they were taking her back to the place CIA recruits were trained, called by the same nickname. Unlike the CIA training compound, this place looked exactly like a farm. Until she entered the barn, she assumed they were going to string her up amongst the hay bales for questioning. Inside, she quickly realized this place was not at all what it appeared.

She hobbled around the tiny space, pacing about like the wounded animal she was. There had to be a way out of here, some way of escape. Maybe she could make up some stuff to tell them when they finally got around to asking her questions. The truth was, she had no idea where Seymour had hidden himself. The only thing she could really offer was a list of known accomplices to his many dark deeds. Surely they had access to that already. Still, there was hope. And if she could not come up with a name, she was certain she could make one up. She needed time, that was all. Just enough time to figure a way out of this mess.

She doubted any escape attempt would work. The place was surrounded by roaming men with guns and radios. Even if she could get out of this room and exit the building, she would be cut down before she made it five feet.

Something. There had to be something.

The drugs they had injected her with to subdue the pain were wearing off. Her leg was beginning to throb. Still, Sara kept up the pacing. Keeping her leg moving was imperative. Leave the thing stationary too long and it would be impossible to move at all.

Move? More like hobble.

She paused a minute to gingerly rub her leg, grimacing from the pain. All at once, she spotted the hope she had been looking for. It was just a tiny thing, but it was hope nonetheless. A mechanical pencil lay on the floor and had rolled into a corner. Perhaps this had been a storage closet for office supplies?

She snatched it from the floor for closer examination. It had a good point and was made with sturdy plastic. Jam it into someone's neck and they would bleed out in short order. Sara Anderson had a weapon. It wasn't much. She didn't need much. She just needed something. Now she had it. Time it just right and Sara Anderson might find her way out of this mess.

She smiled and mumbled to herself. "Should have handcuffed me, you bunch of amateurs.

DJ felt like shooting something, putting his fist through a wall, hurling a stapler across the room, something, anything to release his frustration. He had thought going after all of those men back at the safe house would have acted as a release for his anger and stress. It had not. The only thing to fix this was to find Seymour and Sam and make them bleed. Instead, he did what he become proficient at, burying his feelings. He walked over to the playpen in the corner of the operations room and carefully picked up Cassie. She grinned at him, a single tooth showing through her bottom gum.

DJ tuned back to the room and addressed Agent Ali. "Some of the men at the safe house were employed by the CIA, but what does that mean? Could Seymour really convert that many people to betray the agency and their country? It doesn't make sense. You guys test for things like that when you are recruiting, right? Besides that, the more people he brings on board, the more ways he has to split the money. I can't see any agent abandoning everything they knew for a few million dollars. He would have to offer them more than that. What would each of them want? Fifty maybe? More? It all starts to add up quick. So someone please make sense of this for me."

Ali was about to answer but Carbon jumped in. "I have an idea."

Ali turned to face him, seemingly perturbed that he hadn't had the chance to give his own theory first. "Please, explain. Because I am sure I already know what the answer is. But show us just how brilliant you are, genius."

Carbon stood from his desk and crossed his arms. "Three or four months ago there was all this news about how the CIA was going to get less money. The Senate Appropriations Committee, in defiance of President Neville, decided to cut back the CIA's budget by twenty percent. The President had gone on and on about how we needed to ramp up the war on terrorism. The other party, the majority in the Senate, went on camera and called him a warmonger, saying that this country had spilled enough American blood in too many countries, and that far too many innocent bystanders had suffered the consequences. So, he didn't get his massive increase in defense spending. He got a massive reduction instead. They twisted his arm into signing the thing saying that if he didn't, he wouldn't get his economic package through either. He needed to pick which one he wanted more. The government shut down for nearly three weeks while talking heads from both parties threw little temper tantrums on national television. It was political theater like I've never seen before. I'm with DJ on this. Politicians are nothing but a bunch of D-bags."

DJ spoke up, interrupting Carbon's speech. "Not exactly what I said, but you nailed the tone perfectly."

Carbon, angry now over having to prove himself to anyone, waved off DJ and continued. "Anyway! I think Deputy Director Hartley, or worse, someone over her, has conspired to steal the drive and all of that cryptocurrency. Explains why she is so focused on recovering the drive for herself, and why she was content to release DJ and all of his caveman-like rage after Two-Faced Sam, or whatever we're calling him. Also explains why we still have no clue where he is. It also explains why all of those dead guys DJ killed were CIA. I mean, with over two billion dollars in seized assets, the CIA would be able to fund their little private wars for quite a long time. At least long enough to wait for a new shift in power and sentiment on Capitol Hill." Carbon glared at the rest of the room, daring any to punch holes in his theory.

No one said anything for a long few seconds. Finally, it was Abbi who spoke. "If Hartley is really behind all of this, how come she's letting us go after Seymour too?"

Carbon smiled. "Great question. Glad you asked. She's not. Remember how she initially resisted DJ's demands? She pushed back pretty hard. But in the end, she knew tigers were going to do what tigers do. She knew DJ would never stand down. So, she acted like she was passing her blessing over DJ's pursuit. But think about this: she is also the one who gave us intel on where we might find dynamite chick. She knew full well that I would start looking for power consumption at all of those locations. It's how I figured where that terrorist was hiding that tried to blow up New York City, remember? She's a freaking spy. She did research on all of us. She gave me just enough information to lead me right to her. Then, she sent in her goons only after we were inside. She tried to take us out, all the while acting like she was on the same team. But she's not. She has her own agenda."

Abbi nodded but wasn't convinced. "OK, but why not just come after us here? Why lure us into a trap instead? Why not just kill us all right here at home?"

Carbon took another few steps into the center of the room, looking at all of them. "Because I don't think the whole agency is corrupted. It's a few people at the top and the ones she knows she can count on. Agent Ali has this place surrounded by people he knows and trusts. No way she sends CIA against CIA. She lures us out to that safe house, without backup, and takes out the one person she knows will be there who just can't let this thing go, though God knows why not."

Carbon focused on DJ. "Seriously, DJ, we should let this thing go. Let them have their stupid money and their little wars. Call her up right now. Tell her the team is too injured. Tell her you had a change of heart and want to retire while you can. Tell her whatever, but let this go. We can't win this one."

DJ shook his head. "Because Bounder is dead. Because Coonie is dead. Because Brett has a hole in his heart. Because if you are right, these people will go on killing innocent bystanders, blinded by their own twisted sense of a greater good. If you're right, Deputy Director Hartley is no better than Sara Anderson. You want a big dog to protect your house. But no matter how much you may want that dog around, once they start biting the neighbors, you have to put them down."

DJ looked at Agent Ali. "So, tell me what your theory is. Tell me why Carbon is wrong about all of this."

Ali shook his head. "He's not. Seriously, you do not give the kid enough credit. He's way smarter than he looks."

Cash finally spoke, having sat back absorbing it all. "Then what do we do about it? If Carbon *is* right, and I'm inclined to believe he is, how do we deal with this new development? If we just assassinate her, we'll be wanted for the rest of our lives. That's no way to raise a daughter, DJ. Besides, they'll eventually find us. They'll kill us when they do."

Before DJ could answer, Carbon jumped in again. "What we can't do is stay here. Hanging out behind Agent Ali's chosen troops may have offered us protection up until now, but not anymore. If baiting us into an ambush didn't work, she'll just drop a JDAM on this place from a drone. She'll resign herself to killing her own CIA to get the job done. At this point, she's all in."

Cash agreed, offering the only solution that seemed viable at the moment. "We go into hiding. We vanish before she knows we're on to her. We gather the evidence to hang her and then take her out. We at least go into hiding until we have a solution."

DJ nodded and handed Cassie back off to Abbi. "Fine. Then I know just the place. But, Ali, you need to leave the room while we talk about it. I appreciate all you've done, but it's time for you to walk away. You're better off not being a part of what we do next."

Ali stood straighter and stared DJ in the eye. "Are you fond of shooting your friends? Because that's what you'll have to do to keep me from coming along. I won't work for an agency that has done what they've done. We take them all out. I'm with you. Now, where is that you propose disappearing to?"

DJ nodded, stepping forward to pat his friend on the back. "It's right next to a place I like to call Paradise."

Chapter 15: Fix It

Ali looked at his friend and fellow agent, Hank Rayland, and shook his head. "No, the fewer the people that know the details, the better."

He could see Rayland wasn't happy. "You need backup. I know Slaughter's reputation but look what he's bringing with him. You've got an old has-been sheriff. You've got an ex-FBI agent that I am sure is really good at what he does, but he has a bullet hole in his leg. He's not on his A-game. Slaughter has a few in him as well. As good as he is, he's going to be slower. Period. And then there's a mother and her child tagging along. Or what about Carbon? Don't get me wrong, the kid's smart, but that won't help you in a gunfight. That's not a team. That's a target-rich environment. You know me and can trust me. Let me go along."

Ali nodded. "You're right on all of it. But it's because I trust you more than any other that I need you to get Sara some place safe; someplace no one knows about. She's the only witness we have. We need her alive. Somewhere down the road, there's going to be a Senate Intelligence meeting over all of this, and her testimony will be crucial to keeping us out of prison. Besides, we're dropping Abbi and the baby off on the way. It's with someone Abbi knows. Not really sure who."

Rayland shook his head, placing his fists on his hip. "I don't like this. You're going to get yourself killed."

Ali nodded in agreement. "There's a good chance. That's why we need someone else that knows everything that's gone on and can keep trying to get to the truth. Should we lose, we need someone to avenge us. You will need to fix this if we can't."

Sara felt vibrations on the floor of someone approaching. She stepped back against the wall and slipped the mechanical pencil into her waistband under her shirt. She briefly thought about just going for it and stabbing the first person to open the door, but that was foolish. The place must have fifty armed agents roaming around. Even if she was able to take a gun off her victim, she wouldn't get too far. Besides, she had no desire to kill another good guy and make her problem worse. She had to figure out how to get into their good graces instead. After she escaped, of course. There was no chance at redeeming herself if she stayed locked up in closets until she was sentenced in a tribunal and was shipped off to Gitmo.

The door opened and a well-dressed man in a suit jacket sized her up. He was cute, in a do-gooder sort of way. His brown hair was well-groomed, with a carefully shaped beard and mustache to match. His eyes were dark, mysterious, and seemed to be hiding his real thoughts. She was sure the man was condemning her up one side and down the other, perhaps contemplating the most efficient way to kill her, but he looked like he might be on the way to a meeting in a board room. He would have fit in perfectly walking the sidewalks of Wall Street.

She smiled, innocently. "And who are you?" she asked demurely. She knew flirting wouldn't work, but it was still fun to try.

The man didn't reply with his name. Instead, he tossed over a pair of handcuffs. "Behind your back. Put them on and turn around."

Sara sighed and did as instructed, locking her wrists behind her and facing the wall. The stranger stepped closer and adjusted the cuffs, clicking them tighter to ensure she couldn't wiggle free. "Where're we going?" she asked.

The man wheeled her about, stepped in behind, and pushed her through the door. "Not to a firing squad, if that's what you're thinking, but try anything with me and I'll be happy to put a bullet through your head. We're taking a ride, you and I."

She smiled as she walked down the hallway. "Great, I love adventures, but you still didn't tell me your name."

The man jerked her to a halt, spun her halfway around, and pinned her against the wall with one hand to her throat, squeezing to make his point. "The name's Hank. That's the last question you ask, got me? The next time you go for idle chit chat, thinking to get me to drop my guard, there'll be pain involved. Now shut your hole and head down the stairs at the end of the hall." Hank released her and stepped back. Despite the threat, Hank's countenance was nonchalant, like he had just greeted a colleague at the water cooler.

A trip down the stairs turned into a trip through the front door. The door led to a dark blue sedan. The sedan led to being told to lay down in the back seat and a pillowcase pulled over her head. Then it was a long drive of twisting, turning, hooded darkness. She did manage to get in a good nap, though.

Sometime later, she awoke to the feel of turning into what felt like a parking lot. There was slow driving, a sharp turn, and then a halt. She heard Hank get out of the car, leaving the engine running, and the sound of a metal door being lifted; like that of a metal garage door being pushed up along its tracks. Hank got back in, pulled the car forward briefly, then killed the engine. After hearing the garage door lowered into place, she was finally removed from the back seat and the hood was yanked off.

Sara blinked from the sudden change in light and looked around. They were in what appeared to be a warehouse. The walls were all corrugated steel with no windows. There were two roll-up doors behind the car, and gymnasium-styled lighting hanging from the high ceiling. It may have been an auto maintenance garage of some kind a long time ago. The air had the smell of old oil and grease. It explained the many dark spots staining the concrete floor. It was mostly one giant, dust-filled room. Against the back wall was a closed-in section that had been constructed inside. Perhaps for offices?

She was pushed in that direction and through an open door. Hank flipped on a light switch to reveal a twenty-by-fifteen-foot space with cheap paneling for the walls. There was a couch, a small table with two chairs, a fridge, a five-foot-long stretch of counter space with cabinets above and below, and a stainless kitchen sink on one end. Two other doors were in one corner. As Hank pushed her through one of them, leading into a space converted to function as a bedroom. She could see the other door opened into a small bath with a fiberglass shower. It wasn't much to look at. Sara guessed this must be a safe house of some kind. She had a few of her own that looked worse than this, so she couldn't complain.

Hank made her stop. "I'm going to uncuff your hands from behind you and reattach you to the bed frame. Try something, I dare you."

Sara let out a soft laugh. "You're the one with the muscles and the gun. I'm just along for the ride. Nice place you got here. But, before you shackle me to my new bed, it's been a long time since I went to the bathroom. I kinda hafta pee."

Hank paused, seeming to consider. "Fine. I hope you're not shy because I'm not leaving you in there alone."

As Sara was guided toward the bathroom, she considered a variety of sarcastic remarks she could make about men and their weird fetishes but decided against it. Good old Hank might knock her in the back of the head and let her wet herself while she was unconscious. He marched her inside to face the toilet and then stepped back.

She turned her head to look over her shoulder. "I can't pull my pants down with my hands behind my back." She turned to face him. "Unless you want to do it for me? I don't mind, but I'll need you to wipe me when I'm finished." She flashed him a mischievous grin.

Hank scowled, spun her around once more, and removed her cuffs. She rubbed her wrists. "Thanks," she said. She made to unbutton her jeans, plucked the mechanical pencil from her waist, and spun. His hand went for his weapon instinctively, but she was ready. Her left hand grabbed his wrist, her knee went into his crotch, causing him to hunch, and she pressed the pencil against his jugular vein. "One shove and you will bleed out before anyone can help you. Now let go of your piece."

Hank glared at her, wondering if trying to shoot her was worth the price. Sara could read it in the man's eyes. Gone was the mask he used to fool the world about who he really was. Here was the CIA operative accustomed to killing. In the end, Hank relented, and Sara took his gun for her own. She pressed it to his temple, tossed the pencil aside, and said, "Behind your back, Hank. Cuff yourself and turn around."

He did as instructed. Just like she had once before. What a good little prisoner. "Now lie on the floor and look out the bathroom door. I really do have to pee. Try anything and I'll put a bullet through *your* brain. And, no being a pervert and trying to peek, either."

While she relieved herself, she questioned Hank. He told her what city and state they were in, without fuss. He was less cooperative about what Slaughter's plan was for catching up to Seymour. When she had her pants up, she considered torturing him for the information, but she couldn't risk doing any more damage to her reputation than she had already. Hank also played dumb when she asked where he hid his stash in the building. Every CIA operative had a stash in every safe house they owned: a cache of weapons, money, and alternate identification for vanishing when the need required. After she handcuffed him to a support column in the main warehouse, she searched until she found it. The IDs were useless to her, but the guns and money would sure help.

Now, she wondered, *how does a fugitive from the CIA wanted for murder and terrorism go about gaining forgiveness from that same group of spies?* There was still only one option she could think of.

Time to start working her contacts. Sara Anderson needed to fix this before it was too late.

———

Agent Seymour Sinclair sat on a bench in the East Wing of the National Gallery of Art in Washington, D.C., staring at a priceless oil painting. He didn't know who the artist was, nor did he care. Most art was overrated, anyway. People paid way too much money to hang pictures on the wall. Most of it was a giant waste of capital, including the one hanging in front of him. It was a simple painting of a light blue, curving footbridge over a pond covered in water lilies. Admittedly, it was serene, and staring at it did cause some of his stress to leave, but he imagined he could have purchased a replica image in the gift shop and achieved the same results.

His face was plugged into every facial recognition program around the globe. He was a *very* wanted man. Sitting so casually in one of the most surveilled cities in the world should have been cause for worry. Seymour wasn't. Not in the least. Another program was running alongside his image telling the computers searching for him that he was really a pizza delivery man named Walt Cranzer from Albuquerque, New Mexico. He could catch any plane, travel on any railway, hand his passport over to anyone in authority, and no one would be the wiser. Technology was an amazing thing to have in your back pocket, especially since there was a kill order out for him with every intelligence agency the United States had. The ones that everyone knew about, and the ones that no one knew existed.

Seymour followed the brush strokes around the canvas in front of him with curious eyes. Though he had little appreciation for Renaissance painters, he could tell the creator had approached this work with careful detail. It was, indeed, pleasing to look at. He shook his head, the corner of his mouth slightly turned up in a mostly hidden snarl of disgust. "Waste of money," he muttered.

A woman spoke behind him. It was quiet and soft, just loud enough for Seymour to hear. Her tone was inquisitive but mildly amused. "No fan of the greats, I take it, Mr. Sinclair?"

Without turning, he shrugged, still scrutinizing the artwork. When he replied, he kept his voice low to avoid eavesdroppers. "I guess I'm more prone to office space motivation posters. Like the one with the cat clinging to a limb with one paw, and the caption telling me to 'hang in there.' It's nice, don't get me wrong, but I can think of many other things I would rather spend my money on." He turned to look up into the eyes of the woman who had gotten him into this whole mess.

Despite her age, Deputy Director Hartley had smooth features. He was reminded of the statement he had heard from other people of color: black don't crack. Her naturally tight, curly hair had been straightened and hung about her shoulders like a raven waterfall. It must have been colored to hide the gray, he concluded. Had to be. The woman was in the neighborhood of sixty. She was of medium build, wearing an expensive gray suit. A bright red broach was pinned to her lapel: a rose with a curving golden stem. She wore no other jewelry.

She stood there, her eyes concealing the anger he knew was circulating through her veins, smiling slightly at his opinion of art. "Ah, the amateur's approach to art," she said. "I suppose you have a velvet painting in your living room of dogs playing poker?"

Seymour shook his head. "Elvis," he corrected. "Long live the king."

She smiled broadly. "You are a funny man, Seymour Sinclair. With your gangly appearance, you might have made a good comedian. You still might have a second chance for being one if you were to consider a career change. You certainly don't seem to be very good at the spy game. Perhaps I chose you incorrectly." At this last statement, an evil spark danced in her eyes. Despite her pleasant surface, she was furious. His failures were jeopardizing her well-thought-out plan.

Seymour stood then, towering over her small frame. It wasn't done to intimidate her, far from it. She could have him killed with a snap of her fingers. He glanced around, looking at the few patrons roaming the gallery. Any one of them could be an assassin poised to slay him with a nod of her head. He looked back into her eyes. "You've been in this business long enough to know that a plan consists of multiple factors. They seldom go according to script. We can still fix this. Kill Slaughter and Sam Kenny will hand over the drive. With Slaughter gone, there will be no more threat of retribution. Our problem goes away."

Hartley smiled up at him. "I believe the original plan was for Slaughter to die in the very beginning. His whole team was supposed to be floating around in the ocean and being fed on by sharks. Your man had the jump on them all. It was going to be easy, you promised."

Seymour paused, trying to figure out how to continue this discussion in such a way as he would be allowed to leave here breathing. Say the wrong thing, and she could decide the world had had enough of Agent Sinclair. "Anytime you plan to take out someone, the other party gets a say. Besides, you know the man's reputation. He's good."

Deputy Director Hartley crossed her arms and tilted her head to one side, still beaming her fake smile. "Oh, yes, Slaughter is good at what he does. But *you* said Sam Kenny was better."

Seymour took a deep breath. He was on dangerous ground. What he wanted to do was give the woman a piece of his mind. What he did was assure her a possible solution to get this under control. "Look, why don't we just frame Slaughter for some crime; label him an enemy of the state. Let the FBI take care of him for us."

Hartley shook her head. "Two reasons that's a bad idea. One, by now he knows too much. As soon as his walnut-sized brain starts putting things together, he'll start talking. All it takes is for one person to listen. Remember, Slaughter and his team still have friends in the FBI. And two, that's not the deal we have with Sam. He wants Slaughter dead. He wants to kill him personally. I'm sure there's some macho thing going on in his head. He needs to prove he's better than Slaughter. If we don't let him take care of our Slaughter problem, he won't turn over the drive. We need that money to fund our operations, to get around the Senate Finance Committee. So, I have a better idea. Since you sent in a bunch of our guys on the raid at Sara's safe house, and that failed, *you* are going to assist in Sam Kenny's personal vendetta. Get a team together and lead the assault yourself. This time, if you fail, maybe you'll suffer the same fate as your men. It should incentivize you to get it right this time." She turned and made her way back through the gallery, not giving Seymour an opportunity to argue or convince her of another plan.

Before she rounded the corner and vanished completely, she paused to look back. She spoke again, this time loud enough that anybody close by could hear. "Fix this, Seymour. There will be no more second chances. And don't use our own guys this time. I have enough condolence letters to write." With that, she was gone.

Chapter 16: A+M=BAC

Abbi stood on the second-floor balcony, just outside the front door of a quaint apartment, and gave her friend a warm embrace and smile. She had met Mary Abbot when they had both been at Camp David. Abbi had been rushed away to the presidential retreat when the White House had been attacked. It was where she gave birth to Cassie. Mary had been a PFC in the Marine Corps, assigned there as part of a security force. The two had worked to uncover a traitor within the President's inner circle. They had also managed to free a hostage used for leverage over the President's Chief of Staff. Afterward, they kept in touch.

Mary finished out her tour and then left the Marines, focusing on using her free college tuition courtesy of the Defense Department to pursue a degree in Criminology. According to Mary, she had been inspired by the heroics of Abbi and her team. Abbi assured her it was not about heroics and adventure. It was about doing what was right. Mary wasn't dissuaded and pushed through her degree in record time. The last time the two spoke, Mary had submitted her application to the FBI, attempting to follow in the footsteps of Abbi. Abbi didn't like the hero worship that cropped up from time to time in conversation, but she and Mary did form a tight friendship. Because of the nature of what Abbi did, she had kept this relationship a secret. She was thankful for that choice now.

Mary snatched the baby out of the carrier on the front porch, eager to get her hands on the child. "Aren't you the cutest thing ever?" She turned to Abbi. "Do you know how long you'll be staying?"

Abbi shook her head and filled her friend in on everything that was going on as they went inside. She held nothing back. This was a person she trusted. She didn't have to tell the girl to keep her mouth closed. Mary wouldn't say a thing.

Mary informed her they could stay as long as they liked. The baby could stay even longer, she assured with a grin. Once she showed them to the spare room of her small apartment, she also showed Abbi a small arsenal of weapons in the master bedroom closet. "Just in case you were followed here, anyway," she said with a fire in her eyes.

Abbi could see the girl owning a pistol. It was in solid keeping with Mary's character. She was surprised to see more than a few. Mary explained that she bought the Sig P320 because that was what she had been assigned in the Marines. The AR15, she bought for the same reason, as it was similar to the M4. She had her concealed carry permit, so she needed something smaller to tuck away. That led to the purchase of the Sig P365. Then, she figured she needed something a bit more practical for home defense, so she bought a Mossberg .410 pump-action shotgun with a pistol grip. Finally, since she had committed herself to go into the FBI, and since the Bureau had switched back to the Glock, she picked up a G17 to become familiar with.

Abbi marveled over the collection. "You're like a DJ with pigtails. You and he would get along great. But you better keep your hands off him. That gun-nut redneck is all mine."

Mary laughed and they settled in Cassie for a much-needed nap. The little girl had been rubbing her eyes and fussing. After that, they went into the tiny kitchen to make coffee and chitchat. Mary was excited to tell her that she had been accepted into the FBI and would be starting her training in a month. Abbi gave the girl an embrace of congratulations. That was when the front door was kicked in and plainly dressed men brandishing pistols with suppressors entered the apartment. Five of them.

This was bad news.

The good news was, neither Mary nor Abbi were keen on surrendering. Fighting back was hardwired into their DNA.

The five men apparently had not been briefed on what to expect. One would think the element of surprise would have been on the side of the armed D-bags kicking in the door. It was the other way around of course. One was a trained former Marine. The other was a mother lion guarding her cub and possessing a handful of black belts in various disciplines of martial arts.

Even better news was the fact that these men had been ordered to capture Abbi and not kill her. She could only assume this since none bothered to shoot her or Mary when they had the chance. Abbi guessed they were to take her and her friend hostage and use them against DJ. It was a good plan. It might have worked, too. There was just one fatal flaw in that tactic. They didn't bring enough men.

Abbi broke the nose of the first one with her foot, then moved on to the second one in line. Mary, on the other hand, finished off the first with a jab to the larynx and then smashing a book from a nearby shelf into his temple. That was one down, four more to go.

The second one skittered off to the side to try and clear the path for his friends to step in and help. He was busy fending off a flurry of blows for a good second before the third man came into range. Abbi then began to pivot back and forth between the two, scoring a roundhouse kick on the third that sent him stumbling away, dazed. She returned her attention to the second, stepping deftly out of the way of a jab. She caught the man's wrist, rotated under, and flipped the much larger man over her shoulder, crushing a coffee table in the process. Size didn't matter when leverage was executed perfectly. The ancient physicists Archimedes of Syracuse would have been proud.

The fourth man decided it was time to change tactics. After all, they were getting their heads kicked in by a couple of girls. He aimed his weapon at Abbi's legs, intending to shoot the fight out of her. By then, Mary had confiscated the first man's gun. She put two through the fourth man's face before he could get off a shot.

Mary was far from done. She shot villain number two through the ear while he was recovering from Abbi's roundhouse. She retreated around the corner of the kitchen then, as man number five decided to take out the crazy woman with the gun. Abbi was the one of value, after all. He double-tapped her but only blew holes in the wall as Mary slipped from view. Man number five next focused on Abbi, deciding enough was enough. Killing her was a far better option than capturing her.

Abbi dove across the living room, knowing there was little to hide behind. But she didn't need to hide, she just needed to avoid the first bullet intended to kill her. It was enough time to give Mary a chance to pop back around the corner and finish him off. He dropped his gun and slumped against the wall, clutching the hole in his throat that had suddenly appeared. Next, Mary popped the unconscious form of bad guy number one with a coup de grace bullet to the head, then moved on to bad guy number three. He was still trying to recover from being flipped onto the coffee table.

Abbi shouted at her, "Wait! We need one alive to ask questions."

Mary shook her head. "No, we don't. We know who they work for and why they were here."

Abbi held both hands up, trying to talk her friend down. "But think how quickly he'll roll over on his boss when the FBI offers him a deal."

Abbi could see that Mary was deciding if ignoring her was the better course of action. Reluctantly, she nodded. "Fine," she said and looked to bad guy number four. The man was still slumped against the wall, gurgling his own blood. He might make it if the ambulance got here soon enough. He didn't, of course. Mary shot him in the temple out of sheer spite. She then surveyed her blood-splattered apartment. "By the way, you owe me a coffee table."

Abbi waited for FBI Special Agent Marcus Redman's reply. He looked at her like she had lost her mind. He was ok when she was explaining what all had transpired up till now, but when she asked for her favor, his demeanor changed. "Are you kidding me?" he asked. "You want me to take a prisoner off your hands, stash him someplace until you get this worked out, don't tell anything to my supervisor, then contact the local P.D. and tell them the FBI is taking over the case of dead people in your best friend's apartment just to buy you even more time? Do you hate me or something?"

Abbi rubbed her hands nervously. She knew it was a long shot, but she didn't know what else to do. If they called the cops about the dead men in the apartment, she would be answering questions for days. Deputy Director Hartley would have her dead before twenty-four hours were up. She needed time to put a few things in place first. "I don't hate you." She replied, a frown on her face.

Agent Redman crossed his arms and shot her an unconvinced look. "Really? Looks like it. Do you realize how fired I'll be when all of this comes out? Look, I enjoyed working with you, and DJ, and Brett, and all the others. Brett Foster was the best boss I've ever worked for, but respect and friendship only go so far."

Abbi glanced back at the car and Mary sitting in the passenger seat. Her friend was turned around and talking to Cassie in the back, seat belted into her car seat. "Look," she pleaded, facing Marcus again. "What if I told you that I can personally guarantee that you won't get fired? What if I promised you would get reassigned to the unit back in Texas? And not only would you get your old job back, but you would probably get a promotion as well. How does running your own team sound?"

Marcus shot her a sideways look. "That's a pretty bold claim for someone who was kicked out of the FBI. Don't get me wrong, I heard what you guys did, or at least rumors, and you're all heroes in my book, but you don't have any pull with anyone in power at the FBI anymore. Those days are gone."

Abbi grinned. "Let's just say I have all the pull I need. But you need to trust me. Come on, Marcus, we need your help. I promise, when this all shakes out, you'll help to close one of the biggest cases in FBI history. You'll be able to write your ticket; get any assignment you want. Look at it this way: with great reward comes great risk. But not for you. We'll be the ones taking all the risks. All you have to do is back the cops off for a few days and stash our prisoner. That's all I'm asking."

Marcus still seemed uncertain. "That's all you're asking, huh? And just where is this prisoner?" he asked.

She took a deep breath before replying. "In the trunk."

Agent Redman's eyes narrowed. "The trunk. Of course, he is. Sounds like a great place to put somebody. Nothing illegal with that at all."

Abbi shrugged. "What was I supposed to do? I can't put a murderer in the back seat with my daughter."

After a few more minutes of talking, Agent Redman finally relented. Abbi had always been good at wearing people down. They made the prisoner exchange and Abbi got back into the driver's seat.

Mary shot her a slight grin. "Well, I don't know how you did that, but I'm impressed. So, now where? We meet up with DJ and the others?"

Abbi shook her head. "No way I can tell DJ about this. He'll beeline right back to me. He's got his hands full already. No, we have to take care of this next part ourselves."

Mary seemed shocked, turning over all the options of what that could mean. "You're seriously not going after these guys dragging a baby carrier, a diaper bag, and little ole' me?"

Abbi started the car and pulled away. "Trust me, Contrary Mary. Where we're going will be the most secure place we could ask for."

Mary paused, wondering what Abbi was up to. "And just where might that be?"

Abbi took a right, heading to the freeway. "The White House."

President Tim Neville sat behind the desk in the Oval Office, listening to his campaign manager drone on about how they were eight points behind in polling, but not to worry. The reelection was all but assured, she promised. When the debates hit, Tim's skills behind the microphone would come into play and they would turn this around. If they could manage to negotiate a few bills through Congress, he would be on even better footing.

Tim cared very little about running for President. He enjoyed it well enough to want a second term, for sure. He just hated the running-for-office part. He had landed this job only because he had been named the Vice President and the leading man had been killed. When he had been running as Shane Tibber's running mate, doing his part on the campaign trail had been easy for Tim. He was riding the coattails of someone immensely popular. It had been a cakewalk. This time would be different. Firstly, he wasn't nearly as popular as the dead President. Secondly, he was going to be the front man this time around.

He quietly shook his head as his campaign team began to show potential ads on a rolling TV screen. He never really understood how he, Tim Neville, a worthless, traitorous human being, could end up where he had landed. He had been lucky, nothing more. If there were real justice in this world, he would be behind bars. Instead, he sat in a leather chair behind the Resolute Desk and contemplated what a waste of skin he was. Funny, he thought to himself, how could a person addicted to power, and being appointed to the highest office in the land, be so depressed about his circumstance? And yet, there he was, running for a second term.

He knew the answer to that question, of course. He was a dirtbag. Long ago he made a bad decision for noble reasons. He had tried to keep his family from being murdered. The cost was his soul. Still, that was a story for another time. He should probably pay attention to the presentation. His job was at stake.

A knock came to the door, and his Chief of Staff entered. Marshall Winslow had a worried look on his face. Everyone turned to look at him, and he jumped right in. "I need everyone to leave the office, please. We'll get back to you. We have something important the President needs to address." There were looks of both concern and aggravation. They had been waiting for hours to go over this material.

Tim stood. "Sorry about this, guys. No rest for the weary, I guess. I'll have Margaret reschedule." When they had gone, and the door had closed again, he cast a concerned look at his Chief of Staff. "I don't like that face you're wearing. What's going on? Did the Russian Ambassador come back with an answer already?"

Marshall stepped forward, a cell phone in his hand. "Sir, um, well, I'm not really sure…" He trailed off, unsure of how to proceed.

Tim crossed his arms. "Spit it out, Marshall."

Marshall sighed, seemed to gather his courage for a second, then proceeded. "Sir, there's a woman who just showed up outside the gates of the Eisenhower Building. She showed up demanding to speak with you. She said that if you didn't call her in here in the next ten minutes, she's going to take her story to the press. That if she did, your election would be, in her words, flushed down the crapper."

Tim was curious as to what this could be about. "So, go talk to her. Find out what she wants."

Marshall took another deep breath. "I did that. That's my job. But, Mr. President, she's bouncing a baby on her hip and refusing to talk to anyone but you. Sir, I must ask, is this your child? Because if it is, we have some serious damage control to do."

Tim snorted. "Marshall, I may be many things, but I'm not an adulterer. Did this woman say who she was?"

Marshall nodded. "She said to tell you her name was Abbi Slaughter." He glanced at his watch. "Time's almost up. Should I have the Secret Service hold her until we can figure out what's going on?"

Tim sat down hard, nearly missing his over-priced chair. His heart sank into his shoes. For a long time, now, the name Slaughter had sent chills down his spine and filled him with dread. In a faraway voice, he heard himself say, "Send her in."

Marshall blinked. "Sir?"

Tim snapped, fire flashing through his body, a scowl etched on his face. "I said, get her in here now!"

Marshall put his phone to his ear and began speaking, stepping out of the office as he did and leaving Tim alone in solitude.

What could she want? What could she possibly want from him this time? He had thought he was through with that part of his life. He thought it was over. He had redeemed himself with Brett and the others. Right? Surely that business was finished. Was she coming to blackmail him one more time? Tim didn't know a lot about Abbi Slaughter, but he knew enough. In many respects, she was exactly like her Tyrannosaurus Rex-of-a-husband. She never bluffed, and she was just as likely to snap his neck as DJ was of shooting him. No, this was bad. This was very bad.

The longer Tim waited, the worse the scenarios were that he envisioned. By the time she finally arrived, the back of his neck was sweating, and his palms were clammy. He could feel his armpits soaking his shirt under his jacket.

When Marshall showed her in, Tim pointed his Chief of Staff out of the room. He knew full well that whatever it was, Abbi wasn't going to want people to listen. She waited patiently for the man to leave, calmly bouncing a baby girl on her hip, standing there in her jeans and T-shirt like a common tourist. It was bizarre and frightening at the same time.

He cleared his throat and tried to put on the air of Presidential authority. "Nice stunt you pulled trying to get in here, carrying a baby. Do you know how many rumors we're going to have to kill over that one? I'm sure someone has already called the news as an anonymous source."

She stepped closer, her eyes dancing with evil glee. "Oh, you didn't like that? Hang on to your shorts, Mr. President. You're going to positively *hate* what I have to say next."

And he did.

As Abbi talked, Tim Neville saw his reelection chances spiraling away into a black hole of doom. But then he found a spark of hope. That spark quickly began to burn brighter. Soon, his manipulating mind saw this not as a black hole, but as a guaranteed win for a second term. If he played his cards right, he was a shoo-in for another four years. Abbi Slaughter was not the Matriarch of Disaster he had at first assumed her to be.

Tim smiled inwardly. He had just found those missing eight points.

Chapter 17: Crazy, Trippy, Good

Deputy Director Sharlette Hartley sat in the office of her palatial estate, overlooking her scenic view of the Potomac River, tapping her ink pen lightly on her lips, thinking. It was a good spot for it, and there were a great many things to think about.

When the property had gone on the market, she purchased the place, no questions asked, no walkthrough. The estate was perfect. The gated community emptied onto the Georgetown Pike. From there it was a ten-minute drive into Langley, VA, and work. The neighborhood was well-spaced out, casting a convincing illusion that she was secluded miles from the bustle of Washington, D.C. She saw trees, landscaping, and the Potomac. Her property ran along nearly a thousand feet of the rocky bluff overlooking the river. There was nothing but trees to be seen on the other side thanks to a zoned patch forest along the eastern riverbank. It was like she was alone in the country, but she wasn't. Interstate 495 ran nearby. One could hear the occasional tractor-trailer truck or the errant car horn from time to time. Like living next to a train track, it was easily forgotten. The wind through the trees and chirping birds masked most of the sounds associated with the nearby civilization.

This office was her favorite spot in the whole world. So much so, she conducted much of her work inside her own home. Thanks to her rank and position within the CIA, she had staff working on the property and security to keep her safe. Sometimes she could go a full week without venturing into the office.

A servant came in carrying a silver tray with her afternoon tea. The young woman's pleasant smiled filled the room. The girl always seemed happy and cheerful. It was why Sharlette kept her around. "On the veranda, this evening?" the young lady asked. "The weather's nice today." Sharlette nodded and opened the tall glass doors leading outside beneath a great, sprawling oak. No matter how muggy the summer could get, there was always a comforting breeze coming down the river, keeping this location cool and relaxing in the shade. It was a great spot to watch waterfowl and other birds making their way up and down the Potomac, foraging for food.

The girl set the tray down and politely excused herself, leaving Sharlette to her thoughts once more. She was sure she had everything in place to kill Slaughter and his band of rebels. They would *all* have to die, of course. She had gone too far, now. Any minute, she would receive confirmation from the strike team sent to take out Abbi. Argo had gone on to meet up with Slaughter and the others, so that problem would be taken care of as soon as they arrived in Colorado. She was sure Slaughter had taken Sara with him on his trip west, so that issue would be contained as well. It was unfortunate it had taken this long, but the problem would be taken care of soon. Sharlette hated cleaning up the mess of others, but so be it. Such was the burden that came with her position. She was a problem solver. It was what she was good at.

When Congress and the President went to war over budgeting, and she saw her revenue stream drying up overnight, she was left with little recourse but to come up with a workaround. But she did. Two and a half billion dollars would keep her adequately funded, allowing her to conduct her secret wars and ensuring the safety of this nation. She wasn't going to let a little thing like quibbling politicians get in the way of doing her job.

She was presented with a problem. She solved the problem. It was what she did. And she felt no remorse for doing it.

Almost. She was not fond of having to kill Agent Ali. Ali was a *real* black man. He understood what being black was really like. Not like these urban youths with their du-rags, sagging pants, and rap music. Ali had grown up in the slums of Ethiopia. He knew *real* black struggle. He knew what it was like to see his country starve while white Europeans and Americans either ignored them or used them purely as a photo op. Sharlette had watched her own country's politicians write appropriations bills designed to help, all the while funneling large portions of it through donors who, in turn, funneled another portion right back into those same politician's campaign coffers. It was revolting. Ali had grown up through all of that. And how had he managed to escape? The CIA had used him as a contact within the gangs and mafia of Ethiopia. No, she hadn't wanted to see Ali caught up in all of this. Still, he had been offered an escape path. He had not chosen to join them. Such was life. Everyone was either a victim or a victor of their own decisions.

There was still one pressing matter that needed taking care of: Brett Foster needed to die. This had been tricky for her to work out because Ali had managed to surround the man with those he trusted. The private hospital was secure. It had taken her time to find the right person on his team to apply pressure to. That portion was now complete. She could now sneak an assassin in to complete the job. But who? It needed to be someone local; and it needed to be someone who had demonstrated loyalty to her in the past. This cut the list down to only one. Still, she hesitated to call the man. The job would be risky, and this assassin had special skills that were hard to come by. Not in the killing department. No, that was not what made him so special. He was her secret lover. An exceptionally gifted lover if she were being honest with herself. Try as she might, Sharlette Hartley had developed feelings for him. She hated to send him on a mission where he might end up dead as a result.

There was no other choice though, no matter how many names she filtered through her brain. It needed to be done tonight. He was the best candidate for the job. She had no choice but to risk it. She picked up her cell and made the call. He answered on the first ring. She silently prayed there would be no further complications. She was really looking forward to his next visit to her bedroom.

Brett opened his eyes to the dim lighting of his hospital room and sighed. He was getting sick of seeing the inside of these places. Brett Foster had been a guest too many times of hospitals. It would be nice if people quit trying to kill him. He should have quit a long time ago. He should have quit before he lost the use of his legs. Every addict looks back on their life and says something similar. And that's what Brett Foster was. He was an addict. He was addicted to the job. He was addicted to the rush. When he transitioned to the wheelchair, he had thought the rush was over. It wasn't. He found a new way to do his job and still feel the high he craved so much.

As with every addiction, there was a price to pay. Brett's came in the form of being shot. He silently wondered how many more close calls he would have before the bullet finally did what it was designed to do.

He also wondered how much longer he was going to be here. Open heart surgery usually involved lengthy stays afterward, but he was sure he could put his foot down about that. He had resources. Certainly, he could get hospice to take care of much of this stuff. He would ask the doctor in the morning. That, and the drugs. The drugs were just too much.

Hours ago, he had spoken to DJ. At least Brett thought he had. These narcotics were really doing a number on him. The man had outlined everything going on, bringing Brett up to speed on the problem they were all facing. DJ had told him they were bugging out to lay low and work on a plan to bring Deputy Director Hartley, Agent Seymour, and the others down. This was something Brett should have been called on to do. Figuring out problems like this was where Brett shined. His brain was naturally wired for situations such as this. He felt helpless in this fight, laid up as he was. It was made worse by the painkillers he was on. He was drowsy, his thoughts fuzzy and unconnected. Every time he started placing those file folders in his mind in order, trying to solve the riddle, he ended up falling asleep again. He would have to speak to the doctors about that. He couldn't connect two thoughts together to save his life. DJ and the rest of the team were counting on him.

Brett glanced out of the window and was greeted with city lights and darkness. How long ago had the sun set? It seemed only moments ago he had been sitting here trying to find a pattern to the facts; trying to connect the information in such a way as a path forward could be found. Somewhere along the way, he had drifted off. He was useless. He hoped

DJ could find a way to pick up the slack. Brett doubted he had the ability to even tie his own shoes. These drugs were just too much.

The door opened and a doctor came in carrying a small tray. At least Brett assumed the man was a doctor. He was certainly dressed the part and carried himself like a person in charge. He was older, a black man with a bald spot on the top of his head. He wore the traditional lab coat and scrubs of a physician. He spotted Brett awake and offered up a kind smile. "I see our hero is awake. How are you feeling tonight?"

Brett cleared his throat before replying. "Hero? Do heroe's typically get shot in the heart?"

The man slipped his hands into his lab coat pockets and grinned at him. "Some of them do, but we tend to give them medals posthumously. You were lucky, my friend."

Brett provided a weak smile and tried to focus his thoughts. "Who told you I was a hero?"

The doc motioned behind him and glanced at the door that had swung closed. "All the armed men roaming these hallways. They didn't say anything out loud, of course, but their presence spoke volumes. The only time I've seen that many guns in the building, the patient was handcuffed to the bed. Since they don't appear to be cops, and you aren't wearing shackles, I figured the only other choice was a hero. Since you answered the way you did, mind if I ask what you did to garner so much attention?"

Brett shrugged. "I would think the answer was obvious. I got shot in the heart." His mouth felt like he was talking through cotton swabs stuffed in his cheeks. Could the man even understand what he was saying?

The Doc nodded. "Well, I'm Doctor Brown. I'm the attending physician this evening. How do you feel?"

Brett's eyes narrowed. "Again, Doc, I would think that would be obvious. I got shot in the heart. I feel like crap. Are we clear now? Do I have to repeat that fact again? I got shot in the heart. Please let everyone know I was shot in the heart. The heart." He tapped his chest in case the man didn't understand.

Doc Brown smiled broadly. "We're clear. No more talk about who you are, what you do, or how you came to be here. My apologies. Now, how about we try something different for that pain?"

The doc turned around and removed a syringe from the tray he had carried. Brett held up a hand. "Hang on a sec, Doc. These drugs have me fuzzy. I'd rather not take anything else. I need to start thinking clearly." Again, he wondered if the doc could understand him. It sounded to Brett like his words were dragging slowly out of his mouth. More like a river of molasses than sentences.

The doc nodded but didn't stop what he was doing, filling the syringe from a vial he had brought with him. "You did hear that I said something *different*, correct? You were on the other stuff because we needed you to sleep as much as possible, give your body a chance to do some repairing all on its own. This, however, is Destramethadone. It's formulated specifically to deaden the pain receptors but leave you clear-headed. You're going to like this a lot better."

Brett relaxed a bit. "Sounds like just what the doctor ordered."

Doc Brown chuckled softly. "Nice to see you have a sense of humor."

Brett nodded. "A sense of humor and a hole in my heart. Did I tell you I was shot in the heart? Do you know how much that sucks?" Brett already felt like he was about to drift off to sleep again. They really needed to do something about these drugs. Oh wait, that's what Doc Brown was here for. Good. It would be nice to think clearly. Maybe he should let the doc know he needed a change in painkillers. Wait, had he told him that already? Brett couldn't remember. He was having trouble thinking. DJ had told him of a situation that needed Brett's big old super-powered brain to solve. Being clear-headed was a necessity. But what had DJ told him again? He couldn't remember. Too many drugs.

The door opened just wide enough for a nurse to step in. She was a small thing and wearing a smile of her own. They sure smiled a lot around here, Brett thought. She wasn't looking at Brett, however, she was smiling at the doctor.

Doc Brown barely glanced at her as he prepared to inject the new medication into Brett's IV. "Step out a minute while I finish up, please. You can have our boy when I'm done."

She crossed her arms and seemed to size the doctor up. "I would say you're done, now."

Doc Brown stopped what he was doing and turned to face her. "Excuse me? What's your name, Nurse?"

She shook her head. "Tell me, John, how many women have you slept with that you can't remember who I am?" The doc said nothing, a look of confusion on his face.

Brett blinked at the sudden altercation. What had he gotten himself into? Was he still asleep? Had Brett dreamed himself into a soap opera? These drugs were the trippy cat's meow for seeing things, but this took the cake.

The girl, decidedly younger than the doc, laughed, genuinely humored at the look on the doc's face. "You really have no idea who I am, do you?" She leaned over and looked at Brett. "Your doctor is really an assassin hired to kill you. I wouldn't let him inject that into your IV line. I have a feeling you won't wake up from it." She straightened and returned her focus to the doctor. "I met John here on a job. When he isn't pretending to be a doctor, he's really quite the lady's man. The name's Sara Anderson, by the way."

Doc Brown, quick as lightning, reached behind the folds of his lab coat. The nurse was ready, stepping forward and shoving her foot into the doc's knee. The man stepped back against the bed, retreating from the assault. Brett tried to grab him from behind and felt instant pain from his injury for the effort.

Doc Brown shifted sideways, trying to finish drawing his silenced weapon from behind his back. Sara countered, spinning in place and hitting his gun arm with a swinging leg.

Now that was just exactly like something Abbi would do, Brett thought. Wait… Maybe this *was* Abbi. Maybe she was Karate-Kid-kicking the crap out of someone, and he had hallucinated a new face onto her. Maybe he was just watching TV and had gotten sucked in by the drugs. They really needed to cut down on the amount they were giving him. Shot in the heart or not, this was just too much.

Shot in the heart. Brett had been shot in the heart. Being shot in the heart sucked.

The gun clattered to the floor, and the doc connected with a left across her chin. She staggered back and the doctor advanced to finish her off. She recovered before he could get to her and began throwing a combination of blows, first aiming at the man's middle, then aiming for his head. The doc countered with blocks and strikes of his own.

They danced there at the foot of his bed for a moment, each trying to outmaneuver the other. It was toe-to-toe for a few seconds, with Brett not being able to tell who was going to be the victor. He was really enjoying the show. He couldn't help but watch with drug-induced fascination at the drama playing out in his hospital room. Who would win? Were they even real? Were they merely hallucinations brought on by the pain killers? If so, he was surely going to threaten the doctor in the morning about reducing the amount he had been receiving. This was ridiculous.

Shot in the heart. Brett Foster had been shot in the heart. Being shot in the heart sucked. What sucked worse was these drugs. They were a trippy good time, for sure, but one couldn't think while on them, and Brett really needed to think. DJ had given him a problem to solve. Brett couldn't do it while he was on these drugs. He would talk to the doctor in the morning about them.

Doc Brown hit the nurse hard and she went down. What was the girl's name again? Sara. That's right, Sara Anderson. She wasn't real, of course. None of this was real. It was all the drugs.

Really cool, trippy medication. He would have to order some up for interrogating prisoners. This crap was amazing.

The doctor walked over a few steps and retrieved his fallen pistol. Brett wondered what it was. He bet DJ would know what it was. That guy was a real gun nut. It was freaky how the man cataloged firearm information into the back of his brain for instant recall. It was a talent. Not very practical, but a talent, nonetheless.

Doc Brown stood over the girl as she sat up against the wall, pointing at her head. "Maybe the reason I didn't remember you was because you weren't any good in bed. Pretty enough to interest me, don't get me wrong. Don't feel bad. I have forgotten more of my conquests than I have remembered. It's nothing personal."

Brett shot the man through the ear, the hard crack in the small room sending his ears to ringing. Not really, he was sure. This was certainly all just one giant hallucination. Oh, he really did have his Glock shoved under a pillow just in case. DJ had insisted on the man keeping one handy after the hospital attempt on Argo and the death of Bettie, but Brett was surrounded by men trusted by Agent Ali. He wouldn't need it. So, Brett hadn't really just shot someone. This was just all one big illusion in his mind; his drug-filled mind. He would certainly have to talk to the doctor about changing his dosage. This was ridiculous. First thing in the morning. Top of the list.

Agents from the CIA detail stormed into the room, guns drawn and waving. The nurse had climbed to her feet and began screaming, backing away from the dead doctor at her feet, her hands to her mouth, a look of horror in her eyes. She pointed at the corpse. "He tried to kill Mr. Foster. He tried to kill *me!*"

The agents swarmed the body as the nurse slipped behind them. With their focus on the dead body, the nurse slipped from the room and was gone. What was her name again, Brett wondered? Oh, that's right. Sara. Sara Anderson. Or was it really Abbi?

Too many drugs. Trippy good, for sure, but way too many drugs. He would certainly have to talk to the doctor about that in the morning. DJ had given him a puzzle to solve. He needed to be able to think clearly. Of course, Brett couldn't remember what the puzzle was, the drugs were bathing his brain in fog.

Way too many drugs. He needed to talk to somebody about that. Too many. Way too many. Crazy, trippy, good, but way too many.

Chapter 18: Return to Midget Mine Ranch

Sam Kenny was lounging under a stubby pine, squinting into the west, enjoying the weather and the view. It was picturesque out here. The orange orb of a setting sun was just touching the peaks of snow-tipped mountains and painting the horizon in fire and beauty. Soon, those mountains would cast this area into blue shadow. Below him, the canyon and grass-covered clearings were already there, shifting into peaceful shades of purple. Soon, evening would be on him. While he could, he soaked up the last warming rays of the sun as it methodically pushed its way below the mountains.

He wondered how long he would have to wait out here. He didn't mind it thanks to the weather, but he did have food and water to think about. He had enough for three more days before he had to leave for supplies. He hoped that didn't happen. Sam might never get another opportunity to hike his way in without being spotted. Even if he were able, the moment he was waiting for might have passed. He would have to start all over, if that happened. He wouldn't be happy. All this waiting was making him impatient. There was killing to do, obligations to be met, promises to be fulfilled.

Sam looked into the canyon below, surveying the house on the far side for the thousandth time, wondering how the place became named the Midget Mine Ranch. It was a curious title, and Sam was certain there was a good story behind it. According to what Sam knew about the place, it had been called this since the eighteen-hundreds. The hidden Slaughter homestead nestled into a corner of Colorado was one DJ thought to be out of reach from the information gatherers of the CIA. DJ was wrong, of course.

The CIA knew of Slaughter using a false identity to re-purchase the home he had been forced to run from so long ago. They knew he and Abbi slipped away to their private retreat a few times per year, thinking no one knew. But the CIA knew. They worked hard to know everything. They enjoyed keeping tabs on anyone in their employ. You never knew when you might have to track someone down later. Today's friends were tomorrow's enemies. Deputy Director Hartley had passed the information on to Sam and assured him DJ would eventually show up. All Sam had to do was sit and wait.

Sam was perched over the southern cliff of the boxed-in canyon, overlooking the two-story cabin and the scenic valley of the Midget Mine Ranch. He was about to wonder for the thousandth time how much longer he would have to wait when a set of vehicles emerged from the trees near the small house. There were three of them.

Sam moved forward and slid in behind the rifle already in position. He had taken the opportunity to sight it in before arriving. He had already ranged the distance and knew it to be seven hundred and twelve meters to the front porch. All Sam had to do was spot his target, wait for Slaughter to pause for a moment, most likely when the man unlocked the front door, and squeeze the trigger. It would be a profile shot, a narrower target, but Sam was confident. Besides, he only needed enough of a hit to knock the man down. A second round would ensure Slaughter's death. With no wind currently in the valley, dead still air, Sam was assured of a quick victory. He might take out Abbi just for good measure. Maybe Uncle Argo could raise the daughter as his own. The man seemed to have a fondness for the child.

In the darkening valley, the three SUVs sat motionless. No one was opening their doors. What were they waiting for, Sam wondered?

Sam's satellite phone vibrated behind him. He ignored it. Nothing was going to pry him from behind his scope. After a few moments of buzzing, it stopped, only to start right back up again. Still, Sam shoved the thing out of his mind and concentrated on the vehicles, zooming in closer to see if he could see through the windows. They were black. No way to tell where Slaughter was sitting. At this distance, it would have been hard to make a positive ID through a window anyway. Sam would need to see the man moving about to be sure, recognizing Slaughter from his walk and mannerisms. For a second time, the vibrating sat phone behind him quit.

Finally, a single back door opened, and a dark-haired man stepped out with a hand raised, waving something overhead. From the distance and the pale evening light, Sam couldn't tell who it was, but the figure looked familiar. Not DJ, someone else. The man lowered the hand holding the object, only to press it to his ear. Again, Sam's phone began to vibrate. Frustrated, he rolled around behind him, snatched the phone, then rolled back into position, bringing the scope back to his eye. "What?" he hissed into the mic.

Agent Seymour's voice answered him. "That's me next to the SUV with one hand raised. Don't shoot. I've got new orders from Hartley. We're here to help."

Sam wanted to chuck the phone over the edge of the cliff. "If you didn't want to be shot, you should have never driven into my kill box!" To illustrate his point, Sam pulled the trigger. A satisfying crack split the still evening, and the invigorating smell of gunpowder filled the air. He didn't shoot Seymour, of course, even though it would have made Sam's day brighter, he just passed the round over Seymour's head.

As the gunshot reverberated around the canyon walls, Sam watched with great joy as the curly-headed, gangly CIA man scrambled for cover, looking like an overgrown, uncoordinated spider monkey on a hotplate, going down in the gravel drive once as he raced around to the opposite side of the SUV.

A second later, hidden from view beyond the front end of the vehicle, Seymour shouted through the phone connection. "We're on the same side, you psychopath!"

Sam chuckled. "Still gives me great joy to see you crap your pants. Now, why are you here disturbing my kill box with all of those trucks?"

DJ pulled off the road, taking a left onto a dirt track that snaked into the mountains. These access roads crisscrossed all over the many public lands as a means for fire crews to access and fight forest fires. As soon as he could, he spun the van around and pointed it back toward the blacktop that passed in front of his property. Looking into the rearview mirror, he said, "OK, Carbon, we're close. The entrance to the ranch is about half a mile up the road. Now tell me what's on your mind."

Carbon had been tinkering with some of the toys he had brought along. First, on the private jet they rented under an alias, and then in the back of the van for the hour-long trip to the ranch. For the most part, Carbon had been silent, focused on his task, whatever it was. DJ had enjoyed the quiet. The guy was as sharp as a tack, but he got on DJ's nerves sometimes with his endless yammering. A few minutes ago, Carbon had finally broken his silence to tell him they needed to pull over. When DJ told him they were almost there, instructing Carbon to wait, the guy had a meltdown, insisting that DJ pull over right then.

Carbon had his worried look on as he addressed the group. "How do we know for sure the CIA doesn't know about this place?"

Ali was quick to answer. "I, for one, didn't know. Since I have been your handler since the beginning, it would normally be something for me to follow up on. I would normally do extensive backgrounds on anyone we wanted to use. In this case, I already knew who you were, so I didn't."

Carbon leaned forward a bit. "Yeah, but are you telling me that someone above your head couldn't do it without you knowing? I mean, keeping secrets from each other, compartmentalizing what you know from another department, seems to be the standard operating procedure."

Ali nodded in agreement, thinking about that, trying to decide if it was possible in this case. It was DJ who answered, though. "Yes, but no one knows about this alias except for Abbi and me. We didn't go through you or anyone else to get it, either."

The look on Carbon's face said he was unconvinced. "Yeah, but where did you get it?"

DJ then recounted the story of how he came across a man while entering Charles Kaiser's compound back when his life took a drastic turn and he had been introduced to crime-fighting, albeit via vigilantism. The man had a set of IDs on him and looked a lot like DJ in the photos. He had confiscated them for his own, thinking he could use them later to play keep-away with the FBI. After that, when he had been recruited into the FBI, DJ continued to keep them just in case, eventually using them to repurchase his old ranch in Colorado. Whenever he and Abbi made a trip back home, he used the ID to book passage. They had told no one about them on purpose. They were his safety net in case he ever felt he needed to run again.

Argo asked a question that gave DJ pause. "But can you be one hundred percent positive you weren't followed to the airport when you flew here? I mean, ever? If the CIA paid someone to tail you, and you got on a plane to fly home, they could have reported back on the name you used."

The van went silent; everyone looking at each other, each second-guessing the decision to make the trip out here. DJ slammed his fist onto the dashboard. "Son of a..." he trailed off.

Argo chuckled at him. "Ease up, DJ. Our team leader has a strict no-tolerance policy on cursing." DJ shot the man a lethal look.

Cash spoke up next, asking a question. "What do we do then? We need someplace safe to plan our next move. If she hasn't already, Director Hartley will figure out we're on to her. When she does, we'll need to be hidden well or she might just drop a Predator missile on our heads."

DJ smiled at the group. "We drive around the bend and head to the ranch just like we planned."

Ali sighed behind him. "So, you're going to go all Texas on them and roll the dice, take the chance they don't know about your little hideout. Sounds like you *hope* they have an ambush waiting. *That* sounds like the DJ I know."

DJ shook his head and turned to look at them all. "Look, I know I made a stupid call back at Sara's hideout. I'm not proposing I stage a repeat performance. I got lucky. I know that. Besides, the ranch is set in a boxed-in canyon. There's only one way in and one way out. It's a perfect place to defend. It's also a perfect place for an ambush."

Argo shifted in his seat. "Then what are you suggesting?"

DJ shrugged. "I'm not sure, but aren't you guys tired of being on the defensive? Let's do a little recon first. If we see there's an ambush waiting for us, we figure out how to counter it. And by *we*, I mean we make Carbon come up with some sort of whiz-kid plan to give us an advantage."

Carbon threw his hands in the air. "Oh, sure! Anytime the odds are impossible, you turn to me and expect me to just whip something out. I'll remind you that you constantly refer to me as *kid*, *software dude*, oh, and my personal favorite, *panty-waisted button-pusher*! Well, you want to go grunting and charging into an ambush and show off your muscles, you can do it without me!"

DJ sighed. "Number one, you look like a kid and you play more video games than a ten-year-old. Number two, you know more about software than a person should so consider that a compliment. Number three, I've seen you in your underwear. They're silk briefs. Don't want to be called panty-waisted? Don't wear panties."

Carbon's face went instant crimson. "They're not panties. They're just... shiny. I tend to chafe. I need something slippery."

DJ smiled. "Look, we wouldn't be the same if we didn't have you. Everyone here knows you're the smartest member of the team. None of us could beat you at checkers even if we had railroad spikes in our brains. We would have been toasted twelve times over if it weren't for you."

Before Carbon could reply, DJ's phone started ringing. The number was not one he recognized, and he hesitated before answering. He glanced at Carbon for assurance. Carbon seemed to know what he was thinking. "Go ahead," he said. "After all the precautions I've taken, the CIA couldn't track your phone even if they were using wizard spells and rolled a twenty."

Argo glanced at the hacker. "Rolled a twenty? What does that even mean?"

It was Cash who answered. "It's a Dungeons and Dragons reference."

Argo beamed a grin at Carbon. "And you wonder why we call you kid." The smile vanished and he narrowed his eyes at Cash. "Wait. How did *you* get that reference? Got something you want to confess, blondie?"

Cash shrugged. "It's a game of imagination and endless possibilities. You should try it, Argo. Might make you feel like a kid. It's good for old people like yourself to feel young again."

Chapter 19: The Duelists

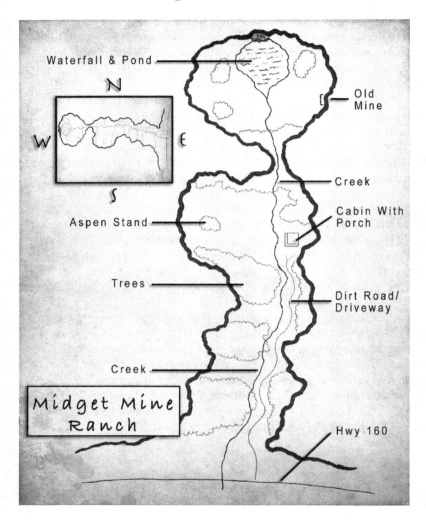

It took nearly two hours to reach his destination, and DJ was winded from the effort. Much of the hike had been uphill in uneven and wooded terrain. Before he reached his target location, the moon was already high in the sky. Even though it was only a crescent, the night was clear, and it was easy to make out the valley below. Laid out before him, in all its grandeur, was the Midget Mine Ranch. The canyon, hand-carved by time, stretched out below like a scene from a Louis L'Amour novel. DJ had been many places and seen many wonderful things, but nothing more spectacular than this beautiful piece of Western Americana. He had thought of it as his own private oasis. Turned out, it wasn't so private after all. Carbon had been right. There was an ambush waiting. It was confirmed when Carbon did a high flyover with one of his drones. The thermal imaging system picked out several people lying in wait around the cabin. Mostly behind it and in the small aspen stand immediately in the foreground.

His mind turned back to a time earlier when other bad men prowled this canyon. It was in that same cluster of aspen that DJ had very nearly lost his life.

The small house sat against the northern cliff face on a small rise. It was a wonderful place to sit on the porch in the morning and watch deer feed in the field on the other side of a small babbling brook. The thin, shallow creek unevenly carved the canyon in half. It too, had a special memory for him. He had flipped his Jeep alongside the banks near the entrance to the property. The crash had dislocated his shoulder. He had to flee from his pursuers across the creek with his arm screaming in pain. All of that was long ago, but the similarity of the situation he eerily found himself in, brought all of those memories into the forefront. Here he was again, about to defend his home. This time would be different. This time, he wouldn't be alone.

DJ found a spot close to the edge and rolled his shooting mat down. The mat would protect his elbows from sharp rocks when he lay across it with his rifle. Next, he set up the rifle. It was a long-range setup made by Accuracy International. The .338 Lapua round would bellow like a great beast when it was finally used, filling the canyon with the crack of thunder regardless of the suppressor. The round would be traveling too fast to be silent. The suppressor was only to hide the muzzle flash and make the gunfire tolerable behind the trigger.

Additionally, if his targets were wearing vests, it wouldn't matter. Stop the round or not, the heavy projectile would put anyone into the dirt if they were the unfortunate recipient of his aim. He would aim low, just in case. A .338 through the middle would take the fight out of anyone.

Since the enemy hiding below knew there was only one way into or out of the canyon, they would be focused in only one direction. They wouldn't suspect that DJ might flank them and start picking them off from the top of the surrounding cliffs. It would be a while before they understood what was going on. It would be like shooting fish in a barrel.

DJ smiled. *Too bad*, he thought. *That's what you get for playing for the other team.*

He keyed his mic. "I'm finally in position. Where are you guys at?"

Cash answered over his earpiece. "We took our time, but we're in position as well. From where we are, we can't see too much. These thermal goggles aren't really helping right now. We'll need you to direct our fire."

DJ spoke to Carbon next. "Carbon, you sure this is going to work?"

Carbon scoffed. "You doubt me? I've hacked my way into the Pentagon. A vehicle is a piece of cake. The challenge was finding a UI that could handle the language. What I had to do was first hack the manufacturer's R&D center. Surprisingly, *they* were nearly impossible. I guess car manufacturers are more concerned with corporate espionage than the Pentagon is of a foreign power. Shame, really. Once I did that-"

DJ cut him off. "Just tell me if you're ready. I don't need a book report."

Carbon's reply was terse. "Yeah. The button-pusher is ready."

DJ had settled in behind the thermal scope on the big gun and started seeking targets. He spotted three straight away. They were parked in the small grove of aspen right below. Their image was subdued in the thermal scope and he almost missed them. They must be wearing heat-dissipating clothing, he thought. Still, from above, he could make them out. DJ called out their position to his team. Next, behind his cabin and to the west, there seemed to be a group of them. If he wasn't mistaken, DJ spotted their vehicles, too. There looked to be three of them concealed in the trees. The combatants were on the other side. He guessed maybe four, but he was uncertain because of how they were clustered and partially obscured. It was exactly as first reported by Carbon's flyover. He called out that confirmation as well.

DJ was as ready as he would ever be. Still, he waited, listening carefully, ears focused on one sound in particular. He checked his watch and continued to wait. He should have heard it by now. The timing was everything on this. Finally, after what seemed like forever, with DJ growing increasingly impatient, he heard what he was waiting for. It was far in the distance, barely detectable. He called out over the mic. "Let the games begin. Carbon, you're up."

Again, DJ had to wait. The gravel road leading into the ranch was long. A few minutes later and he could see headlights coming through the trees. In short order, it pulled through the wooded drive and slowly came to a halt in front of the Cabin. The headlights stayed on and the vehicle just sat there with no one exiting. DJ scanned through his targets. None were moving. His enemy could not afford to jump the gun until they were sure who was driving the van. If they sprung their trap, and the occupants were not DJ and the others, they would have to deal with the trouble of collateral damage. So, they waited.

DJ did not. He spoke one word to Carbon. "Now."

All at once, in the back of the cabin, the three hidden SUVs began flashing their hazards, blowing their horns, and lighting up the surrounding area with their bright LED headlights. Carbon's hack into their remote systems had worked. The enemy hidden close by began moving, surprised by the sudden commotion.

DJ went to work.

His first round had one of the men in the back of the cabin crumple to the ground, the crack of his rifle carrying through the canyon. It was like an angry god of mythology snapping a whip. DJ cycled the bolt and picked another target: one stationary and partially obscured behind the hood of an SUV. The round punched through the top of the hood, passed through the fender, and took the man out anyway. Now that DJ had started firing, it was his team's turn. Argo and Cash opened up from the tree line on the eastern edge of the clearing, aiming into the stand of aspen, peppering the small grove with rounds from their .300 blackout assault rifles.

DJ glanced back to the front of the cabin and saw Ali streaking from the van and into the house, barreling through the door without pausing to unlock it. Someone hidden on the other side of the drive, an enemy missed on their initial survey of the canyon, broke from hiding and tore after him, trying to follow Ali inside. DJ clipped the man with a well-timed shot, and he went down in front of the door. A follow-up shot ended Ali's pursuer for good.

Going for the cabin had been a risk. There was a possibility people were inside, but DJ had a sophisticated alarm that would have notified him via a cell signal through an app. There were no notifications. Nor did any of the inside camera views show anyone inside. It was assumed the ambushers had not entered for fear of accidentally alerting DJ remotely to their invasion. With the risk being minimal, Ali elected to go in. The reason was apparent a few seconds later. Floodlights located on all four corners of the cabin flipped on, completely illuminating the surrounding area. DJ could see the enemy scrambling in all directions, the cover of night suddenly gone for them.

DJ grinned. Six rounds left in the box magazine. More people to shoot. With a smile on his face, he went back to work, focusing on the front and back door to keep Ali covered inside.

Sam was focused on the van in front of the cabin, gleefully waiting for Slaughter to pop out. When the SUVs stashed behind the cabin in the trees fired up their lights and started honking their horns, he was at first confused, angry that some idiot had set off the alarms and tipped off their adversary to the ambush. When a heavy-caliber rifle opened fire from somewhere to his right, somewhere on the top of the cliff near Sam, he realized what was going on. Slaughter had flanked them. Carbon had hacked their trucks. They had been caught with their pants down. The man firing the rifle to Sam's right could only be DJ. The team leader was a far superior shot to the rest of his group. He would have appointed himself to make the hike in and set up overwatch, initiating a little ambush of their own.

Sam had to hand it to the guy, it was a first-class move.

He stood and shouldered his pack, leaving his own rifle in place. Unholstering his pistol, he backtracked into the trees and began circling around behind Slaughter. DJ didn't know Sam was up here with him. He thought himself protected and secure, focusing on picking apart the men in the valley.

Sam was in no hurry, and he didn't care about the people dying below. He had no interest in protecting them. If they lost this fight, Sam was at peace with it. His focus was on DJ. He moved slowly through the trees, carefully watching where every foot was placed so as not to alert Slaughter of his presence.

This was going to be fun. He would shoot the man, show him what a real shooter could do, then vanish.

Agent Ali charged into Slaughter's home at full speed, nearly tearing the door from the hinges, swinging his pistol up, and sweeping the living room. He had chosen to forgo the use of a rifle, knowing he would be inside. His movement speed would have been hampered by the .300 Blackout AR rifles that the rest of Slaughter's team had chosen to carry. There was no doubt they packed a wallop in the short-range they were intended, but Ali needed speed. If this went according to plan, Ali wouldn't ever leave the safety of the house.

The room was clear, so he sprinted forward through the wide entrance marking the dividing line between the living room and the kitchen. On the back wall, he spotted the switches he was after, four of them in a neat little row next to a doorway leading into the workshop at the back of the cabin. He flipped them on and was instantly rewarded with the sound of swearing outside the home. Through the windows on the south wall, overlooking the large field, bright floodlights had turned night into day around the house. Toward the east, he could hear Cash and Argo engaging the suddenly target-rich environment. Farther away, he could make out the harsh crack of DJ's big rifle as it reverberated around the canyon, causing Ali to chuckle. He was sure the big man was having a great time lighting up the enemy as they scurried for cover.

Ali peeked into the workshop, checking for bad guys, just as the back door crashed open. Someone had decided to enter from the back and shut off the lights before they were all killed. It was a good idea, but Ali shot the man through the nose for his quick thinking. A second man was right behind the first. He died as well, Ali killing him in much the same way. The CIA trained their operatives to shoot for the head. It had been ingrained into Ali's thinking from the very beginning. A third man hung a rifle around the corner, spraying the inside of the house with automatic fire. Ali dropped to the floor and put three rounds through the wall near the doorway. The shooter dropped his weapon and the firing stopped. All Ali had to do was hold the building until the helicopters arrived and this would all be over.

He got to one knee and looked behind him, glancing at the front entrance just in time to see someone trying to come up behind him. The man didn't make it. What could have only been a bullet from Slaughter's .338 passed sideways through the man's neck, nearly taking his head off in the process. The man collapsed into the entrance on top of another that DJ had capped. It was shocking to see but rewarding as well. Ali was constantly impressed by DJ's unnatural talent for feeling his way around a firearm. It was as if Slaughter could sense what the projectile would do even before he pulled the trigger. It was an extraordinary gift with only one brutal purpose.

Ali turned back to the rear entrance just in time to engage yet another brave soul. Ali didn't kill him, only a flesh wound to the side of the face, but it certainly made him change his mind on entering.

Not much longer now, Ali thought to himself.

Carbon sat hunched against a tree behind Cash and Argo as they fired into the field, picking off the enemy who was currently in a state of confusion. Carbon wasn't a shooter like the others, so he positioned himself on the backside of the tree and faced the rear. In fact, he would have liked it better if the tree he was against was about ten times wider. The more cover the better.

So far, everything was going to plan. His plan. This whole counter-ambush had been Carbon's idea. In fact, if it weren't for him making DJ pull over, they would have waltzed right into this valley and be dead right now. Instead, they were making the bad guys pay a heavy price for, well, for being bad guys. *Not bad for a button-pusher*, he thought to himself.

In the distance, he could make out the sound of an approaching helicopter. He hoped there was more than one coming. He hadn't been surprised when Abbi called to tell them she had decided to take matters into her own hands and gone over the CIA's head to the President of the United States. She was bold like that. Besides, they knew the man. Well, Carbon didn't, but the others did. They didn't like him too much and there was some apparent bad blood between them. Still, Abbi had somehow managed to get into a room with the leader of the free world and strong-arm the man into helping them out. It was thinking like this that proved Abbi and Carbon were the real brains of this operation. If it weren't for them, and Brett, of course, these guys would think the solution to every problem could be found in the act of switching a weapon off "safe" and into "full-auto."

As Carbon consulted the screen of his tablet, he could see things were definitively going their way. The drone feed showed that DJ was picking people off from above, the three or four guys that had hidden in the stand of trees in the middle of the field were no longer moving, and Argo and Cash were nailing anyone foolish enough to step out from behind the house. When the helicopter landed with well-armed troops on board, this would be over. The remaining enemy would find themselves against overwhelming odds and start throwing their hands into the air.

Carbon felt the whiff of a bullet past his ears and flinched. Another one smacked into the bark above his head, peppering him with wooden shrapnel. That made no sense. All of the gunfire was behind him in the field and around the house. Carbon rolled onto his belly, desperately trying to become one with Mother Earth herself, and repositioned the drone overhead. What he saw had him slithering across the ground like a frightened lizard and hunching up behind Cash. "*Behind us,*" he screamed. "There's more coming from behind! Four of them!"

As if they could read each other's mind, Argo stayed focused on the field and Cash spun to engage the enemy to the rear. How in the world had he missed the ones behind them, Carbon wondered? For that matter, how had they managed to walk right past them and not get shot? Carbon didn't know. Carbon didn't care. Carbon should have stayed in town and gotten a hotel room and had pizza delivered. Why did they always insist he come with them? He wasn't a combat soldier. He was a button...

Carbon swore out loud as he watched Cash take a bullet to the left arm and roll over to hide behind the tree. Cash grimaced in pain, sucking in deeply and shouting at Argo for support.

The older black man, who moved far quicker than his age suggested, spun about to focus on their rear. He fired off a few shots then barked at Carbon. "I think I got them. Double-check with your toy."

Carbon looked at his tablet. "It's not a toy. It's a highly sophisticated, state of the art, piece of engineering. Yeah, I don't see anyone else. I think you got them all."

Cash was quick to correct. "Then he only got one. I got the other three."

Argo shot Cash a look. "Oh, so it's a competition, now, is it?"

Uncharacteristically, Cash smiled. "It always has been. I'm still winning, by the way."

Carbon swung the drone around and shifted over to the southern wall of the canyon. The helicopters, he could now tell there were two of them, were close. He needed to make sure the drone was clear. In doing so, he spotted something that made his heart sink. He could see DJ standing with his back to the cliff. He wasn't alone. Someone else was holding a gun on him, standing nearly twenty feet away. Carbon swore again. "DJ's in trouble."

Argo refocused on the field while Cash had begun to bandage his arm. On hearing this, Cash stopped what he was doing and crawled over to look at the screen. "Who is that? Which one is DJ?"

Carbon pointed at the screen. "That's DJ. I have no idea who that is."

Cash seemed less certain. "How do you know who's who?"

Carbon replied angrily to the man. "Because DJ hiked up there only carrying his rifle bag. That person is wearing a backpack."

Cash smacked the ground with an open hand. His standard stoicism was gone. "Sam Kenny! It has to be Sam!"

Carbon looked closer at the screen. The man with the backpack was Sam. Carbon dropped his tablet and dove for his pack laying nearby, tearing into the contents, tossing things out in his haste to find what he was looking for. "Somebody shine a light!"

Argo was looking at him then, confused. Over the roar of the two big helicopters that suddenly passed low overhead, he shouted at Carbon. "What are you doing?"

Carbon screamed at them; his thoughts focused on what he had to do but too hurried for a detailed explanation. *"Give me a friggin' flashlight!"*

Seymour Sinclair swore at the sudden turn of events. What was intended to be a straightforward ambush had turned into the biggest screwup he had ever been a part of. The problem was it was all his idea and planning. Not only was he losing men left and right, but this fiasco was also a gut punch to his ego.

Over the blaring horns of the SUVs next to him, he shouted at two of his men. "Get in that building and shut off those floodlights! We're getting picked apart!" He pointed at two more. "You two, pop the hoods on these things and yank the battery cables!" There were two hidden vans stashed further down the road near the entrance. With them was a small force of backup shooters just in case. He hoped and prayed they were on the way. He would have loved to call them, but their coms had gone dead. Maybe some sort of jamming device? The answer to the suddenly broken coms and their vehicles going crazy had to be related to that hacker Carbon. If they managed to get out of this, Seymour would make it his life's goal to personally choke the man to death.

The two men he had ordered into the cabin died as soon as they swung the back door open. Seymour swore and tasked another to enter. That one hung his rifle around the corner and blasted the inside with automatic gunfire. A second later, he was dead too. A bullet smashed through the wall and clipped the man in the back of the head.

Where was Sam? he wondered. Why wasn't that man using his battle-proven sniper skills to level the playing field? Had they gotten him too? Seymour could only imagine the answer to those questions. He needed to do something to end this chaos. He needed to get those floodlights shut off.

Seymour looked up at the building in desperation. There was an upstairs window above him. If he could enter from the second floor, he might be able to surprise whoever was on the first. He rotated the selector switch on his rifle to full-auto and aimed, blasting out the window with a long burst. He switched mags and moved forward. Pointing at a member of his team, he fired off an order. "You! Give me a boost!"

The man responded and darted to stand next to the wall, interlocking his fingers in front of him and crouching. Seymour put one foot into the man's hand, and the man shoved Seymour up just high enough for him to grasp hold of the windowsill. After a second of struggling, he was able to pull himself up and over, thankful for his gloves keeping him from getting sliced up by the shards of glass poking out from the framing.

The room was a bedroom and spanned the length of the back, with windows that faced the rear of the house and the lit-up field and creek to the south. Choosing his pistol instead, Seymour moved forward to the door, padding as lightly as he could. Not that anyone would hear. The chorus of blaring horns behind the house would drown out any sound of his movement. The hallway was clear, so he moved cautiously to the top of the stairs. Spotting no one, he edged down. Surprisingly, the living room was clear as well. This only left the kitchen and backroom for hiding spots. Seymour wondered which Slaughter team member he was going to get to kill. He was silently hoping for John Argo. The man's sarcasm and condescending face were annoying. It was too much to hope for Slaughter himself. Seymour was sure the man was the sniper responsible for the carnage outside. Slaughter must have somehow spotted Sam on the cliff and had taken the man out with the first shot fired, then focused his attention to the valley below.

Seymour paused. The blaring horns suddenly quit, leaving only the sound of sporadic gunfire. And something else. Seymour's heart sank. A chopper was approaching, low and fast. The unmistakable sound of Blackhawk rotor blades was rapidly filling the air. No, he realized, two of them.

Seymour came to the undeniable conclusion that this fight was over. More troops were coming in. It was either tactical teams from the FBI Field Office in Denver, or worse, it was an assault team from the Fort Carson Army Base. That would mean door-mounted, belt-fed, rotating barrel, M134 machine guns capable of leveling this entire canyon. They were dead. This was over.

Seymour swore silently to himself. No, not yet. He could at least take out one of Slaughter's team, giving the man even more reason to grieve. It was to be a last parting gift to a man who had become a colossal pain in his... Seymour cut off in mid-thought. The man standing on the other side of the kitchen, watching the back door, was none other than Agent Ali. The very same man Seymour had asked to join in on this endeavor. The very same man who had turned him down. The very one who had somehow freed himself and killed more of Seymour's men in the process. He was the agent who had rescued Abbi and the baby, derailing Seymour's plans and allowing the unmitigated disaster in this canyon to take place. Agent Ali, the self-righteous do-gooder, had become just as much of an annoying problem as Slaughter himself.

Agent Ali seemed to sense trouble and darted into the backroom, crossing over to the southern wall. Seymour fired two rounds in haste. One passed through the doorway and out the back. The other went into the door jam, nearly taking Ali's head off. "You've got nowhere to hide, Agent Ali. Might as well come on out and take a bullet like a man."

Ali was quick to reply. "You come in here and get me, Seymour. I've got something I want to show you." Ali hung his pistol around the corner and began to rapid-fire without even bothering to look. Seymour dove left across the living room, seeking cover on the other side of the wide opening leading into the kitchen. Thankfully, every round missed, but it made Seymour smile. The man had wasted an entire mag of ammo in the process.

Seymour sucked up against the wall, took a breath, and stepped around the corner, firing steadily into the wall Ali was hiding behind, walking methodically forward and through the kitchen, watching each of his rounds punch neatly through the sheetrock and into the room beyond. Just before his own mag ran dry, he hot-swapped another while still aiming and continuing to move forward. "You should have taken me up on my offer, Ali!"

Ali pressed against a bookcase in DJ's workshop at the back of the house, watching Seymour's rounds punch through the wall, spraying the air with sheetrock dust in front of his face. He was pinned. He needed to do something desperate. He needed to think outside of the box. If he charged forward and around the corner into the kitchen, he would likely just walk into a bullet. Still, there had to be something he could do to even the odds.

The bookcase. Cash had said something sarcastic to DJ about the bookcase and DJ being a Rambo-like gun collector as DJ explained the layout of the house and the light switches Ali needed to locate. Ali hadn't been paying attention because Carbon had been talking in the background, insisting he stay back so he could run his surveillance drones without fear of being shot. Ali had tried to tune both of them out so he could pay attention to what Slaughter had been saying. Pinned against the bookcase as he was, he suddenly felt like he had missed something important, something vital to his survival.

Ali spun quickly and looked at the shelves of books lined up behind him, ever mindful of the bullets passing by a mere twelve inches away. The books were mostly technical manuals about reloading, or biographies written by former military snipers the world over. Nothing unique. Nothing out of the ordinary. Except for the large volume sitting to one side. It had War and Peace stenciled down the spine. An ambitious read, Ali thought. It also didn't seem to match the theme of the bookcase.

Like a spotlight being switched on in a cave of black, the memory of what Cash had said popped into his brain. Ali hastily grabbed the book. He hoped this worked. He was out of time. Seymour was going to step around that corner and punch holes through him at any moment. What was happening to the wall separating him from his former coworker was about to be happening to Ali.

Seymour stepped around the corner and stopped firing. Ali was gone. The rear door was still open, and thanks to the spotlights, he could see the remainder of his men focusing on the field as the helicopters touched down in the tall grass. A few were tossing their weapons aside and preparing for capture. Most were uncertain of what to do. Seymour wanted to shoot them for their cowardice and stupidity.

He looked around the room, wondering where Ali had vanished to. He couldn't have run out the back. Surely, Ali would have been cut down by the armed men outside. Still, there was no place to hide. On the wall where he had suspected Ali to be was only a bookcase. A few of the books showed where bullets had ripped into them. On the opposite side was a large gun safe and a workbench. Still, no Ali.

Wait, he thought. Had Ali somehow darted across the doorway without being seen and hidden in the safe? Surely not. Still, it was the only answer he could think of. Pointing his weapon, he advanced across the room, eyes locked onto the safe. "Come out, Ali. I know you're in there. Those steel walls won't help you. I have a brick of C4. Doesn't sound like a fun way to go. You should kick that door open and come out blasting. Die fighting for your life, Ali. Not like a coward hiding in a box."

There was a noise, then, accompanied by a vibration on the floor under his feet. Seymour made to spin about, suspecting he had been set up, somehow. He froze halfway through his turn, his head finishing the spin before his body did. A section of the bookcase had swung open to reveal a small hidden room. It was lined with various firearms hanging from the walls. Slaughter had a hidden gun room, and Ali was standing in the middle of it holding a large rifle. No, not a rifle. The barrel was too big around. It was some sort of tactical shotgun with a boxed magazine like an AR15. Ali was pointing it right at him.

Seymour sighed and dropped his weapon, slowly turning to face Ali fully. "Fine," he said. "You win. I surrender. I'll tell you anything you want to know. I'll testify."

Ali smiled. "Just like a coward. Ready to spill your guts and hope to plead a deal, escape some of that jail time?"

Seymour nodded. "Something like that."

Ali pulled the trigger three times fast. Seymour was pushed backward into the gun safe, pain ripping through him as buckshot tore through his body, the sound of thunder filling the room and deafening him. Seymour didn't feel himself fall, yet there he was, slumped against the safe, watching his life pour out of him in throbbing gushes of crimson onto the wooden floor. Seymour struggled to speak, to plead for help. Instead, blood erupted from his mouth in one ragged cough, blocking his words. He reached out a hand, a symbolic gesture of mercy. Ali did nothing to assist. He only watched as Seymour's universe slowly faded away.

———————

DJ was having fun, gaining great pleasure from finally taking it to the enemy who had plagued his life, who had stolen his friends from him, who had betrayed him. He cycled the bolt one more time, already seeing his next target as the sound of approaching helicopters filled the canyon below. Then a voice spoke behind him. It was one he recognized. In an instant, his joy was replaced by seething anger and rage.

Sam Kenny called out loudly behind him, his voice calm and confident. "Stop shooting and roll over slowly." DJ hesitated, contemplating his next move, thinking of rolling hard to his left and drawing his pistol with his right. It was a foolish move, he knew. There was little doubt Sam had a gun pointed at him. Sam was a seasoned killer. Sam was fast. DJ didn't stand a chance. The traitor seemed to read DJ's thoughts. "Go for it, DJ. Give me a reason to kill you. Please."

DJ did as instructed, keeping his hands clear from the heavily modified Sig X-5 series pistol he lovingly referred to as "MP." He rolled over and looked toward his feet to find Sam standing nearly fifteen feet away. Moonlight filled the cliff, and even though DJ had removed his night vision goggles to use the scope on the rifle, he could see the man bathed in pale light. Sam had his own gun raised, standing with his feet shoulder-width apart, wearing a backpack and looking through the sights. His own goggles were pulled down around his neck. No doubt the man had stood there for a moment watching DJ while his eyes had grown accustomed to the light before speaking. Sam was planning something here. It was clear.

With anyone else, DJ would have thrown caution to the wind and gone for it. The man was fifteen feet away. There was a good chance any adversary at this distance would miss on the first shot in such low light. But Sam wasn't any ordinary gun thug. DJ had stood behind him on the firing line for nearly thirty days straight and watched the guy shoot. If DJ so much as flinched, he would surely die as a result. "What now," he asked. "You want me to be looking at you when you kill me?"

Sam chuckled. "Close, but not quite. Keep your right hand up. Use your left to get to your feet and face me. Slowly, please."

DJ chuckled. "You said, please. How nice of you. Manners from a murderer."

Sam didn't move, focusing on DJ's head through the sights. "What can I say, Momma raised me right." DJ stood and faced his enemy, raising his left hand to match his right. Sam nodded his head. "Now turn around and face the cliff. Keep your hands up."

DJ turned carefully, wondering what the man was thinking. Surely Sam had something in mind or DJ would be dead already. Did Traitor Sam think to capture him and bring him to his boss like a trussed-up prize? Surely the man had to realize this fight was over. The helicopters should have informed the man that the powers that be were on to Deputy Director Hartley. When Abbi had called, the Justice Department was on the way over to pick her up. What was the idiot thinking? No matter what it was, as long as DJ was breathing, he had a chance. When he got that chance, he was going to kill Sam Kenny.

DJ faced the valley, flipping through options in his mind. He could dive left or right and draw, firing on the way down. The right would be the best choice as it would allow him to bring the gun into line with Traitor Sam's face the quickest. He prepared to do exactly that when Sam spoke, surprising DJ with a new set of instructions, trashing those plans, and presenting DJ with new options. "Lower your hands by your side. When I tell you to, you're going to turn back to face me. I'll give you the option to draw facing away from me or in the middle of your turn. You won't stand much of a chance if you do, but you're the one making the decision. If you manage to get turned all the way back around, we get to see who the fastest really is. I've never actually had a chance to see you at your best, but I'm still pretty sure I can take you."

DJ lowered his hands, slowly, at a snail's pace. If Traitor Sam was going to let this be a test of skill, then so be it. He didn't want to lower his hands too quickly and let the man get the jump on him. "You sure you want to do this, kid?" DJ asked. "If I were you, I would just shoot me while I had the advantage. Because when I turn around, we're going to be on a level playing field."

Sam laughed, his tone suggesting he wasn't concerned in the least. "You're getting old, DJ. Being a professional duelist is a young man's game. I'm ten years younger and ten years faster than you are. Plus, you're overly cautious. All that thinking about not coming home to your wife and baby. But we'll see. I'm ready whenever you are."

DJ blinked, looking out over the canyon, watching the Blackhawk helicopters pass low and then bank around, preparing to land. "Nice job, trying to get in my head bringing up my child. But I promise you, Sam. Nothing you say is going to stop me from killing you."

DJ took a deep breath and cleared his mind, knowing what happened next would take all his focus, skill, and determination. He turned carefully, taking his time, not giving Sam any reason to shoot him before the fun could begin. Traitor Sam was still standing in the same position but had dropped the backpack to the ground behind him. The man was standing relaxed with both hands down by his side, his gun holstered.

From the glow of the moon, DJ thought he saw Sam smile. "Go ahead, big guy," Sam instructed. "I'll let you pull first." DJ took him up on his offer, his hand reaching for MP.

Time slowed.

He always found it amazing how this worked, his brain firing electrical impulses so fast that time seemed to take a step back from the laws of physics. He had heard that only gravity and speed affected the passage of time, but DJ was living proof that those were not the only variables. For DJ, it wasn't the perception of time slowing; it was a physical trait unique to his brain chemistry. In this slowing of time, DJ had the chance to reason things through, look for advantages, see the best course of action to take. Right then, as he was sliding MP from his holster, he could see that despite starting his pull first, Sam was going to clear quicker than he was. DJ was going to lose this battle.

Maybe lose wasn't the right prediction of the outcome. Sure, Sam would clear his holster first. Sure, Sam would likely pull the trigger a microsecond before DJ did. But there was still accuracy involved here. Oh, to be sure, DJ understood just how deadly his adversary could be. Still, both men weren't aiming for the body. Both men would be going for a four-inch imaginary circle placed on each of their faces. DJ had only one option available to him to try to decrease Sam's odds of hitting his target. He shoved himself to the left, pushing off with his right foot, providing a moving target for Sam.

Traitor Sam seemed to come to the same conclusion. Even though he would beat DJ to the trigger, there was no way to avoid being shot. Sam was fast, faster than DJ, but not quick enough to avoid dying. Sam Kenny shoved off with his own right foot, shifting sideways and in the opposite direction of DJ. Both men were going to pull the trigger while in motion.

This was another factor that might work to save DJ's life. Still, the odds were only slightly reduced. Sam was as adept at firing on the move as DJ.

DJ then turned his attention to little Cassie. Wondering how Abbi would do raising the girl without him even he didn't manage to walk away from this. Fine, he was sure. Abbi was amazing at anything she set her mind to. The girl would be in good hands. Still, DJ had to make sure his round flew true to his target. He had to do his best to shift his body just enough to avoid the same fate himself.

DJ could see Sam's gun tilting up while still being held low. Sam was going to shoot from the hip as well, relying on instinct and his familiarity with his weapon of choice just as DJ would. Both men were bringing their barrels into alignment. As DJ had first detected at the beginning of his pull, Sam was going to fire first. Suddenly, a blinding flash of light erupted from behind Sam, silhouetting the man, instantly illuminating the surrounding area in a dazzling white that quickly morphed to yellow, then orange, then red. At first, DJ's rapidly firing brain thought this to be some sort of hallucination. Maybe his weird superpower, his abnormal brain chemistry, had fired so fast that it had caused some sort of aneurism, an eruption of blood vessels bursting inside his skull, causing him to see lights that weren't there. Maybe Sam had already fired, and the projectile was ripping through his frontal lobe, sending a shockwave through his brain, making him hallucinate for a fraction of a second before he died.

Time returned to normal, and DJ's understanding came into focus. An explosion of light, sound, and shrapnel tore into Sam from behind, rending his body into pieces as if he had been placed into a giant Margherita mixer. Shrapnel struck DJ next, crossing the distance faster than thought, peppering him with debris that lacerated his face and arms, and sending something thick and pointy to lodge in his leg. The blast pushed DJ backward, rolling him along the ground. He came to rest inches from the edge of the cliff.

He pushed himself up into a sitting position and looked at what was left of Sam. DJ sat there bleeding, dazed, unsure of what exactly had just happened. Not really caring too much anyway.

DJ was alive.

Sam Kenny was blown to pieces.

Poking out of the front of DJ's upper leg was a piece of bone, Sam's bone. It was a vicious reminder of the pain and anguish the traitor had done to the team. DJ yanked it out, ignoring the proper medical procedure of leaving it in and wrapping it in place. He discarded it to one side and crawled over to his rifle bag. Inside was an emergency pressure dressing. As he bound his leg to stop the bleeding, he watched the helicopters touch down.

It was finally over.

Carbon stared at his tablet. Argo and Cash looked first at the screen, then at Carbon, then back to the screen. Argo pointed at the tablet. "What was that? What happened? What did you just do?"

Carbon blinked, staring at the screen, not really sure what to say. Instead, he held up the small cylinder in his hand to show them.

Cash smiled and shook his head, but Argo still didn't understand. "I don't get it. What is that thing?"

It was Cash who replied. "Remember when we retrieved the data drive? It came in a booby-trapped box. There was plastic explosive lining the inside. That cylinder is the detonator. You know Carbon has a problem with discarding any piece of technology. After Sam stole the box, our little hacker here, probably thought to reuse the detonator for something else later. He still had it in his pack."

Argo looked at the cylinder, then to Carbon. "So… you saw the backpack on Sam and took a chance the box was inside?"

Carbon nodded, shocked by what had just happened even though he was the one responsible. When he replied, his voice sounded small and far away. "When I pulled out the detonator, I saw that the LED on the bottom was on, indicating there was a signal."

Argo turned his head, eyes focusing off into the darkness and the cliff far away. "That means you blew up the data drive, too."

Carbon nodded. "Probably. Unless Sam stashed the drive somewhere else. But why would he do that and still keep the protective case it was stored in? So, yeah, all of that money is gone now."

Argo began to laugh. Carbon looked at him like he had lost his mind. There didn't seem to be anything humorous about what had happened. DJ had barely escaped with his life. Argo gripped Carbon's shoulder and shook it slightly, leaning forward with a big grin on his face. "Soooo…. what you're saying is, you just saved the day by… *pressing a button*?"

Carbon blinked. Cash started laughing too. Argo, still on his knees, sat down hard and pointed at Carbon's nose. "DJ was right. You *are* a button pusher!" Argo rolled on the ground, clutching his sides, laughing hard. "Oh," he howled. "I think I'm going to pop a stitch, but I don't care! That is *soooo* funny!"

What Cash said next had Argo redouble his efforts at laughing, causing the man to wheeze into the dirt and lose his breath. "To be accurate," Cash corrected, "Carbon is a button-pusher in silk underwear. He is, quite factually, a panty-waisted button-pusher!"

Carbon stood, glaring at them as they laughed at his expense. "I told you," he said with his voice raised, not only in frustration but to be heard over the loud helicopters landing in the field. "They're not panties! I need them because I tend to chafe! You're both seriously going to laugh at a man's *medical condition*?" His eyes stared laser beams at them, wanting to punch them both in their noses. Carbon turned on his heels, clutching the tablet to his chest and heading back to the entrance of the canyon and the van that waited down the road. He fired off one more shout of anger as he stomped into the underbrush. "*SHUT UP*! The both of you just shut your faces!" Carbon stormed into the night, the sound of laughter and helicopters behind him.

Chapter 20: The Fine Line

DJ couldn't help but laugh. It was fun to watch two children play. One was his daughter, the other a man-child. Carbon was driving an ATV in slow circles in the field next to DJ's cabin. One hand on the wheel, the other on little Cassie. The child was giggling uncontrollably, blowing snot bubbles out of her nose, thinking the open-air ride was the absolute greatest thing ever. DJ could hear her rolling laughter non-stop on the other side of the shallow stream. The sound was infectious, causing everyone sitting on the porch to join in. He wasn't sure what the child found so entertaining about driving in the ATV, but for Cassie, it was apparently something only a toddler could comprehend.

It had been nearly a month since this valley had been the scene of a war. Bullets had flown. Blood had been spilled. But the passage of time has a way of snuffing out the pain of struggle. Despite having lost Coonie and Bounder, DJ was happy. The rest of his friends had made it through. It could have been a lot worse; it very nearly had been.

Brett sat in his wheelchair at the end of the porch, capping off a long line of his friends and loved ones. Argo, Cash, Brett, and even Agent Ali all sat in rockers and camp chairs, watching the sun set on a Colorado summer, listening to the sounds of laughter dance through the canyon. Yes, DJ thought, it could have been a lot worse.

Everyone here had decided to help DJ and Abbi restore the cabin from the many bullet holes that pockmarked the building. Agent Ali took some much-needed time off and vowed to replace the shattered front door. DJ had given the man the keys to enter on that eventful night, but the agent had decided that entering the building in the quickest way possible was the way to go, using his body as a battering ram. DJ, of course, could not have cared less. What was a broken door in the grand scheme of things? Nevertheless, Agent Ali was insistent on fixing the thing he broke.

He asked if DJ minded if he stayed here for a while. The last place he wanted to be right then was Washington. The CIA was in disarray The President had fired the director and appointed a new one. Countless investigations were underway, scrutinizing the entire agency; answers being demanded on a great many things. Until all of that shook out, Ali was content to spend some of his accrued time off at DJ's ranch.

Brett was recovering quickly. The man was tough. No matter what the guy went through, he always seemed to bounce back. As soon as he was fully recovered, he had been promised a spot for an experimental treatment to restore the use of his legs. DJ had thought the promise made by Deputy Director Hartley was considered null and void after all of this, but once Brett had learned of the procedure, he wasn't going to be denied. There were quite a few people in D.C. who owed Brett favors. The President of the United States was one of them. DJ was unsure of what markers Brett had called in, but Brett was enrolled in the program and couldn't wait for his turn to go under the knife and fix his legs. The poor man had never truly come to terms with being confined to that chair, and this promise of being able to walk again had caused his countenance to improve.

Speaking of Deputy Director Hartley, the woman had vanished into thin air like a magic trick. Agents from the Justice Department had arrived at her house only to find she had escaped moments before. A cold glass of lemonade, the ice still in the glass, was sitting on a table on the back patio. She couldn't have been gone for more than a few minutes. She had somehow been tipped off and fled. There was a massive hunt for her, but to date, no information on her whereabouts had been discovered.

Even more curious, the data drive hadn't been inside the debris field that was Sam Kenny. Carbon had not blown it to pieces as first suspected. They did discover a clue, however. It looked like a key to a bus terminal locker. Once cleaned up from the blast, it had an identifying marker. The back part where you turned the key was covered in yellow plastic. On it was stenciled with what looked to be a crashing wave and the number 23. DJ was sure someone was at this very moment on a treasure hunt to solve the mystery, but if they had discovered anything, no one was talking. DJ hoped they would never find it. That much money was nothing but trouble. That much money always involved bloodshed and innocent people caught in the middle.

Abbi rounded the corner with a pitcher of iced tea and a stack of plastic cups. She paused to watch Carbon and Cassie for a minute, admiring the scene across the creek. DJ looked at his wife with deep admiration and love. She was quite a woman. Abbi was warm, vibrant, intelligent, and could love like there was no tomorrow. If it were not for her bold play in going directly to Tim Neville with their problem, they might not all be here. Their wounds might have been deeper. Not only had she saved the day, but she had managed to get their old jobs back. As soon as Brett was at full strength, they were to head back to the base near Jasper, Texas. They had all been reinstated into the FBI, their records cleared, and Brett was to reprise his role of Special Agent in Charge.

As if Argo could read DJ's mind, he asked Brett about taking over the position. "So, Brett, how does one step in to replace a leader of a field office who hasn't been promoted, nor have they done anything to get in trouble? How do you establish yourself with the people who are new and have never met you without making waves, making the transition as smooth as possible? After all, this isn't your typical FBI Field Office we're talking about."

Brett shrugged and seemed to think about it. "It's tricky. You try to present yourself in such a way so you don't hack off the people who liked the old boss, but you still have to firmly establish that you're the person in charge. It's a balancing act. If you don't get it right, you won't get the best productivity out of your people until they've formed some sort of relationship with you. Still, in the end, these people are all professionals. They'll fall in line, no matter what."

Argo wasn't agreeing. "I say rip the bandage off and get it over with."

Cash looked at him. "What do you mean by that?"

Argo began talking with his hands as he tried to explain. "You know, you just go in there, put on your boss's voice, bark out a few orders, don't smile at anyone. Let everyone know you're the new sheriff in town. Just rip the bandage off. Get all the hurt feelings out of the way right in the beginning. As you said, they're professionals. They'll fall in line behind whoever's been appointed over them, whether they like the change or not. So, establish your authority right off the bat. Get it over with. Don't mess around."

DJ laughed. "Remind me to quit if they ever put *you* in charge."

DJ turned to see Carbon heading back toward them, crossing the stream and driving far faster with Cassie than DJ was comfortable with. He stood and prepared to issue a rebuke for the man's recklessness but stopped. Carbon had a look on his face that said something was wrong. It was a look DJ had seen far too often.

Carbon stopped barely twelve inches from the porch, nearly ramming right into it. Holding up his cellphone, he said, "We have a hit."

DJ dropped down off the porch. "A hit on what?"

Carbon held the phone out to show the contents on the screen and DJ had to squint to see the surface in the sun. Carbon didn't wait for DJ to figure it out. He plowed forward with an explanation. "Hartley! I have her. I know where she is right now!"

Argo was first to speak. "So, you have your own algorithm thingy running in the background trying to find her," he asked?

Carbon nodded. "Instead of using facial recognition to spot her if she walked in front of a camera somewhere, I started putting out feelers with some black market people I know. The kind that specializes in rock-solid identifications. I passed her photo around and offered a substantial bounty if anyone came across her trying to buy a new life. By the way, DJ, I hope we have some petty cash still lying around for emergency issues because this is going to be expensive."

DJ took a deep breath. "How much?"

Carbon offered a sheepish grin. "Um, well, see, these people have reputations to uphold. To get them to compromise that reputation costs money."

DJ took a step closer. "I asked you how much." DJ sucked in when he heard the amount, ready to tell the man to come up with the money himself. It wasn't the amount that irked DJ so much. Covering it would be easy. It was the fact the kid ran behind their back and made a deal without asking for approval.

Before DJ could reprimand the hacker, Argo spoke up. "You don't seriously want to go after her, do you? Just hand off the intel to Justice. Let them deal with her."

Brett held up a hand to get everyone's attention. "We can't do that. We have to do this ourselves, and I can give you two very good reasons why. First, doesn't it seem odd that our intelligence agency hasn't caught a whiff of her yet? We supposedly have every intel agency and resource devoting serious assets to find her, but no one has come up with anything. Not a hint. And Carbon finds her just by asking questions and throwing a little money around? I don't think so. I think she still has friends out there covering for her. Maybe she had dirt on them, or they see her as some kind of hero. I don't know which, but I do know someone is intentionally looking the other way. No, if she's to answer for everything that's happened, it has to be us to do it."

Abbi was next. "That's one reason. What's the second?"

Brett looked at them all, a determined look on his face. "We were betrayed by her. She used us as expendable pawns on her bloody chessboard. She lied to us. She treated us like the enemy and got a few of us killed in the process. I'm not one for vengeance, but in this case…" Brett let the sentence hang for the others to digest.

Cash spoke next, leveling a question at Carbon. "Where are we headed? Should I pack for a warm climate or cold?"

Carbon looked around the group, but no one was offering any objections. They were simply waiting for Carbon's answer. "Spain," he said. "My contact met her in a house there to hand off the documents. She's outside a town called Conil de la Frontera."

Everyone looked at DJ for approval. He wasn't sure why. It seemed like they had made up their minds already. Plus, DJ knew himself. This chapter of his life would never be closed until Hartley was either being questioned at Gitmo, or dead. Preferably, the latter.

DJ looked around the group and nodded. "There's a fine line between justice and revenge. We've crossed it so often, why should today be any different?"

Chapter 21: Poof

The plan was to recon the area, learn the routines of the enemy, develop a plan, and then take the woman into custody. They would get her out of the country and back to the States before the locals even knew what happened. Once in the U.S., they would hand her over to the FBI. However, things seldom ever went according plan in the world in which DJ lived. Tonight, was normal. Why should he expect anything different?

DJ and the team had just arrived in Spain and located the house in which former Deputy Director Hartley was staying when things went sideways. Having just arrived in the small seaside town, the whole team was doing a late-night drive-by in a rental van to get an idea of what the place looked like; to spot what was easily visible from the narrow street in front of the four-story building. What they found was troubling. It instantly derailed the normal routine of observation, formulation, and execution.

Four men in suits were loading bags into three sedans. Two more were standing in the entry to the place, staring intently at the van as it drove past. Judging from the bulges under their coats, all of them were armed. The implication was obvious: Sharlette Hartley was leaving. As it was 12:30 PM local time, this was odd. One would have thought that a planned trip would begin in the morning, allowing for time to drive long distances or to catch a plane.

Sharlette Hartley had either been tipped off, or a sixth sense was warning her to get out.

DJ pulled around the corner and stopped. This part of the town was old with a noticeable European atmosphere. The cobblestone streets were narrow, and the buildings pressed in close to the edge with only the narrowest of sidewalks on both sides. The buildings stretched three and four stories tall, sharing a wall with their neighbors. There were no yards, with many having a rooftop terrace if one wanted to enjoy the outdoors. Many of the windows were darkened. Most who lived in this town had a quiet lifestyle, and the night scene was almost nonexistent. Even though the van windows were up with the air conditioning blowing, DJ could smell the saltwater from the nearby Atlantic. One block over was a lengthy, ancient stone dock that ran for nearly a mile along the water, allowing boats to park right up against the town. Most were small commercial fishing boats.

DJ turned to look at the others. Only Abbi had stayed back at the ranch with her new best friend, Mary Abbot keeping her company. There would be no intel from her on this trip. This had not been sanctioned or coordinated with any intelligence team, so she would not be huddled up to monitors and watching from above via satellite. Only Agent Ali knew what they were doing, and he was keeping his lips sealed. He had wanted to tag along but DJ had insisted the man not get caught up with anything they might get into. He would be more valuable to them on the outside if they got into trouble.

"What now?" DJ asked. "Going in with no intel will be risky. Follow and see where she goes? Maybe ambush her on the way?"

It was Cash who replied, shaking his head. "Even if we're able to ambush them on the way, we have no exit strategy. We would alert the locals. Without them knowing what was really going on, if the local authorities get involved, it might mean getting ourselves into a shootout with the police. Can't risk it. We need to get in and get out. For that, we need a plan."

Argo jumped in, adding more pessimism to the problem. "Yeah, but if we do nothing and just try to follow her, she might slip away. With no satellite intel, we might lose her completely."

Brett killed the mood even more. "Then there's me. I was supposed to be in the background, helping to coordinate the capture with Carbon. Any spontaneous assault we might try on the fly will be hampered by me and my wheelchair. You can't be quick and clean if you have to include a guy on wheels."

DJ shook his head. "There's really only one option. We go in now, take out the guards, and throw her into the van. We can be in and out in two minutes. If we hit them hard and fast, we can be back on board our plane in forty-five and winging our way out of the country in an hour."

Carbon didn't like it. "That's if nobody is looking out a window and call in the license plate to the police. If that happens, we'll be in a Spanish jail. I have very little hope of Ali being able to get us out of that. And I don't see President Neville vouching for us to the government of Spain. In fact, he may even say nothing at all and just let us rot here for the rest of our lives, extradition treaty or not."

DJ was done talking. He had made up his mind. He pointed at Brett. "Crawl yourself to the backseat. Find us alternate routes out of here in case we make more noise than necessary. Carbon, get behind the wheel and stay on coms. Turn the van around. When we call for you, pull up to the front entrance fast and then slide over to the passenger seat. I'll be driving us out. Argo, Cash, silenced pistols. Let's move."

Sharlette Hartley was about to move to another alternate location. It was purely out of an abundance of caution. So far, her moles within the CIA, and a few others in the FBI, had not informed her that the search for her had yielded any results. Still, it was prudent to stay on her toes. One particular sympathizer within the CIA had programed the computers to disregard any match that facial recognition software might find as they scoured the millions of cameras across the globe. That wouldn't last forever. Eventually, someone would catch on to the "glitch" in the system and she would be found.

Sharlette had money stored away in case she ever needed to go into hiding, but it was finite. What she needed was a permanent location to live out the remainder of her days. With the new IDs in hand delivered just this afternoon, the first step to this was in place. Next, she needed to find a safe haven and purchase property under her new alias. She had a few candidates in mind but was still making her decision. She was thinking someplace in the Pacific might be good. There were few connected camera systems for the CIA to hack, and politicians were easily pliable. For the time being, she would jump from place to place until those details could be finalized.

She stood at the window on the fourth floor, watching her hired men load bags and prepare for the next leg of her journey. They had no idea who she was, and this was intentional. If they learned her true identity, one of them might sell her out. Worse, they might just tie her up and hand her over for the bounty the U.S. had offered. She sighed. All she had wanted to do was protect her homeland. She had only done what had needed to be done to achieve these goals. Sure, innocent people had died, but this was the cost of war. Always had been, always would be. It wasn't fair she was being hunted for being a patriot but she couldn't change that. All she could do was wash her hands of the situation and find a quiet place to retire.

As she watched the men below perform their duties, something hit the windshield of the first car in line, causing shards of glass to fly. There was no wondering if a rock had been thrown. She knew what it was. Someone had just shot the driver in the head from somewhere to her right.

They had found her.

Sharlette spun around and grabbed a small travel tote. Inside was her new alias and everything she needed to start her new life. She also snatched the small Walther PPK from the dresser along with the two spare mags. It might not be the best weapon for a shooting scenario with its less powerful .380 ammunition, or magazines that only held seven rounds, but it fit her hands and she was quite comfortable in using it.

She hit the hallway running. Instead of heading down the stairs, she turned left and went for the roof. She had chosen this home for its escape routes, not for the aesthetics. There were two she could choose from. One was in the basement, the other was the roof. Since going down would lead her into trouble, she climbed the stairs two at a time heading up. Despite her age, she kept in good physical shape, and climbing the stairs didn't slow her in the least.

One of the first things she had learned in the clandestine services was the importance of having backup plans. If her men below were even close to being competent at their job, she would be long gone by the time her pursuers could clear the building.

———————

DJ stepped around the corner and didn't wait. He put one round through the driver's head in the lead car, and then picked off two more before the rest of his team went into motion. Behind him, Cash and Argo swung wide around the corner to his right, clearing the way for them to engage as well. The three of them made quick work of the men outside save for the two standing in the entranceway to the building. Both had the wisdom to duck inside and stay there. How many friends were inside with them, DJ didn't know. He just hoped their weapons were silenced or this was about to get real loud, real quick.

DJ charged the doorway, not wanting to give them any time to pop back out and spray the street with bullets. There was nothing in the way of protection out in the street other than the three sedans parked in front but DJ and the others had to get there first. It was a good idea, and very nearly worked. A solitary figure hung a silenced pistol around the corner and began hammering away just before DJ could make the doorway. DJ dropped and slid forward on his side. The sidewalk, slick from decades of foot travel, offered little resistance and he came to rest in front of the door. He killed the man at the corner with little effort. Unfortunately, there was more than one there. The other guard had decided a pistol was not good enough. He was waiting for DJ with what looked to be an old Uzi sub-machine gun with a fat suppressor hanging off the end. The man fired a long blast from the hip, and DJ was hit. Three of them planted into his vest. Another grazed his shoulder. The rest smacked into the top of the two steps leading into the house, and ricocheted over him.

Stunned by the impact, DJ could offer little in the form of return fire. He tried anyway, missing with two rounds of his own. Thankfully, Cash showed up in the last second and double-tapped the man in the head from the edge of the door. Cash stayed where he was, looking for more targets as Argo arrived, hauling DJ to his feet and looking him over. "You good?" the man asked. DJ nodded, admonishing himself for not being smarter. He went past Cash, sweeping right and into the building. Argo was right behind, sweeping left.

The room beyond told DJ they were in the middle of the building. Archways to either side led to a study and a small living room. Both were clear. DJ took the time to hot-swap his magazine and looked around the living room where he stood. A doorway to the back of the building seemed to empty into a dining area and he reported it to Argo who was in the study. Argo reported another door that was closed on his side. Both men eased forward to investigate while Cash watched the stairs leading up.

There was no one else on the bottom floor. However, a creaking board above DJ's head told him there were people above.

When you cleared a building, if you were given the choice, you always cleared from the top down. The reason was simple: It was always harder to shoot your way up a flight of stairs than down. Having the higher ground was always an advantageous position to be in. They didn't have that luck. So, they were going to have to do this the hard way. And, since it was his stupid idea to assault now, with no knowledge of the building or intel on the exact number of forces expected, DJ led the way.

DJ confiscated the Uzi, swapped the mag for a fresh one from the dead body, and started up. He aimed and fired with his left hand, pointing it at the top of the stairs, releasing short bursts to prevent his enemy from peeking the corner. He moved quickly, skipping two steps at a time, his friends right behind him. On the second floor, he ran dry and dropped the Israeli-made weapon to the floor, quick-peeking the corner.

The second floor was arranged like the first, with rooms spreading out in both directions from the stairs. He came face-to-face with another enemy on his left, staring down the barrel of a pistol. DJ jerked back just in time as wood and plaster fragmented and dusted the air with debris. He answered in kind, hanging his own around the corner at waist level and squeezing off two shots into the man's middle, firing blind. He stepped around, pressed the barrel of MP to the man's forehead, and dropped him.

Eighteen rounds left. Two full mags at his side. One partial. Sixty-eight rounds in total.

Argo went right, clearing the room across from DJ, who was prepared to clear his own portion, but Carbon called out over the coms. "I've got four people exiting the roof. One looks like our tango. They're crossing to the next roof, west side."

Argo answered before DJ could respond. "*Tango*, Carbon? *Really?* So, you're a Green Beret now?"

DJ was already charging up the stairs, ignoring the conversation between the two. He wasn't about to let Hartley get away. With weapon raised and pointing, he snapped orders to Cash and Argo. "Argo, with me. Cash, meet them on the bottom floor. We'll pinch them between us." DJ ignored the third floor, anxious to get to the roof. Behind, he could hear Argo's heavy footfalls trying to catch up.

DJ had to hand it to Carbon. The kid was always looking for a high-tech solution to a problem. DJ hadn't instructed the kid to launch a drone, had never even considered the option, but Carbon did so anyway. It was more than likely the small one he kept in his backpack called Scotty. DJ had assumed it was a Star Trek reference. Carbon had corrected him, saying it was the identity of Ant-Man. DJ wasn't sure what an Ant-Man was, so Carbon was happy to tell DJ of the storied comic book hero named Scott Lang.

DJ met no more resistance on the way up, but just before reaching the door to the roof, Carbon alerted him to an ambush waiting. "You've got two guys waiting for you on the roof. They're pointing right at the door."

DJ came to a halt. The door was already slightly ajar, inviting whoever came up the stairs to just step on out. "Carbon, can you give me a distraction?" Behind him, Argo came to a halt, finally having caught up. The man wasn't even winded. DJ hoped he was in as good of shape when he was that age.

Carbon laughed. "Distraction coming up. But if this goes bad, you're paying for the replacement. Wait for it. Wait for it. *Now!*"

DJ burst through, swinging right and going wide, Argo right on his heels. Both bad guys were in front on the opposite flat roof, hunched over from having to duck. The buzzing sound of Carbon's drone was already fading into the background, having dropped low and raced right between the two enemies, causing them to recoil in surprise. DJ dropped the man on the left. Argo took the one on the right.

DJ and Argo darted forward, hopped the small wall dividing the two buildings, and quick-peeked the doorway leading down before entering. Below, DJ heard the sound of a door splintering and then Cash called out over the coms. "I've got nothing here. Between us, maybe?" DJ eased down with Argo following, hunting for the ambush he was sure awaited them. "Wait," Cash said. "I heard something. Not above me. Deeper inside." DJ paused on the stairs. Were Hartley and her last remaining henchman on the first floor? Was there a way out the back? On the satellite imagery they studied on the way over, the back of this building butted up against a row of similar homes behind. Was there a doorway connecting the homes? DJ voiced his concern and Carbon replied that he was watching from above for movement out of those houses. Finally, Cash called out. "I've got an open door and stairs leading below street level. I think they're in the basement."

DJ and Argo bounded down the steps, with DJ ordering Cash to wait for them before entry. They were on the alert for a setup on the way down, but as expected, there was none. Hartley was on her way out of here, and she wasn't leaving her last shooter behind to fend them off and strike out on her own. She was taking him with her to use as a last resort. Which meant they weren't holed up in the basement preparing for a last stand. If the woman jumped to the next building, then descended all the way to the basement, it meant there was a way out below their feet.

DJ was right. After meeting up with Cash, they proceeded cautiously down into the dark, using small flashlights to see. The power was off in this building and none of them had thought to bring their thermal vision goggles. In the basement, they found a square, wooden hatch on the floor. Argo grabbed the latch and waited for Cash and DJ to pick two sides and aim. He jerked it hard, throwing it open and standing back. Nothing. There was just a black void below.

DJ stepped forward carefully, waiting for someone below to hammer them with gunfire. Instead, he found a floor roughly ten feet below with a ladder laying off to one side. The only way down was to jump.

DJ reported the find to Carbon and Brett. "Looks like it goes into the sewers. Break out the rest of your drones and start spreading out. They have to come up somewhere. We're going in. I suggest you take the van and move just in case someone has called this in."

Brett replied back. "Maybe it would be best if we got out of here while we can. We'll find her later."

DJ wasn't in the mood for retreating. There was a chance to put the last nail in this coffin and he was going to get it done. "Not a chance." With that, he dropped through the basement floor and into the sewers.

———————

Sharlette held on to the arm of her hired guard to not get separated, or worse, stumble and go down. She didn't even want to imagine that. It might be considered a fate worse than death. She didn't even know the man's name. She didn't care. She needed him and his gun to get out of this mess. That, and his arm to keep her on her feet in the foul-smelling sewer she found herself in.

She moved quickly but carefully, using the light from her cellphone to navigate. She did her best to not touch anything, or step in anything that her feet might sink into. Regardless, she was going to smell like a dog kennel after a three-day weekend when she got out of here. She tried not to think too hard about the random piles of rubbish and waste littering the sewer floor. She knew what most of them were from the intense odor that hung in the air like a putrid fog.

She knew precisely where she was going, what turns to take, how many feet it was to the next one. She had memorized the route just in case she had to use it. When selecting this location to hide, she had considered it a smart move. With a smell so intense it was causing her to gag, she questioned just how smart she actually was.

Sharlette went down, her feet losing traction in something sickenly slimy. She lost her grip on the man's arm, one leg went one way, one leg went the other, and Sharlette landed on her butt on the wet floor with a splat. She wasn't hurt, but she was horrified by what she was sitting in; what was soaking through her pricey slacks and her panties. The very idea that she was sitting in someone else's feces caused bile to rise in her throat, and she coughed to try and keep it down.

She cursed under her breath and held out a hand to her bodyguard. He hesitated, not wanting to get any of it on him. She scowled at him with a rapier-like glare and spoke to him in Spanish. "If you ever want to see the rest of your payment, you better wipe that disgust off your face and help me up." The man shifted in behind her, reached under her armpits, and lifted her to her feet.

She motioned for him to be quiet and strained her ears, listening. There was movement somewhere behind them; a splashing sound. Whoever it was that attacked her, they were headed this way. How could they know which way she had gone in this maze? she wondered. Shining her light at her feet, she figured it out. They were leaving footprints in the layer of muck on the sewer floor. She cursed again, seized ahold of the bodyguard's arm, and hauled him forward. She picked up the pace. Not much farther to freedom.

Brett watched Carbon stare at the drone feed, shaking his head. "They could come up anywhere. We've got nothing to go on. Seriously, they could have another access in any building or follow the sewers out to what must be a hundred different locations. How are we supposed to help?"

Brett was frustrated. He had years of experience at this sort of thing and a superpower that allowed him to solve riddles. Yet, there he was, stuffed into the back of a van twiddling his thumbs like a passenger in a taxi. His surgery couldn't get here soon enough. The doctors had said that while it was likely he would regain full mobility, it might take years of physical therapy to accomplish. He would make them out to be fools. No one could be more motivated to recover his freedom than him. No one.

Brett snapped his fingers a few times at the hacker, leaning forward in his seat. "Pass that thing back here. Let me take a look."

Carbon looked at him like Brett had been popping pills. "This is a highly sophisticated bit of hardware. Flying it takes hours of practice."

Brett snapped at the young man. "If I have to come up there and take it from you, you're going to need a rolling chair of your own."

Carbon swallowed, hesitated, but held it across the seats gingerly. "Be careful. Now, the stick on the right, that controls… *Hey*! Not so aggressive! You have to massage it, feel your way gently, treat it like a lady. Don't manhandle it like a teenage boy trying to get to second base."

Brett didn't look at him when he answered, focusing on the screen. "How do you know what second base is? Relax, Marvin, she handles like a luxury car."

Carbon's growl sounded like tires on a gravel road. "Don't use my real name!"

Brett's eyes stayed glued to the screen, searching for answers, trying to discover where Sharlette Hartley would exit the sewers. "Our little secret, my hacking friend." All at once, Brett spotted something and all of the little file folders in his brain lined up to flash a pulsating green. He pointed at the screen. "There! Get me there. Quick as you can. Move it."

This wasn't the first time DJ had been in a sewer. The last time involved him running for his life and waist-deep in blue, treated, icy water. This time he was the one doing the chasing. At least he wasn't wading through crap like before. It didn't make it any better, however. The smell made him want to vomit. Cash said little as they navigated the low ceilings, but Argo had plenty to say about the environment. He threatened to send the cleaning bill to DJ and to beat the crap out of Hartley when he caught up to her for making him have to endure this place.

They moved as quickly as they could, hampered by the low ceilings and slick floor. DJ was concerned about the prospects of an ambush. They had no thermal goggles and they kept having to point the flashlights at the ground to follow the obvious footprints. An enemy could just stand there and wait until they got close before attacking. DJ and the others wouldn't be able to detect them until they had walked into the snare. He could only hope the ex-Deputy Director was more concerned with escape than ambushing her pursuers.

At one point, they came across a spot where it looked like someone went down in the green and black gunk. It made DJ smile to think Hartley might have faceplanted in the stuff. The prim and proper, well-dressed woman lying face down in poop was a fitting demise for the woman. Capturing her and making her remain in her soiled clothing for days on end while they took their time transporting her back to the States was an even better one.

They rounded a corner and a familiar sound hit his ears that made him pick up the pace, sprinting forward as best as he could. He could hear the sounds of waves breaking. Sharlette's makeshift escape tunnel led her to the long dock on the ocean side of the town. There was a good chance she had a boat in position to whisk her out of here in case of an assault. She was going to get away.

The three of them moved forward and rounding a bend, they could suddenly see the night sky at the end of the tunnel. Gratefully, the smell of sewage was rapidly replaced by salty air wafting through the space. Within seconds, their shaft finally ended. The sewer dumped straight into the ocean. There was no beach below, just black water of undetermined depth. Where had she gone? DJ wondered. He leaned out and looked around, spotting a steel ladder protruding from the stone wall of the dock. He killed his flashlight, tucking it away. Grabbing hold of a rung, he scrambled up, his head working back and forth, searching for his quarry.

The dock area was a two-tiered system. The street-level sat higher up, overlooking the lower level, the actual dock on which he was standing. Boats, mostly fishing, were tied up alongside with bumpers hanging over the railing. Many of them had rope ladders hanging down to access the ones with decks closer to the water. Only a few lights stretched down the dock to provide visibility. It was obvious tourism didn't reach this ancient seaside town. The fleeting light and dim shadows didn't allow DJ to make out detail at any great distance.

The sound of an engine and tires on cobblestone suddenly appeared on the street above. DJ looked up to see their van pull up right next to the iron fencing, skidding to a halt. The sliding door opened and Brett looked down on them. DJ held his arms out. "We lost them!" Behind him, Argo and Cash had ascended to the worn stone dock, looking in both directions, killing their flashlights as well.

Above them, Brett was searching as well. Suddenly, he pointed. "Five or six boats down!" As if on cue, the sound of a powerful boat motor roaring to life could be heard in the same direction. Brett took aim from where he was, carefully firing off one round at a time. The muffled shots were like handclaps echoing through the night, reverberating down the long and pitted dock.

DJ took off, eager to catch up, his friends on his heels. He only made it a handful of steps when the boat motor revved to full power. DJ's frustration reached new levels as he could see a lengthy ocean-going powerboat peeling off into the night, its bow tilting up at the sudden thrust of the engines and then slowly dipping as the speed increased, curving toward deeper water. DJ slid to a halt and raised his weapon. In the low light, he could barely make out two figures near the wheel, draped in shadow and hunched low. He took aim, let out a breath, and tried to time the rise and fall of the craft as it cut through the waves. He squeezed off a shot.

One round. Two rounds. A third.

Sharlette ducked even lower into the boat as a round whiffed through the air above her head and struck the windshield. Her bodyguard leaned across the wheel trying to push the throttle even further, willing the vessel to go faster. A second smacked into the dash to her left and she practically buried herself, her smelly self, into the shoulder of her last remaining man. She wrapped an arm around him and squeezed herself into him. When this was over, she was going to learn his name and give him a sizable bonus. Besides, she needed someone to accompany her for as long as this journey would take her.

A third round went further to her left, clipping the edge of the fiberglass hull. The rapidly increasing distance was making it harder and harder for whoever was shooting at her. Soon, whoever was shooting wouldn't have a chance of connecting with one of their bullets. Sharlette was going to get away.

Already, her mind was racing ahead, thinking of how to vanish. She was sure the CIA had sent in a team to take her out. If this were true, then somewhere in orbit was a satellite tracking her location. At a terminal on the other end, was an operator relaying her direction and speed to the team behind her still shooting. She was getting away from them, but she only had so long to dock this thing at the next town and vanish. They wouldn't be able to stay on the water for long.

Impossibly, a fourth round connected, smashing through the shoulder of her driver and new best friend. Hugging the man as she was, she felt it strike as the bullet sent a rippling shockwave through his body. The man flinched and groaned, jerking the wheel slightly and causing the boat to rock back and forth. She took a look and could see it was nothing life-threatening. She shouted over the roaring engines and crashing waves. "You're going to be fine. Just a flesh wound. I'll get you patched up; I swear. Turn south."

The man said nothing, rotating the wheel at her order and sending the powerboat in a southern heading. To the north was a U.S. Navy base at Rota. There was a good chance they had ships pointed this way at the direction of the team on the docks.

She glanced behind her, watching the docks growing smaller. The shooting had stopped. All Sharlette had to do was put some more distance between them and she was home free. She laughed. Killing someone as seasoned as her would take better planning than what she had just seen. "Children, all of them," she said out loud.

———————

DJ holstered his weapon. He had failed. Carbon and Brett had driven the van further down to stay close to the rest of the team. He turned and looked up at Brett. "See if you can get Ali on the phone. We need him to try and access satellite imagery and see if he can find out where she's gone."

Brett nodded and then pointed down the dock. "There's some stairs and a ramp that will lead you back to the street. We need to get out of here."

Another voice spoke behind him, a woman's voice. "Leaving so soon?"

DJ drew and spun. Cash and Argo responded in kind, rotating their weapons in the same direction. Sara Anderson stood on the deck of a small fishing boat; her hands raised.

She eyed them all. "I'm not armed. Well, I mean, I am, of course, but I left it behind me in the cabin. You know, you guys are like ticks. You just keep showing up in the worst places."

DJ wanted to shoot her. He wanted to end her right then. She had killed a member of his team. True, she had been set up to believe they were the enemy. True, she had saved Brett's life. It didn't matter though, the woman was psycho. While her targets were usually deserving of assassination, she had no issues with taking out innocent bystanders in the process. Her sense of morality was warped. She was beyond rehabilitation. She had a sick, twisted habit, and she just needed to go. And yet, he didn't just shoot her in the head and walk away.

He re-holstered. He needed to. The urge to shoot her through the nose was overwhelming. Besides, Cash and Argo could take her if she tried anything stupid. He was curious. She could have hidden; they would have never known she was there. She could have ambushed them, maybe taking them all out, but she didn't. Why, wasn't the real question. The real question had to do with her presence on this dock in a small fishing village in Spain. So, he asked her. "Why are you here, Sara Anderson?"

She lowered her arms but kept her hands visible. "Same reason as you, handsome. To kill Sharlette Hartley. I figured if I could do this, it might put me back in good graces with the CIA. If I could serve her head up on a platter, maybe I could get my old job back. This whole thing has had me reevaluating my life. I've made some bad choices. You made me see that. I want to try and make it right. If I could get my old job back, I would be placing myself in a box to make sure the good I do isn't overshadowed by the bad." She shrugged. "That was the thought, at least. Then you guys come in waving your guns around like a bunch of Army recruits fresh out of basic and ruin everything. It was all under control until *you* showed up."

Argo stepped forward. "You were going to blow her up, weren't you?"

She nodded. "I had every one of those sedans she was about to flee in wired with explosives. The plan was to wait until she got to the outskirts of town and then…" She held her fists together and then separated them, extending her fingers. "Poof. Like the woman never existed at all."

Sara looked at DJ. "Any chance you're going to let me live? I tracked her down once. I can do it again. You just have to let me go."

DJ envisioned scenarios with her running and back and forth on his gun range, using her for target practice. He thought of tying her up to some of her own explosives and making her go poof, like she never existed at all. But suddenly, DJ had a better idea. One that would ensure she really did turn over a new leaf.

He crossed his arms and sized her up. "I have a better idea. You come to work for me."

In unison, Cash and Argo turned their heads and looked at him like he had just renounced steak and vowed to become a vegan. "*What?*" they both cried out in shock.

DJ nodded. "This way I get to keep a close eye on you. This way I get to make sure that you try to make this right. Coonie, that was the person you killed, had family back in Louisiana. They live on this little farm out in the swamp, raising pigs. She sent the majority of her pay back to them. Her dad's sick and her brother is autistic. You're going to step into that role. You're going to help them out now that she's gone. You'll earn a paycheck working for me, and you'll send the bulk of it to them. They'll never know where it's coming from, but you'll help them all the same. Carbon will take care of the logistics. You miss a payment, you give me any reason to doubt that you've turned over a new leaf, I'll chop you up into little pieces and feed you to their pigs."

Sara blinked in surprise, genuinely dumbfounded at the offer. She looked at them all, overcome. Finally, she stepped off the boat to stand in front of DJ. "I won't let you down, I promise. And I'll take care of her family. I'll do whatever I can to make this right for as long as it takes." She reached into her pocket and DJ felt himself tense, ready for her to try something. She didn't. She pulled out her cellphone and tapped twice on the screen. Handing it over, she said, "While I was casing this place, I found the boat she had prepared in case she needed to get out here quickly. I wired it with explosives too. Dial that number and Sharlette Hartley will go up in a brilliant fireball out on the water. I'm sure she's still in range of a cell signal."

DJ looked at the phone, and then at her. "You had this the whole time but didn't say anything. Why?"

She shrugged. "Insurance."

DJ looked at the phone. He dialed the number. He watched with great satisfaction as Sharlette Hartley's boat blew up exactly as Sara said it would. They all stood there for a moment, enjoying the show. Then they left. They could finally get on with their lives and put this story behind them.

Poof, DJ thought. *Like she never even existed at all.*

Chapter 22: New Sheriff in Town

DJ, Abbi, Cash, Argo, and Carbon exited the van that had transported them to the place they had once called home and would now do so again. The old Air National Guard base outside of Jasper, Texas, had extensive renovations and additions since the last time they were here. The place was disguised as a company performing electronics and flight control upgrades for military aircraft. The cover story allowed for transports from every branch of the service to fly in and out with little suspicion from the people who lived nearby. All who worked here were employed by the government and held the highest security clearance. It was a top-secret facility stationed in plain sight; a cooperative endeavor by the Pentagon and the FBI, and vigorously secured by tight-lipped Marines.

DJ held mixed emotions in coming back. Their leaving had not sat well with him. They had only tried to do the right thing and prevent a global war. Their government had fought them, not believing the concern was real. Politicians had been more concerned with their imagery on the global stage. DJ and the team had been ordered to stand down. They had ignored that request and conducted unsanctioned and armed actions in the politically neutral country of Sweden. The Swedes were not happy, and DJ and the others were blackballed in the process. DJ supposed it could have been far worse. They could have all ended up in a foreign prison.

Since leaving, DJ had enjoyed his freedom. His team called the shots. They did what they wanted to do and how they wanted to do it. The CIA made their living on keeping things secret. So, when DJ decided to break the rules, his CIA friends tended to turn a blind eye and pretend nothing happened, happy as clams to get the end result they were after, more than willing to cover up the team's exploits and make it go away.

Coming back within the fold of the FBI came with certain restrictions. DJ was still able to operate without the normal level of bureaucracy that was found in an FBI Field Office, having only to answer to the Director. Still, politics within an organization of this size could not be eradicated entirely, and politics was something DJ detested with a white-hot passion. But, that wouldn't be his problem to deal with and navigate. That was part of Brett's job. It was something the man was good at.

DJ had required Sara Anderson to undergo FBI training at Quantico. He did this to ingrain rules and procedures back into her brain. She had been a rogue operator for far too long. He felt she could use a refresher course in discipline. Sara would have company as well. Mary Abbot, Abbi's good friend, had already been accepted. Should Mary pass her training, and DJ had every belief the fearless ex-Marine would, he had already planned to bring her into the fold. As such, he had given her a mission already. Mary had been instructed to keep an eye on Sara and report on how she was coming along. Brett had even made a call and arranged for the two women to be roommates, just to make sure. If Sara was half as good at playing the game as DJ assumed, he was sure the mad bomber would figure out she was being spied on. Still, he needed good intel on her and how she was faring, being constrained as she would be.

As they walked the corridors of their building, heading for the nerve center of their new operation, Carbon was an endless chatterbox of complaints and threats. He warned them that when he took over his department again, he was going to have heads rolling if they "messed up" his lab or tinkered with the computers he had left behind. He claimed that he didn't like any of the people who were here when he left, and if they were still here, they had better get on the same page as him or he would be doing a fair amount of firing. Brett politely reminded Carbon that all hiring and firing decisions went through Brett first, and to not get carried away. Carbon should settle in, evaluate all of the changes, understand the existing department dynamics, and then come to Brett with any changes he wanted to make. It wasn't like they had left yesterday. There were bound to be many new processes and procedures in place since the last time they were here.

Abbi was a chatterbox as well, though far less annoying. She smiled and bubbled with excitement, anxious to return to her role. After all, she was the one who had dreamt up this place and had shaped it into being. She couldn't wait to see what improvements had been made, and meeting up with old friends and making new ones. She led their procession with a bounce in her step and her ponytail wagging back and forth like a happy dog.

As they rounded the corner of the short hallway that would take them to the center of the building, an open concept, two-story giant room with workspaces in the middle, and offices and meeting rooms around the two-level outside edges, she came to an abrupt halt. This caused a small collision of the team following close behind. In a flash, her mood changed from upbeat and pleased-as-punch to simmering fury. She stammered her way into a question. "I... I can't believe... Who...? Just *who* do these people think they are?" Her back stiffened, her chin jutted forward, and she marched with purpose to the desk outside the double doors and the solitary guard stationed in front.

DJ was confused and tried to get an explanation out of her. "Abbs, what's wrong?"

She held up a finger over her shoulder to silence him and then pointed that same finger at the guard. "Open it up! Open those doors right now!"

DJ shook his head, worried that this was about to get ugly. The guard was not to let anyone pass without scanning everyone's I.D. card first. Luckily, the guard knew who they were. More specifically, he knew who Brett was. In the guard's mind, the new boss was coming in and one of his entourage was giving an order to open the doors. He hesitated only a moment, looking straight at Brett, and then complied, swinging both doors wide.

Abbi stormed through the entrance and struck a Drill Sargent's stance: her feet shoulder-width apart and her fists on her hips. "I need everyone's attention right now!" she shouted to the room. All eyes turned her way, looks of confusion and wonder on the people's faces gathered beyond, waiting to greet their new boss. They weren't exactly expecting a ranting woman in slacks and a ponytail. "My name is Abigail Slaughter. If that name doesn't mean anything to you, I'm the one that *built* this place. I designed every aspect of this facility. I'm also the one that hung the Batcave sign above the doors outside of this room. I don't know which one of you knuckle-draggers, pencil-pushers, or data-crunchers took it down, but if you know what's good for you, you'll get it back up there in the next five minutes or you'll need to call the janitorial staff. *Why*, you wonder? Because someone will be needing to mop blood off the floor. Now, put my sign back, *right freaking now*!"

Argo stood next to DJ, his body shaking with barely controlled laughter. The ex-sheriff slapped Brett on the shoulder and smiled, pointing at Abbi. "Now, *that's* how you let people know there's a new sheriff in town!"

DJ closed his eyes and shook his head. Today was going to be a long day. Not quite the return he was hoping for.

Chapter 23: Right Click, Select All

The water park outside Dallas, Texas had few permanent staff. Aside from the management team that oversaw day-to-day operations, most of the people who worked there were seasonal employees. This meant, of course, many older teenagers in polo shirts roamed around gathering trash and cleaning bathrooms. There were plenty of similarly dressed college-aged adults that worked there as well. They were off for summer break and eager to make a few extra bucks. They blew whistles to keep the kids from sprinting barefoot around the pools and waterslides, ran the ticketing booths, and supervised the water slides.

Of course, when your workforce was mainly kids, a few bad apples were bound to slip through.

Tommy was working here to save a few bucks for a new gaming system that was coming out in the fall. His old one was on its last legs anyway. He had asked his dad for the money, but dad had a better solution. He told him to get his sixteen-year-old butt off the couch and get a job if he wanted the money. Quick math told him that this part-time, seasonal job would still land him far short of what he needed. So Tommy was looking for ways to supplement his income. Since Tommy was a bad apple, he had no problems engaging in petty theft to reach his goals. Customers were always leaving things behind. Mostly, this meant suntan lotion, tennis shoes, or the occasional pair of gas station sunglasses. Tommy took anything he thought he might be able to sell.

He was making good progress swiping the things left lying around. Twice, he snatched a few wallets stashed under customers' towels. He had managed to even get a few pairs of expensive designer sunglasses that he sold to friends. Once, he even got his hands on some pricey high-tops bearing the trademark of a popular basketball superstar. All of that was well and good, but today, Tommy had set his sights on a bigger prize.

He had paid close attention to the routine of the shift manager and saw an opportunity. He would swipe the master key to the customer rental lockers when the guy went on break and raid them for any valuables found inside. If he was lucky, he could come out with a big enough haul to carry down to a pawn shop and get everything he needed, plus a little extra. Since the lockers were in the dressing room, there were no cameras to watch Tommy engage in larceny. If his score was big enough, he would quit this job and spend the rest of the summer hanging out with his friends.

Getting the key was about as easy as expected. Next, he grabbed a cleaning cart and headed to the dressing room. Once the room was clear, he set up cones outside the door, hung the "closed for cleaning" sign, turned the deadbolt to avoid surprises, and set to work. It took him all of five minutes to run through it all, emptying everything into a trash bag and shoved it into the cleaning cart. His plan was to stash his loot until it was time to leave, but with a surprising number of wallets, cell phones, and other odds and ends in his haul, he decided today was a great day to quit. He said nothing to no one. He just walked through the gate like it was no big deal and drove the used car his dad bought him to a pawn shop.

One thing was for certain: bad apples know bad apples. Tommy knew of one that ran a pawn shop not too far from his house. The man inside had bought stolen goods from him before, asking no questions. Today should be no different.

It wasn't.

Phillip Lansky was a pot-bellied man who had to be in his fifties. He was balding, smoked way too much, and generally looked like he needed a shower. Phillip was happy to see the garbage bag when Tommy walked in. "What you got for me today, T?"

Tommy grinned. "I hope you got a stack of Franklin's for me. Today is going to be a good day."

They went through the pile piece by piece with Phillip quoting prices on the things he wanted. The ones he didn't, went back into the bag. There were several wallets, most not worth anything. Tommy had already stripped them for cash, but two were nice enough he scored five bucks apiece. There were three sets of high-dollar sunglasses, eighteen phones that Phillip said he could wipe and sell, one wedding ring that earned Tommy $200 by itself, and an expensive-looking portable hard drive.

Phillip scrutinized the last piece, turning it over in his hands. "Who brings a portable drive to a water park?" he asked.

Tommy shrugged. "Who cares? How much you gonna give me for it?"

Phillip didn't answer. Instead, he said, "I wonder what's on it."

Tommy was exasperated. "Some old lady's recipes, some dude's porn vids. Again, who cares? What's it worth?"

Phillip looked at the drive, squinting to read the text on a small label stuck to the back. "These things don't go for much used, and I don't recognize the brand. Looks Korean or something. Hmmm... Let's see if it works, first." He walked over to a beat-up laptop that was yellowing with age and nicotine smoke and plugged it in.

Tommy leaned across the counter to try and see. "Well, does it work?"

Phillip nodded, staring at the screen, and firing up a cigarette. "Looks like it. I think it has Wi-Fi too. Battery's dead on it. Probably just needs a charge. Moves quick, so it's solid-state. That's good. But the files are locked with some security program."

Tommy drummed his fingers on the counter. "Like I said, probably porn. You can wipe it though, right?"

Phillip leaned in closer to the screen, taking a long drag on the cigarette. "Maybe," he said, blowing out a white cloud of foul-smelling smoke. "Let's see." He turned the laptop so Tommy could see better. "If I can wipe it, and if that kills the password protection, then I'll give you ten bucks for it."

Tommy was mad. "Dude, that's robbery! You know that thing's worth a few hundred."

Phillip paused and glared at him. "Maybe, but I can't get more than fifty for it, used. You want me to try or not?"

Ten bucks was better than nothing, so Tommy begrudgingly nodded. Regardless, he had made the money he was looking for. He watched as Phillip went to the root directory, right clicked on the drive and hit the delete button. A second later, Phillip smiled. "Done. Ten more bucks added to your pile. What you gonna do with all that money, T?"

Tommy leaned on the counter with one arm and began to tell him about the video game console that was coming out. He went on and on about how fast it was, the graphics capability, the storage capacity, and anything else he could think to include. He couldn't wait to get it in his hands. He even listed off the games he was looking forward to buying. Phillip listened while he counted out Tommy's money, puffing on a cigarette, thinking of how much money he was going to make off of Tommy's stolen goods. Both of them dreamed of cash and what they could buy with it. Neither knew of the mountain of it they had just thrown away.

The End. Or is it?

You can help me out tremendously if you would leave a review for this book. You have no idea how that helps us authors. It will take you seconds. It will help me tons. Thanks in advance.

Sincerely,
James Beltz

To my wife: There is no one like you.
Thank you for encouraging me to pursue my dreams.
Thanks for listening to me drone away
about the silly stories in my head.
You are a true gift from God.

Special thanks to the hard-working people
who proofread my work,
shred my stories,
and correct my mistakes.

Susan Bieser Steckenfinger
Bert Gevera Piedmont
Ken Daniels
Sara Engle Anderson
Susan Coy
Jennifer Verzosa
Suzy Perry Weinrich

Copyright

Betrayal
By: James Beltz
ISBN:
Published internationally by James Beltz
James@JamesBeltz.com
405-613-6279

© James Beltz 2021

Made in United States
North Haven, CT
25 April 2023

35871080R00095